www.MinotaurBooks.com

The premier website for the best in crime fiction.

Log on and learn more about:

The Labyrinth: Sign up for this monthly newsletter and get your crime fiction fix. Commentary, author Q&A, hot new titles, and giveaways.

MomentsInCrime: It's no mystery what our authors are thinking. Each week, a new author blogs about their upcoming projects, special events, and more. Log on today to talk to your favorite authors.

www.MomentsInCrime.com

GetCozy: The ultimate cozy connection. Find your favorite cozy mystery, grab a reading group guide, sign up for monthly giveaways, and more.

www.GetCozyOnline.com

MINOTAUR BOOKS

THE COLD LIGHT OF MOURNING

ELIZABETH J. DUNCAN

St. Martin's Paperbacks

This is a work of fiction. All of the characters, organizations, and events portrayed in this novel are either products of the author's imagination or are used fictitiously.

THE COLD LIGHT OF MOURNING

Copyright © 2009 by Elizabeth J. Duncan.
Excerpt from *A Brush with Death* copyright © 2010 by Elizabeth J. Duncan.

For information address St. Martin's Press, 175 Fifth Avenue, New York, NY 10010.

Library of Congress Catalog Card Number: 2009004487

EAN: 978-0-312-53345-8

Printed in the United States of America

Minotaur hardcover edition / May 2009
St. Martin's Paperbacks edition / July 2010

St. Martin's Paperbacks are published by St. Martin's Press, 175 Fifth Avenue, New York, NY 10010.

10 9 8 7 6 5 4 3 2 1

For Lucas

ACKNOWLEDGMENTS

The idea for this story began with a wicked little item in the *Toronto Sun* newspaper. A few months later, friends Fred and Margot Parker kindly gave my son and me a lovely lunch in a small North Wales village, and with that, I had a starting point and a setting.

My deepest thanks go to the wonderful people of Llandudno and Llanrwst, North Wales, for their interest and help with the factual details.

Thank you to Harriette I. Sackler and the members of her committee, who awarded this work the 2006 William F. Deeck–Malice Domestic grant for unpublished writers.

In Toronto, heartfelt thanks to Madeleine Matte for the chapter-by-chapter encouragement and to Carol Putt, who introduced me to Malice Domestic and went on to provide wonderful content editing, along with cups of tea and those nice little empire biscuits. Thank you, Carol, for your insight, expertise, and practical suggestions that made everything come right in the end.

I am grateful to everyone associated with the St. Martin's Minotaur–Malice Domestic competition for best first novel: Luci Zahray for short-listing the manuscript, Ruth Cavin for the phone call on a cold March afternoon that every writer dreams of, and Toni Plummer, who, with patience and good humor, turned a pile of paper into a book. It was lucky for me that New York literary agent Dominick Abel came along at just the right time and agreed to take me on. I know how fortunate I am.

Several established mystery writers—notably Carolyn Hart and Maureen Jennings—have been very supportive and I appreciate their kind words.

And finally, special thanks to dear Dolly for those endless lakeside rambles where we do our best thinking. I wonder how many bodies would remain undiscovered were it not for "a local woman walking her dog."

CHAPTER ONE

Emma Teasdale had been ill for some time and on a cool evening in early June, alone and peacefully, she died.

Those who gathered at lunchtime to set the world to rights at The Leek and Lily, the local pub, were saddened to hear of the retired schoolteacher's passing and remembered their long-ago school days with the reflective kind of nostalgia that is the gentle gift of time.

But one person, hearing of Emma's death, knew there was something to be done that only she could do.

Pulling on an ice-blue cardigan, Penny Brannigan turned the door sign to CLOSED, pulled the Happy Hands Nail Care shop door shut behind her, strode purposefully down Station Road, and turned left into Market Square.

A few minutes later, mildly out of breath, she arrived at the sedate façade of Wightman and Sons, the town's undertakers for more than a century. She paused for a moment to take in the familiar shop window that had been carefully draped in faded green velvet, framing a stiff arrangement of dried, dusty flowers.

Then, bringing her focus back to the purpose of her mission, she pushed the door open. As the overhead bell tinkled, Philip Wightman emerged from the back room, wiping his hands on a small yellow-and-white-striped towel.

Tall and slightly stooped, with thinning white hair, Philip was impeccably dressed in a sober black jacket and striped trousers. He smiled when he saw who it was and was just about to greet his visitor when Penny spoke.

"Philip, I've come about Emma Teasdale," she burst out. "To get right to the point, I'd like to do Emma's nails before she goes. Emma would have wanted me to do this for her. She always liked her manicure, Emma did, and was most particular about it. I'll use her favourite colour, Altar Ego. It's a light pink laced with lavender and it will be just right for the occasion."

With a sympathetic smile, Philip asked Penny to take a seat.

"Hello to you, too, Penny. How are you, then? Holding up all right? No time for the pleasantries anymore?"

Penny started to apologize, but he shook his head dismissively.

He thought for a moment as he carefully finished drying his hands and then nodded his agreement.

"Well, now, I think you're right. Miss Teasdale would have liked that very much," he said. "Why don't you come back tomorrow morning, after eleven, say, and bring your kit with you. We'll have Emma, ah, Miss Teasdale ready for you then. I'll stay with you while you do it, if you like.

"The visitation will start at two tomorrow, so that should give you enough time." He paused and looked at her sympathetically. "And you're quite sure you want to do this?"

Penny nodded. "I am, Philip, but thank you for your concern. I've never done a manicure before on someone who is . . . who has . . ." Her voice trailed off, and Philip supplied the word she couldn't bring herself to say.

"Died."

Penny thanked him, turned to go, and more slowly than she had come, made her way back along the narrow street to the small manicure shop she had opened more than twenty years ago.

The day, which had started out fine, was now threatening to rain. Low, dark clouds scudded across the sky, and the wind was picking up. Empty cups, plastic bags, and bits of paper blew along the street, washing up against the curb.

As she reached her shop, she paused for a moment to enjoy its unique setting. Hers was the third of three businesses in an old stone building; the premises beside hers had been empty for some time and a photographer had recently opened a studio in the third space. The charm of her shop lay in the small stream that ran merrily alongside it, bouncing over slippery, smooth stones to create the soothing yet energizing sound of rushing water. A curved wrought iron set of stairs led from the narrow pavement to her small flat on the first floor. She rarely used the stairs, though, because it was usually faster and more convenient to access the flat through the interior stairs tucked behind a discreet door at the rear of her shop. And, as she had learned the hard, bumpy way one rainy morning, the narrow steps could be very slippery when wet.

She unlocked the shop door and stepped inside, thinking as she often did when she turned the door sign from CLOSED to OPEN, how fortunate she was to be able to earn her living, small though it was, doing something she was good at, and which other people seemed to value.

Her manicure salon was clean, tidy, and well laid out. Bottles of nail polish, ranging from rosy pinks to vivid reds, and deep burgundies and browns through to vanilla creams and pearly whites were neatly arranged beside the small worktable where women, girls, and even the occasional man, always a tourist, sat to soak their nails, have their cuticles trimmed, and then their nails shaped, polished, and painted.

Penny prided herself on being able to suggest the perfect colour for any woman, any occasion. A job interview? You want to look professional, so why not try Japanese Rose Garden. A first date? Wow him with Big Apple Red. Over fifty? Steer clear of deep, dramatic colours and opt for something that flatters aging hands. Sonora Sunset would be just the thing for you.

As she thought of Emma, she smiled. Emma, who had never married, was in her seventies but her favourite colour, Altar Ego, was from the bridal collection.

Drawn together despite the differences in their ages and backgrounds, the relationship between the two women had grown steadily over the years into a close, affectionate bond. Penny adored Emma as the loving, kindly aunt she had always wished she'd had and knew that Emma returned her affection.

Although Penny didn't love music the way Emma did, she willingly accompanied her to the odd concert or recital, and Emma, in turn, went with Penny to visit art galleries or touring exhibits, once as far away as Manchester.

As Emma grew older, and the illness began to take its toll, Penny did everything she could to make her elderly friend comfortable while they both struggled in their own ways to come to terms with the inevitable. And now, the day Penny had been dreading, with its devastating news, had finally come.

Like Emma, Penny had come to Llanelen from another place. As a Canadian backpacker in her twenties, she had arrived in the village by chance on her way to

Betws-y-Coed and stopped for lunch. She had found her way into St. Elen's churchyard where she sat, legs outstretched in front of her as she munched an apple and admired the brilliance of the green fields in the middle distance as they rose to meet the craggy purple hills above them. For the first time she realized the significance of the phrase "breathtaking view." She was staggered by the depth and vibrancy of the velvety green fields that rose all around her, sloping higher, up and away, until they blended into the purples and greys of the trees on the hills above. And in the foreground, adding dimension, sound and movement, was the sparkling River Conwy. After a few minutes, she decided to capture the awesome grandeur around her and reached into her backpack for a small sketching tablet and pencil. While she worked, head bent and oblivious to time, the light began to change. As the sun slipped lower in the sky, the light brightened and intensified into that magic hour that announced the coming of dusk. Glancing at her watch, she decided it was too late to make it to Betws-y-Coed; she would try to find a place to stop for the night. In the town square she approached a smartly dressed mature woman in a light green spring coat carrying an old-fashioned wicker shopping basket and asked if she could recommend an inexpensive B&B. Although the woman was clearly in a hurry to get to the shops before they closed, she took the time to suggest in an educated English accent a place that might do. The next morning Penny bumped into the woman, this time wearing a head scarf and carrying a couple of schoolbooks. Recognizing her, the woman greeted her warmly and asked if her accommodations had been all right. The woman, of course, had been Emma. Penny spent a second night at the B&B and on the third day, had gratefully accepted Emma's kind offer to stop for a couple of nights in her spare room. The sketch Penny had made that first afternoon, now a small, framed watercolour, had been given pride of place for almost thirty years in Emma's cozy sitting room.

Such a simple meeting, Penny thought, as her eyes filled with tears. She doubted that many people today would extend such kindness to a stranger.

At first, Penny had worked whatever jobs she could, the way you do when you're young and your future stretches out endlessly before you—waiting tables in the dining room of the Red Dragon Hotel and chopping vegetables in the kitchen of the old people's home. One day, she offered to give an elderly resident a manicure as a birthday treat and as the other ladies gathered around to watch and then admire the result, they asked if they could have one, too, and offered to pay. Soon she was doing manicures at the residence every Saturday. Word got around, and before long she was booking appointments. Within six months, she had opened her own nail salon on a little side street and was living in the small rented flat above it.

She had kept her Canadian accent and over time the villagers had come to regard her affectionately as one of them, even if she did talk a bit funny. Now, in her early fifties, and older than Emma had been when they met, her hair was still an eye-catching, vibrant red that she wore tucked behind her ears. Her figure was not quite as trim as it used to be, but the comfortable casual clothes that had become her signature style hid those extra few pounds that inevitably find their way onto middle-aged waistlines. She liked tan or black trousers, worn with a neatly pressed white blouse and V-neck jumper or cardigan, always in soft colours like beige, white, pale pink, or ice blue, which, she had read in a fashion magazine, complement an over-forty face.

Settled and mostly content, she thought her life had turned out reasonably well.

The rector, who had called at Emma's request to finalize the arrangements for her funeral, had found her body in a small upstairs bedroom of Jonquil Cottage. On the bedside table, under an old-fashioned glass paperweight in which delicate purple flowers hung suspended for all time, he had found the meticulous notes she had made in preparation for their meeting.

"That was so like her," Rev. Thomas Evans said to his wife, Bronwyn, later that morning in the rectory's sunny kitchen, as he gently placed the two handwritten pages on the table. "She always thought of everything right down to the smallest detail and kept everything in her life so tidy and well organized. We could all learn a lesson from her."

He smiled affectionately at his wife, slipped off his jacket, and hung it casually on the back of a chair.

A short, slightly overweight man in his early fifties, Rev. Evans had managed to hang on to some of the good looks left over from his youth, although his jaw-line had slackened noticeably, and his bushy sideburns were definitely dated. His wife was a practical, down-to-earth woman with fading blond hair streaked with grey worn in the serviceable pageboy style that she'd had since she was a girl. Her comfortable clothes with their too-long skirts hung loosely on her small frame, and if her parishioners thought her wardrobe as outdated as her husband's whiskers, she took no notice. With her warm, compassionate nature and unfailing knack of saying the right thing, she was well suited to her role as the rector's wife—one she had filled for almost thirty years. She'd grown up in the village and considered herself fortunate to have spent many happy years of married life in the comfortable stone rectory that adjoined St. Elen's churchyard.

In the matter of Emma's funeral, as in most things, she agreed with her husband.

"I'm glad we know the music Emma chose," she said, gesturing in the general direction of the documents on the table. "She loved music so much, and having just the right hymns would have been so important to her. We'll make sure she gets the service she wanted." And, she thought as she paused to admire Emma's old-fashioned penmanship, perhaps we can add an extra special touch of our own, as a fitting tribute to the quiet Englishwoman who gave us so much over the years.

The small Welsh market town of Llanelen, nestled in the heart of the Conwy Valley, had welcomed Emma many years earlier, and for decades she had taught generations of children in the village school. While the children were actually in her classroom—fidgeting or gazing wistfully out the window at the lush green hills that encircled the town—they thought she was strict, humourless, and much too English; but when they got out into the world, running a sheep farming operation in the valley, working in offices as far away as Cardiff, forging successful careers in prestigious professions or even serving in Parliament, they remembered her with gratitude and respect, not only for teaching them many of the things they needed to know to be successful in their chosen careers but for encouraging them to aspire to those careers in the first place.

"I'd better put the kettle on," Bronwyn said as she walked over to the sink, adding over her shoulder, "you'll have a busy few days coming up." As the sound of running water filled the kitchen, the rector nodded absently and reached for his pocket diary. Opening it to the current week, he nodded again. "Yes," he agreed, "it is going to be busy. I've got the Gruffydd wedding on the Saturday at four. I think the funeral had better wait until the Monday. It just gets too crowded, and a lot of brides don't like the idea of getting married on the same day we've had a funeral in the church. They think the atmosphere isn't right, but how they can tell is beyond me. Too much leftover doom and gloom hanging over everyone, they say. Still, half the time it's the same crowd that goes to both and who wants to go to a funeral in the morning and a wedding in the afternoon? I certainly don't, and the last time I looked, neither one can start without me."

The rector pointed at the sturdy brown teapot that sat warming on the counter. "And will there be biscuits with that?" he asked hopefully.

Sliding a few chocolate digestives onto a plate, his wife shook her head, sighed, and then turned around to face her husband.

"The Gruffydd wedding! Emyr could have had anyone—anyone!—but he takes up with her. Now, I know I'm not supposed to think or talk like that—being judgmental they call it these days—but I'm only saying what's true and what everyone knows. That Meg Wynne Thompson's a right little madam, and she'll make his life a merry hell. In this day and age, I don't know why he would think he has to marry her." And then, after a moment's reflection, she added, "That didn't come out quite the way I meant it. I haven't heard any talk of her being pregnant or anything like that, so I'm sure that's not . . ."

Her voice trailed off as she gave the tea a brisk stir, slapped on the lid, placed the teapot and biscuits on the table with a bit more emphasis than usual, and then sat down opposite her husband. As a comfortable silence descended on them, the rector reached for a biscuit with one hand, then fumbled in his jacket pocket for his pen with the other. There was much to do, and he needed to make a few notes.

A few moments later Bronwyn took a delicate sip of her tea and looked at him. "Listen, Thomas," she said. "I've had an idea. It's about the funeral. See what you think about this."

Like the rector, Penny was thinking about the Gruffydd wedding, because she, too, had a role to play. The bridal party had booked appointments for Friday afternoon weeks ago, but the bride had decided to have her nails done on the morning of her wedding, so Penny, carefully disguising her reluctance, had agreed to take Meg Wynne Thompson on the Saturday at nine.

Penny always advised members of the bridal party to come in for a pre-wedding manicure a couple of weeks before the big day to choose and coordinate their colours and then to get their nails done the day before the wedding. There were always too many things to do, and too little time to do them, on a wedding morning.

Fortunately, Meg Wynne hadn't wanted a pedicure, as many brides did, so their feet would look their sexy best in strappy sandals, and because of the timing, Penny hadn't dared suggest one.

Glancing at her watch, she decided there would be just enough time for one of those sandwiches from the Spar that she loved—prawn mayonnaise this time— and a cup of tea before her afternoon clients began to arrive.

First would be Evelyn Lloyd, coming in for her regular Thursday afternoon appointment. Like many of Penny's regulars, Mrs. Lloyd regarded a professional manicure as a bit of pampering richly deserved after a lifetime of hard work and, since she had given up smoking, a little treat she could easily afford, although every now and then she would suggest to Penny that her over-sixty clients really ought to get a senior's discount.

Penny laid out her work tray, turned the shop sign, closed the door, and headed upstairs for lunch.

CHAPTER TWO

Penny returned to the shop a few minutes before Mrs. Lloyd was due to find her waiting on the pavement peering in the window.

"Oh, Mrs. Lloyd, I am so sorry to have kept you. Do, please, come in. May I get you a cup of tea or coffee?"

Mrs. Lloyd entered the shop and, after the preliminaries were over, settled herself into the client's chair. A robust, well-kept woman in her mid-sixties, with tightly permed grey hair and always conservatively turned out in a pleated skirt with a matching cardigan and a white blouse with a bit of detailing on the collar, Mrs. Lloyd had been the village postmistress for years. In her day, she believed, the job had been essential to the smooth running of the village. After all, it was she who made it possible for money to be transferred, bills to be paid, and anniversaries and birthdays to be remembered. Now, of course, with mobile telephones, e-mail and the Internet, all that had changed. But the one thing that hadn't changed was her love of what she thought of as useful information but others might well have considered plain old gossip, and she liked to think she was almost as well informed of village doings in her retirement as she had been when she stood behind the counter with her weigh scales and currency conversion charts.

"I guess you heard about Emma Teasdale, did you, Penny? Of course you did. That was too bad, really it was. But still, at her age . . . she did have a good, long life. I wonder what will happen to the cottage. Be worth a bob or two what with the price of property these days. Bought that long before single women were buying houses, Emma did. I don't know if she had any relatives left in England."

Mrs. Lloyd paused for a moment to gather her breath and her thoughts.

"I think there was someone once, though, but nothing ever came of it. They certainly never married, did they?"

Penny, who had never even thought about Emma having any kind of romantic involvement, was astonished, but couldn't bring herself to say anything. Because Emma had never volunteered any details on this part of her life, Penny felt it would be disrespectful to her memory to push Mrs. Lloyd for details.

After a few moments of silence, Mrs. Lloyd moved on to the other main topic of conversation in the village, the Gruffydd wedding. Like the rest of the villagers, Mrs. Lloyd was not impressed by Emyr Gruffydd's choice of a wife.

The son of a wealthy landowning family, Emyr was well liked and respected in Llanelen. In his early thirties, he had been living in London for several years, but six months ago, with his father in failing health, he had returned home to oversee the family's business interests, which included real estate, farming, haulage, and investments.

The Gruffydd family lived about ten kilometres outside the village in a large stone house with spectacular views over the valley to the Snowdonia mountain range, and it was to this house, formally called Ty Brith but often referred to as the Hall, that Emyr was planning to bring his bride.

"I don't really know that much about her," Mrs. Lloyd confided as she soaked her nails in a small basin filled with hot, herbal-scented water, "but I do know that people here haven't taken to her. Folks in the shops say that she's rude to them and comes across like Lady Muck. Much too grand for the likes of us! I've heard that the staff at the Hall, what's left of them that is, aren't looking forward to having her there, but of course, they have no choice in the matter, see. She's from London, you know, and very posh with it. That's where he met her. What she does there I don't know. I think all the young people in London work in advertising or mass media—whatever that might mean—or some such."

At a nod and gesture from Penny, Mrs. Lloyd pulled her right hand from the basin. Penny dried it carefully, as if it were a fragile porcelain heirloom, before beginning work on her nails.

"I haven't met her yet," Penny said, "this Meg Wynne Thompson, but Emyr's mother used to come in regularly. She was a lovely woman."

"Indeed she was," agreed Mrs. Lloyd as she leaned in for a better look at her hand.

"There was something about her that always reminded me of a Hollywood film star you'd have seen back in the 1940s. Every now and then I see an actress in one of those late-night black-and-white pictures that reminds me of her. Beautiful wavy hair, she had, and huge blue eyes. She was always impeccably turned out and carried herself with such dignity. And yet, she came from a simple background, see." Mrs. Lloyd nodded for emphasis. "Oh yes. Her father was the village black-smith." She gave a little snort, and then continued. "A blacksmith! That's going back a ways. You'll not find many blacksmiths around these days. Still, even ordinary folk had much better manners in those days and knew how to eat properly and speak respectfully to their betters."

She thought for a moment, and then withdrew her hand, giving Penny the other one to work on.

"Some people, like Emyr's mother, are just born with that kind of poise or grace you might call it," she went on. "I honestly don't know what she would make of this wedding, but I suspect she would have wanted Emyr to marry a local girl. Still, times have changed, and who from around and about these parts would have suited him? And besides, he's been away so long, he doesn't really know anyone from Llanelen anymore. Of course, there is my niece, Morwyn. She and he used to be sweethearts once, but then he left for London.

"Of course, it's the same all over, now. The young people think they have to go to Cardiff or London or Manchester to get a decent job. What nonsense! There's plenty of perfectly good jobs to be had in the towns, if only they would consider it."

"Perhaps it's more the nightlife they're seeking," suggested Penny. "Not everyone likes the quiet life, especially when they're young. And you must admit, Mrs. Lloyd, there's nothing to do here in the evenings, except go down the pub. Even the cinema has been closed for years."

"That'll be that clubbing you hear so much about," agreed Mrs. Lloyd. "No one under forty stays home with the telly and a good book anymore. Not nearly exciting enough, I guess.

"Now, that Meg Wynne, I can't see her settling down

to a quiet life in the Hall. Even though Emyr's mother made a great success of it, you really need to have been brought up to it, been to finishing school so you know how to arrange flowers and sort out a dinner party with the cook and all the rest of it. I don't think she's cut out for it, so it'll be interesting to see what happens." She gave it a few more moments thought, and then shook her head gravely. "Poor Emyr. No, she's not the right girl for him. It'll all end in tears, you'll see. And as for his chum, that cheeky Williams lad, don't get me started! Charm to spare, that one, but very short on substance, if you ask me. And I don't think he's a very good influence on Emyr. Used to lead him astray something awful when they were young. Emyr was never one to stand up for himself. Needs to grow a backbone, he does."

She glanced over at the bottles of polish and then brought her attention back to Penny.

"Where was I? Oh yes, Emyr's friend. Well, I can tell you that some of us—and that includes your Emma— were surprised he turned out as well as he did. He was a real troublemaker. Always up to something but with those good looks of his, he got away with it."

She looked expectantly at Penny.

"Well, Mrs. Lloyd, to change the subject, what colour would you like today?" Penny asked.

"It's my bridge night as usual, Penny, so I think a nice rose shade would be appreciated. How about that one?" she said pointing to a bottle in the front row.

"Oh, that would be good, Mrs. Lloyd. It's just in. Very new. You'll be the first to have it."

Mrs. Lloyd leaned forward to watch as Penny carefully applied a base coat, and then followed it with two coats of the chosen lacquer, and finally, a finishing, protective topcoat.

"You know, Penny, I always like to get my nails done

on a bridge night. I consider it a gift to the table so everyone can enjoy them!"

"That's a nice way to look at it, Mrs. Lloyd." Penny smiled. "The job should hold up for the wedding on Saturday. You are going, aren't you?"

"Oh, I wouldn't miss it. I don't suppose that you . . ."

"No, I wasn't invited, but I will be doing the bridal party's nails if you want to consider that a gift to the congregation."

Mrs. Lloyd laughed good naturedly, stood up, patted down her skirt, and gave her finished nails a final blow. She gathered up her few belongings and prepared to leave the shop.

As she reached the door, she turned around and passed on one more observation.

"Why do you suppose it is that young people aren't taking up bridge? You never see young people playing bridge anymore, do you? Well, cheerio. See you next week!"

With that, she was gone. Penny made a few notes on Mrs. Lloyd's client card and began to set up for her next customer.

CHAPTER THREE

Penny woke up early Friday morning to the sound of rolling thunder and heavy rain lashing against her bedroom window. Turning on her side and pulling the bedclothes up around her shoulders, she watched for a few moments as fat, lazy raindrops cascaded down the fogged windowpane. She sighed, stretched, pushed the covers off, swung her legs over the side of the bed, and reached around for her slippers. She sat on the edge of her bed, looking around the familiar room, with its sloping white ceiling, sketches and watercolours on the pale yellow walls, bookcases, and much-too-small closet. Still, it was home and it was hers.

As she made her morning cup of coffee she decided that before she threw herself into the day she'd have a decent breakfast so she put an egg on to boil and found a relatively fresh slice of whole wheat bread that would do for a piece of toast.

After finishing her breakfast with the morning paper for company, she opened the shop and did two rather impersonal manicures. When the second client had left, she flipped the shop sign to CLOSED, gathered up a few tools and bottles into a carrier bag, and fetched an umbrella from the small cupboard under the stairs. Closing the door behind her, she opened the umbrella and set off on the short walk to Wightman and Sons, where Philip would be waiting for her.

He greeted her on the step, and asked how she was holding up.

"Usually, I would take care of her nails as part of her hair and makeup, Penny, and if you want to change your mind, just give me the polish, and I'll get on with it."

"No, Philip, but thank you anyway," Penny said as she shook the rain off her umbrella into the street. "This is something I can do for Emma, and I would like to."

"That's fine, then, Penny. She's ready for you. Follow me."

He led Penny through the premises, past the visitation room, to a small, white-tiled workroom at the rear of the building. Emma was lying on a stainless steel table, dressed in a tailored navy blue dress with white buttons. A crisp white sheet covered the lower half of her body, and her hands had been placed on top.

"In your own time, Penny," Philip said.

Penny cautiously approached the table, looked carefully at Emma, and then turned to smile timidly at Philip.

"It's a cliché, but it's true . . . she really does look peaceful. You did a good job, if that's the right thing to say."

Philip brought a stool to the table and set it down beside a worktable covered with a green surgical-type cloth on which he had thoughtfully placed an empty glass, a bottle of water, and a box of tissues.

"You might find it easier to sit on this side," he said, "do her left hand, and then take the chair and table around the other side of the table and do her right hand."

Penny sat gingerly on the stool and looked expectantly at Philip. He nodded gently and said, "It's up to you, Penny. I'll stay with you while you work, or if you prefer, I'll leave you alone with her."

"I think I'll do this on my own, Philip, thanks. Give me about half an hour."

He nodded again and quietly left the room. Penny reached into her carrier bag and set out the contents on the worktable.

She reached for Emma's hand, lifted it gently, and placed it on the small white towel she had brought with her. At the first touch of Emma's cool, still hand, her eyes filled with tears. She knew those hands so well. She had seen them hand her an icy gin and tonic, make the most delicious biscuits, fit in the last piece of a jigsaw puzzle, eagerly open a Christmas gift, and gently brush the hair from her forehead on a hot day as she worked in her garden. Penny had held them in her own hands almost every week for more than two decades. And over the years, she had seen them change as time did its cruel work. Brown spots had developed on the thinning skin as its elasticity was lost. The knuckles had become more pronounced and dark blue ropey veins had surfaced. How Emma had hated the way her hands looked! But despite all the hand cream, manicures, and wearing of cotton gloves to protect them from the sun, her hands had aged along with the rest of her. And, thought Penny, they told the story of a long life lived with truth and dignity.

She pulled a tissue from the box that Philip had thoughtfully left for her, and began to work on Emma's nails for the last time, telling herself she could have a good cry when this was over. Half an hour later, just as she was finishing, Philip returned.

"They look lovely, Penny. You were right, Miss Teasdale would have wanted you to do them for her. Well, just a few more things to tend to and she'll be ready for this afternoon's viewing. Will you be coming in?"

Penny shook her head.

"No, Philip. I'm doing the Gruffydd wedding girls this afternoon so I'm going to come this evening. Thank you for letting me do Emma one last time. It was sad, and felt strange, but at the same time it was, I don't really know what the word is . . . helpful?"

"It may have helped you accept Emma's passing. You were a lot alike, you two, and she thought the world of you."

Penny felt the sharp sting of new tears pricking her eyes and turned away.

With the sensitivity acquired over many years in his line of work, Philip said simply, "You probably don't feel like a coffee at the minute, so we'll save that for another time and I'll just show you out, shall I?"

Penny nodded, and they made their way in silence to the shop door.

He put a reassuring hand on her arm and smiled down at her.

"Good-bye, Penny. See you later, then."

Putting up her umbrella, Penny bent her head against the rain and headed home to a sad and solitary lunch.

Her afternoon began with the sound of noisy giggling as the two bridesmaids, Jennifer Sayles and Anne Davidson, made their entrances. They were approaching their late twenties, and while each appeared to be expensively groomed, Jennifer, the taller of the two, looked as if she came by her toned, fit body naturally. Anne, on the other hand, would find herself betrayed within the next few years by the body she was working so hard now to maintain; with youth on her side she was winning the battle, but eventually, she would lose the gravity and collagen wars.

Both girls wore expensive designer jeans but not with trainers or sensible country walking shoes. They were wearing Jimmy Choo sandals with extremely high stiletto heels, and Penny could barely conceal a smile as she thought of the comments those silly and unforgiving shoes were sure to be inspiring around town.

Seating herself at Penny's worktable, Jennifer said she would go first, so Anne took a seat in the small waiting area and pulled the latest *Tatler* from her bag.

"We picked our colours last week when we were in town," Jennifer reminded Penny. "Anne and I have chosen Embrace, and I think Meg Wynne is having something else when she comes in tomorrow."

"How is Miss Thompson doing?" Penny asked. "I expect she's been awfully busy trying to organize a wedding here when she lives in London. Can't be easy."

"That's true," Jennifer agreed. "Ordinarily, I guess, they would have had the wedding in London, but with Emyr's father not being well, it seemed like a good idea to hold the wedding here. I must say, it's been great fun for us getting out of the city and coming to North Wales, of all places, for a few days."

"What do you do in London?" Penny asked casually.

"We, that is Anne and I, work together at a PR agency. Meg Wynne works at a graphic design studio, her company did some work for us, and we all just got to know one another through our work, the way you do, really. And then Emyr and his friend David Williams were regulars in the wine bar in Covent Garden where we go after work, so we all just naturally formed a little group. And that's how we all met up."

She looked over at Anne, who was flipping through her magazine.

"Anne, how did it happen that Emyr and Meg Wynne started going out together?"

"Yeah, well," drawled Anne, looking up. "I think he sent us over drinks one night, but you could tell it was really Meg Wynne he fancied. And she led him on for a bit and played it cool. For a while, we thought it was David she was after but I think one night she invited Emyr around for a meal or whatever and that was pretty much it. After that they were just together. They've been going out for about two years now, wouldn't it be, Jenn?"

"Yeah, it would be about that," Jennifer agreed.

"And will Miss Thompson's family be coming to the wedding?" Penny asked.

The two girls exchanged glances, and then Jennifer, apparently by some unspoken understanding, was elected spokesperson.

"I think so," she said carefully. "Meg Wynne doesn't like to talk about her family. Her brother died about a year ago, and the family has been struggling ever since. Apparently he got in with some bad company, and drugs were involved. He used to come along for dinner with us sometimes when he came down to London to visit Meg. He was only about eighteen or nineteen, I think. Good-looking lad, he was. Meg Wynne said her mother took it really hard. Well, she would do, wouldn't she? But I'm sure her parents will be here to see her get married."

Penny murmured sympathetically as she reached for the topcoat polish.

"You're almost done, Miss Sayles," she said. "You obviously keep your nails well looked after in London, so there wasn't too much for me to do today. Miss Davidson, just give me a moment to set up for you, and then it's your turn!"

Anne handed off her magazine to Jennifer as the two girls changed places.

What are your dresses like?" Penny asked as she started work on Anne's nails.

"Well, what they are definitely not is puffy and

covered with bows," replied Anne. "They're just, well, like evening dresses, but not over the top, you know? Meg Wynne always wants everything to be in the best possible taste and I guess it's the designer in her, but she likes everything to be sleek and sophisticated, if you know what I mean. Minimal. Modern.

"By the way, I was wondering, what part of America are you from?"

"I'm not from the States, actually, I'm from Canada. Most people make that mistake, because the accents can sound quite a bit alike. I'm from Nova Scotia. Nice little place called Truro."

"Oh, I was just wondering, because Emyr and Meg Wynne are going to America for their honeymoon. New York. Have you ever been there?"

Penny said she had, many years ago, as part of a university trip. While her classmates had spent their days at the Museum of Modern Art, she had found it difficult to tear herself away from the old masters in the Frick Collection.

"I haven't been yet, but one day!" Anne enthused. "I love everything about America and I can't wait to go there. I was just green with envy when Meg Wynne told me about New York. I think I was even more jealous about that than I was that she'd landed such a great catch as Emyr!"

Penny smiled at Anne's open and eager charm.

"I was wondering which of you is the maid of honour," she said.

"That would be Jennifer," said Anne. "There are just the two bridesmaids, and Emyr is having David as his best man, and there's one usher, Robbie Llewellyn. They all grew up here, apparently. Went to school together and been friends almost all their lives. The wedding is quite small, only about fifty people, and most of them are Emyr's people. But you'd expect that, wouldn't you, when the wedding is being held in his village?"

"Yes, I guess you would," Penny agreed. "It's been quite the topic of conversation around here lately. Everyone certainly wishes Emyr and his bride every happiness."

"They've sent the most wonderful presents, Meg Wynne says. They are all on display up at the Hall, and we'll get to see them all tonight at the dinner."

The two girls exchanged excited smiles.

The dinner to be held at the Hall on the evening before Emyr's marriage had been the talk of the town for weeks. The award-winning chef-owner of an exclusive nearby country house hotel, with her culinary team, had been hired for the evening to cater it. Besides the wedding party, a few select guests—mostly longtime friends of the family—would attend. No expense had been spared for food or flowers, and preparations had been under way for days, with much coming and going of tradesmen's delivery vans.

The groom and his supporters were staying at the Hall, while the bride and her party had rooms at the Red Dragon Hotel, with its easy access through a side door to the picturesque walkway along the River Conwy that led to the church. Penny had offered to nip along to the hotel in the morning to do Meg Wynne's nails but had been told that Meg would prefer to come to her.

All arrangements for the bridal party's nail care had been made over the telephone, and Penny had been instructed to submit her bill for the bridal party's nail care to the Hall.

When the bridesmaids' manicures were finished, Penny suggested they might want to sit quietly for a few minutes to make sure their polish was completely dry before setting off. Impatient to get on with their day, however, they said their good-byes, gingerly opened the door, and pranced off into the street.

Penny finished her work for the day and, leaving the shop clean and ready for the next morning, went upstairs for a light supper before setting off for Wightman and Sons. She didn't expect too many people would be at the evening visitation for Emma, just a few old friends, and that was how it turned out. The rector and his wife, Bronwyn, were acting as unofficial family, greeting the few people who had dropped in. Penny quietly made the rounds, speaking briefly and politely with everyone, and then made her way home for a quiet cup of cocoa and an hour or so struggling to concentrate on a library book as her thoughts kept drifting back to Emma and the meaning of a life fulfilled. And, as waves of grief began to wash over her, she realized how dearly she would miss her friend because as of today, her own life had begun to move slowly forward, leaving Emma frozen in the past.

And then she smiled as she thought how Emma would have enjoyed hearing about the bridesmaids' shoes.

CHAPTER FOUR

The private road leading to Ty Brith wound its way up the hillside for about three kilometres. At first narrow and flanked on each side by trees and brush, the road widened as it got closer to the Hall and the trees gave way to lush, green fields.

On this night, from the bend in the road where the trees ended and the fields began, lanterns had been placed alongside the fence to light the visitors' way to the Hall and to let them know that a magical evening was about to unfold.

It seemed that every window in the Hall was aglow, and the welcoming sound of excited party voices greeted visitors as they emerged from their cars on the warm summer evening and crunched across the gravelled forecourt to the porte cochere.

Emyr Gruffydd, with Meg Wynne Thompson by his side, was standing just inside the front door to greet his guests. Tall, with dark wavy hair, a determined chin, and deep-set blue eyes, Emyr was good looking in a way that would have been better appreciated thirty years earlier. But the woman beside him was definitely of her time, and by anyone's standards, she was exquisite.

Meg Wynne, dressed in a strapless emerald green

vintage Valentino gown, was tall, with the perfect posture and long legs that suggested a pampered childhood filled with ballet and riding lessons, and holiday visits to London for the pantomime, followed by a walk down Regent Street to see the Christmas lights. Her shoulder-length, frosted blond hair was brushed softly back from her face and held in place with a diamond clip. Chandelier diamond-and-emerald earrings, a wedding gift from her soon-to-be father-in-law, almost brushed her bare shoulders. Her smile was polite but superficial, and if she felt any excitement, she did not show it. Her calm, poised presence was reassuring but discomfiting at the same time, as if she was deliberately holding something back. The aura around her was not of happiness, but of triumph.

At twenty-eight, she seemed on the brink of a charmed life: adding great wealth to her great beauty. She had worked tirelessly for both.

The daughter of a lorry driver father and a shop assistant mother from Durham, Meg Wynne had set about early to reinvent herself. As a fourteen-year-old schoolgirl she worshipped the princess of Wales, knew the names of all the best designers, and dreamed of the day she would travel with Louis Vuitton luggage, wear Armani and Versace, and have closets filled with Chanel shoes and Prada handbags. She devoured fashion magazines and used them to carefully plan her escape from working class to first class.

She instinctively knew she would have to find a way to get into the orbit of the people she aspired to join, and this meant finding a suitable career that would put her in all the right places and in touch with all the right people. Bright and talented with an innate sense of colour, proportion, and design, she easily won a scholarship to Central Saint Martins College of Art and Design where she graduated top in her class. And since she was moving to London where no one knew her anyway, she thought that would be a good time to change her name from the simple Sandra that her mother had chosen for her, to Meg Wynne, which she thought would grant her more acceptance in the world she was about to join.

Snapped up after graduation by a high-end London graphic design firm, she met fashion-magazine editors and advertising and public relations creative directors. Her world expanded to include international contacts and, as she became more polished and sophisticated, with the help of an acting coach, her accent went from Durham to Duchy. She sought out the best cosmetic surgeon in London and redefined her body. She learned about table manners and paid attention to the smallest detail of everyday etiquette. Let other women be common and vulgar. She would be elegant, sophisticated, and professional. Her designs at work were award-winners, but in the end, her best design was herself.

Of course, this upward mobility came with a price. She shed friends and lovers along the way as they outlived their usefulness. This she did without regret or remorse as she set about finding the man who could take her life to the next level or, even better, the level above that.

While she accepted that a lifestyle on the Beckham scale was probably beyond her grasp, she did think that a man who came with a large, beautiful house, a generous income, and a title was not too much to ask for.

And when she met Emyr, she decided that two out of three wasn't bad and who knew? One way or another, the title could always come later.

When he asked her to marry him, she accepted without hesitation. She knew that he loved her, would be devoted to her, and would always give in to her. When he suggested she might like to have his mother's engagement ring, she said that was so thoughtful and sweet, but really she would prefer something more modern in platinum from Cartier.

When he asked if she would mind if they married at his home in Wales, she was glad to agree. She had come too far, and accomplished too much, to have her wedding in Durham, with all its ugly, embarrassing, working-class associations. It was bad enough that her parents would be coming to the wedding in Wales, but if they weren't invited, or for some reason didn't go, eyebrows might be raised and questions asked.

Her timid, withdrawn mother, she knew, would be so socially overwhelmed by the scale of events surrounding the wedding that she would be more than content to hover silently in the background, hoping no one would notice her or speak to her. But her father was another story. How would she manage the situation if he drank too much, got loud and boisterous, and started shouting the odds?

When she tucked her arm through Emyr's as they turned to join their guests inside, she caught a glimpse of her parents across the entrance hall. Her father's flushed face, as he raised his glass to take a long drink, worried her. I'm going to have to have a word with him about that, she thought. I can't let him ruin this night. Earlier, she had left instructions with the serving staff that her father was not to be offered anything alcoholic to drink, but that if he asked for something, it should be well watered down and slow to arrive.

Dinner was announced, and the members of the party made their way to the dining room. The large, gracious room, seldom used anymore, had been thoroughly turned out, its panelling and furniture polished, curtains aired, and the rugs and carpets shampooed.

Every piece of silverware and crystal had been polished until it gleamed, and in the warm, rich glow of dozens of candles, the table settings glittered like they might have done fifty years earlier. The heady fragrance of fabulous flowers filled the air as the sideboards overflowed with spectacular arrangements of old-fashioned pink roses and white peonies. The centrepieces were scaled-back versions of the same arrangements, placed precisely along the length of the table.

At Meg Wynne's request, the evening was black tie, and as the guests took their places, everyone agreed that reviving the long-abandoned custom of dressing for dinner had been the right thing to do.

As he looked around the room, Emyr's father's face lit up.

"It's wonderful to have so much life in the old place again," Rhys Gruffydd said to Meg Wynne who was seated on his right. "Thank you, dear girl, for organizing this. I know it's terribly old-fashioned of me, but I do miss the days when people used to dress for dinner."

He looked admiringly around the table and then back at the woman who, by this time tomorrow, would be his daughter-in-law.

"Everything looks so beautiful. And it's so good to have the house filled with young people and overnight guests again. I just wish that Emyr's mother could have . . ." His voice trailed off as he contemplated his water glass. After a few moments, he looked at his companion again and continued. "We've been too quiet here, for too long." A wistful smile softened the angular contours of his face. "I hope all that's going to change once you and Emyr have settled in. I know you'll be good for him. No, better than good for him. You'll be the making of the man. You'll give him the strength he needs and be his rock."

"I'm glad you're pleased," Meg Wynne replied. "It's such a beautiful house, and I know it's seen many wonderful parties. We'll bring some of that energy and excitement back."

She smiled at him and lightly touched his hand before turning to have a few words with the guest on her other side.

As the waiters entered to serve the starter, a tomato, red pepper, and orange soup, Meg looked across the table to Emyr who was deep in conversation with David Williams, the old friend he had chosen as his best man.

Suddenly, the sound of Meg's father's voice, raised in alcohol-fuelled anger, registered with the guests and the conversational buzz died away as everyone stopped what they were saying and turned their attention to Bill Thompson.

"I'm telling you, no good will come of it!" he was shouting at his wife. "She's—" He broke off as his wife put her hands to her face in despair and he realized that everyone was watching him.

After a moment of stunned, embarrassed silence, the guests turned back to the person beside them and did their best to pick up conversations where they had left off.

"Take no notice," Rhys whispered to Meg Wynne's profile, covering her hand with his. "He's in his cups and doesn't know what he's saying."

But as Meg Wynne sat staring straight ahead, a dark look of undisguised hatred clouded her face.

The meal continued through the fish course of turbot with lobster sauce, champagne sorbet, main course of roast saddle of Welsh lamb, followed by cappuccino mousse, and finally, a cheese board. Out of consideration for Rhys Gruffydd's failing health and to allow everyone to get to bed by a decent hour, coffee, liqueurs, and Godiva chocolate truffles were served at the table, rather than in the drawing room.

The dinner drew to a close about eleven, chairs were pushed back, and guests gathered up their belongings and made their way to the front entrance where a small van was waiting to give anyone who had been drinking a lift back to the village.

Thank yous and good nights were called back to Emyr and Rhys Gruffydd as they stood in the doorway, lit from behind by the warm glow of the entrance hall, with David standing behind them in the shadows. As the last of the guests departed, Rhys made his way slowly back inside and David and Emyr stepped outside and lit cigarettes.

"Big day tomorrow," David said, blowing smoke at the stars. "Are you up for it? Sure you want to go through with it? It's not too late—you can still change your mind."

"Why on earth would you say that?" Emyr asked irritably, glaring at him. "Of course I want to go through with it and I've never been more sure of anything. I know what I'm doing. I'm not stupid. And it's her I'm marrying, not the parents. When this is over, they won't be coming back. They're only here now because of her mother."

David shrugged and dropping his cigarette, ground it into the gravel with the polished toe of a Gucci evening shoe.

"Of course not. Well, I just thought I should say something," he said smoothly.

"David, for God's sake, if it was the money she was after, she'd have picked you."

David touched his friend on his shoulder and gave him a loose, easy smile.

"In that case, I'm here to support you in every way I

can. You've only to tell me what you want me to do, and I'll do it."

"Well, I'm glad of that," replied Emyr. "Because there's a lot to be done in the morning. We're going to be really busy."

As the exchange hung in the air between them, with its awkward, unpleasant undertones of thoughts unspoken, they silently turned to go back into the house. Emyr paused for a moment on the doorstep and turned back to look at the cloudless sky. Later, a full moon would rise over the valley, drizzling it with a pale honey light.

The van made its way into town, dropping off a few guests along the way before pulling up in front of the Red Dragon.

The two bridesmaids, Jennifer and Anne, delicately pinching the skirts of their evening dresses to lift them up, got out first, followed by Meg Wynne, who helped her mother disembark. Her father was the last one off, but no one waited for him or spoke to him. The little group of women went on ahead and entered the small lobby.

Subdued good nights were said as they made their way up the blue-carpeted stairs to their rooms. The bridesmaids waited as Meg Wynne said good night to her mother at her door, bending down to kiss her on both cheeks, and then the three continued on down the corridor.

"Shall we come in for a bit to help you get settled?" Jennifer asked when they reached Meg's room.

"Mm, I could use some help with the zipper," Meg Wynne replied.

Her father's drinking had spoiled what should have

been a charmed evening, and Meg Wynne was glad of the girls' company as they entered her comfortably furnished room.

With the door firmly closed behind them, Meg Wynne turned to face her friends and released the pent-up emotion of the past hours.

"Bloody typical," she exploded as she threw her beaded evening bag on the bed. "Leave it to him to ruin everything. I wish to God he were dead!"

Behind her, the two bridesmaids exchanged worried glances.

"Look, Meg Wynne," Jennifer began. "I know this is really difficult for you, but I wonder if you should have a word with your dad in the morning and ask him again if he could just try, for one day, to leave off the drinking. Tell him it's ruining your wedding and maybe even let him know that if he starts drinking in the morning that you won't let him attend, let alone walk you down the aisle. That might get his attention."

Jennifer handed Meg Wynne the burgundy leather case for her earrings.

"Stand still," she said to Meg Wynne as she moved around behind her. "I'll undo your dress for you."

Anne, seated in the wing chair beside the window, got up from the chair to close the curtains.

The room overlooked the street, and, glancing down, she saw a shadowy silhouette across the street looking up at the window. She felt a small frisson of anxiety, but shrugging off the feeling, pulled the curtains closed, shutting out the night and the light from the street.

"I'll sleep on it, Jennifer, and do what I think best in the morning. You're right about one thing, though. If I don't do something, he will ruin this wedding, and I'm not going to let him do that. He's only here because of my mother. And I've promised Emyr that this is the one and only time he'll ever be invited here. I don't want him anywhere near me, ever again."

She moved into the bathroom to change into an oyster-coloured satin nightgown and emerged a few minutes later.

"Well, thank you both very much for everything you did this evening. I have to get my face ready for bed now, but before you run along, let's just go over the arrangements again for the morning. I'm getting my nails done at nine, so I should be back here by about ten, and the hairdresser is coming at eleven, so why don't we all meet here at, say, ten-thirty to start getting ready? But we'll change later.

"I'm having an early breakfast in my room because I want to go running. Be sure to bring the checklist and all the planning details, Jennifer, so we can make sure everything is buttoned down.

"Right, off you go. Emyr's going to ring any minute now to say good night, so I'll see you in the morning."

She started to turn away, but remembering the burgundy leather case, held it out to them.

"You're still dressed . . . would you mind awfully walking this downstairs and asking them to put it in the safe? And here," she added, handing them another small box, "might as well keep everything together and give them this one, too. It's the hair clip."

Jennifer and Anne closed the door quietly behind them, just as Meg Wynne's mobile rang. They smiled at each other and started to make their way down the hushed corridor. But as Meg Wynne's voice from behind the closed door got louder, they stopped and looked at each other.

"No, I don't want to do that," they heard her say in a raised voice.

As she broke off, apparently to listen to her caller, Anne and Jennifer, uncomfortable with overhearing what was obviously a private conversation heading into confrontational territory, set off again on their errand, each holding a small box of Meg Wynne's jewellery like magi in a Christmas pageant.

CHAPTER FIVE

Meg Wynne woke early and stretched luxuriously under the light warmth of a summer duvet. She had slept soundly, and was enjoying the sense of well being that a good night's rest often brings until the real world intrudes. This morning, however, felt different and after a moment, she smiled as she remembered it was her wedding day.

Dressing quickly in her running gear, she let herself out of her room and quietly made her way downstairs. The night porter was sitting sleepily behind his desk with a cup of tea and a morning paper as she dropped off her key and made her way out into the cool freshness of a June morning.

After stopping briefly to do a few limbering stretches, she struck off at a fast walk across the square in the direction of the old three-arched bridge that spanned the River Conwy. Forty minutes later, damp with exertion and her face flushed from the intensity of her exercise, she passed by the desk, picked up her key, and returned to her room.

As she stepped out of the shower, a light tap at the door announced the arrival of her breakfast: vanilla yogurt, tea with lemon, a slice of unbuttered whole wheat toast, and half a grapefruit.

Bundled in a soft white towelling robe, her long legs tucked under her and a towel wrapped turban-style over her wet hair, she sipped her tea while looking over her list of things still to be done. She and Emyr had assigned tasks to every member of the wedding party, and the morning would be busy for all of them. She crossed off a few items, added a few more, and then sat quietly for a moment. As the expression on her face changed from one of contemplation to troubled determination, she walked over to the desk, picked up a yellow notepad, and returned to her chair. She began to write, confidently and quickly.

When she had finished, she re-read what she had written and gazed thoughtfully in the direction of the window. Then, with a small, resolute sigh, she folded the paper in half and tore it into small pieces as she walked over to the wastepaper basket. Opening her hand above it, she released a short shower of jagged pieces of yellow paper that fluttered gracefully into the bin. After a quick glance at her watch she began to get dressed and at twenty minutes to nine she set off to keep her appointment.

Promptly at nine the door to the Happy Hands manicure salon opened and Penny looked up as a beautifully groomed young woman entered. Penny smiled, stepped forward to greet her customer, and ushered her into the shop.

"You must be Miss Thompson. Please, have a seat. I've been looking forward to meeting you."

While Meg Wynne had been nibbling on her toast, the groom and his supporters had been tucking into a rather more substantial breakfast at the Hall. Gwennie, who had been working for the family for years and was stopping over for a few days to help out with the wedding, had left cold cereal, yogurts, and juices on the dining room side table, along with a tempting spread of kippers, scrambled eggs, bacon, sausages, and hot buttered toast in silver warming dishes. One by one the men had arrived downstairs, hair still slightly damp from the shower, and lifting the heavy covers of the warming dishes, eagerly helped themselves.

"That was wonderful," said David as Emyr went around the table, coffeepot in hand, offering refills. "Have you thought of doing B and B? You'd look very fetching in your pinny."

Emyr joined good naturedly in the loud laughter as he sat down again.

"Let's hope it won't come to that," he said as he looked around the lovely dining room. "Somehow I can't see Meg Wynne running the valley equivalent of a seaside boardinghouse.

"Now listen, you lot," he said, taking a sheet of yellow paper from his pocket and waving it at them. "Here are our latest marching orders. We've got a lot to get done today, and the girls will kill us if we don't get things right. And they've added more things to the list, it looks like." He studied the page for a moment. "Someone has to get down to the florist to pick up the buttonholes. Oh, and you might as well take the Land Rover. It needs petrol, so you can get it filled up while you're out. Any volunteers?"

The men looked at one another.

"I'll do it," said David. "As the best man, isn't it my job to do your bidding today?"

"As a matter of fact," agreed Emyr amiably, "I think it is."

Tall, blond, and reassuringly well built, David looked like a man who had the money to hire expensive personal trainers, and the time and motivation to follow the regimes they created for him. In contrast, Robbie Llewellyn was short and dark, with the kind of Celtic good looks that had distinguished Welshmen for generations. He had studied law at Cardiff University and after a few years of practice there, had returned home to the Conwy Valley where he was doing well in a general practice.

The men spent the next few minutes dividing up the errands that should keep them occupied all morning, and making plans to meet back at the Hall for a light lunch around one.

"By the way, I heard that Miss Teasdale's died," Robbie Llewellyn said as they pushed back their chairs from the table. "Do you remember her? She was a wonderful teacher, wasn't she? They don't make them like that anymore. You wouldn't believe the clerks we get in these days. Couldn't spell to save their lives and couldn't care less. She really drilled things into us. Hated it at the time, but I'm grateful now."

Emyr and David looked at him.

"I didn't know," said Emyr. "That's too bad."

David murmured sympathetically.

"She was always on at you two," Robbie added. "Telling David he'd have to change his ways if he was ever going to amount to anything and as for you, Emyr, remember how she used to tell you to stand on your own two feet and that you didn't have to do everything that Williams boy told you to?" He had mimicked an English accent in a high-pitched voice for the last part of the sentence and they all laughed at his bad acting skills.

"Well," shrugged David, "what can I say? I guess I've done a whole lot better than they thought I would. But enough about me. Let's get ready to roll." He reached over to take the last piece of bacon, and then, thinking better of it, withdrew his hand and turned toward his friends.

"If it's all right with you, Emyr," said Robbie, "I've got rather a big real estate project on at the minute, so I'd just like to pop into the office for an hour or so this morning. I'll be back in time for lunch, though."

Emyr nodded and tapped him lightly on the chest.

"Just make sure you get through the things on your list. Everything has to go off exactly the way Meg wants it. Exactly."

The men left to go their separate ways and a few minutes later Gwennie crept into the room carrying a large tray on which she began piling the breakfast remains.

Such waste, she thought as she scraped the plates. It's a good job someone in the kitchen knows what to do with that tasty bacon.

Just before ten, as the muted Saturday morning sounds of buses arriving and leaving, parents calling out to children on their way to the swimming baths or library, and shopkeepers greeting customers crept in the open window, Penny began the final stages of the bridal manicure.

"You're done," Penny announced a few minutes later. "Your nails are going to be a bit tacky for the next hour or two, so do be careful. But if anything happens between now and then, come back and I'll give them a quick touch-up. Oh, and good luck, today!"

Penny opened the door, thanked her customer, and stood in the doorway watching as her client started to make her way down the street. A few steps later, the elegant young woman slowed, then turned and returned the way she had come, as if she had forgotten something.

"Was there something else?" Penny asked.

"There is a small thing I'd like you to do for me," she said, offering her bag to Penny. "Please reach in there and get my mobile out for me. I need to make some calls, and I can't be digging about in the bag with wet nails."

"Of course," Penny said as she reached into the bag, pulled out the phone, and handed it to its owner. "Thank you, Miss Thompson, and good luck, again!"

Penny stood on the pavement and watched as she set off in the direction of the hotel. A few moments later she turned the corner and Penny stepped back into her shop.

By eleven, when Meg Wynne was at least half an hour late and there was no response to their repeated knocking on her door, Anne and Jennifer began to feel the first pangs of rising anxiety.

"This isn't like her," Anne said. "Still, anything could have happened. Maybe the manicure lady was backed up and she had to wait. She could have bumped into someone, Emyr maybe, and gone for a coffee and forgotten about the time, or maybe it slipped her mind that we were supposed to be meeting up now. Maybe she's with her parents. She could be anywhere."

The two girls looked at each other and Jennifer shook her head slowly.

"It doesn't feel right, Anne," she said. "You know Meg Wynne. She's meant to be getting married today, for God's sake. Forgotten about the time? I don't think so. She would have phoned if she was going to be late. You'd better ring her and see if you can raise her."

Anne reached into her pocket for her mobile, pressed a key, and listened. After a few moments she shook her head, and began speaking.

"Hey, Meg Wynne, it's Anne. Where are you? You're late and we're getting worried. Ring me. Bye."

She ended the call and replaced the phone in her jacket pocket.

"Right, then, Jennifer. Let's start at the desk and see if anyone's seen her, or maybe she left a message for us there and they forgot to deliver it. Maybe it's as simple as that."

As relief flooded their faces they headed down the stairs and made their way quickly to the reception desk. The night porter was long gone and the quietly efficient Mrs. Geraint, who had been daytime receptionist at the hotel for years, looked up at their approach from behind her official nameplate. Her stiff, heavily lacquered black hair, rigorously applied blue eye shadow which had not changed in decades, and uncompromising navy suit gave her a grave air of respectability left over from an earlier era when unmarried couples, barely able to keep their hands off each other, would sign the register as Mr. and Mrs. Jones for the sake of appearances.

"Yes, hello," Anne began. "We're wondering about our friend Meg Wynn Thompson. We think she went out earlier this morning but she should have been back by now. We can't find her and she doesn't seem to be in her room. We wondered if perhaps she left a message for us?"

"Just a moment, please, and I'll check." Mrs. Geraint riffled through a couple of pink message slips, and then looked up at the two anxious faces.

"No, I'm sorry," she said sympathetically. "There's nothing here for you. No one really leaves messages much anymore; they just ring everybody up on their mobiles. Shall I check and see if her key's here?"

"Yes," the two responded together.

"Her key is here, so she must have gone out."

Anne and Jennifer looked at each other, and then back at Mrs. Geraint.

"She was down to have a manicure at nine," Anne told the receptionist. "Please, just give us a minute," she added as the two friends stepped away from the desk.

"Look," whispered Anne, "there's bound to be a simple answer to this. We'll see if her parents or Emyr know anything, and if they don't, the next logical thing would be for you to leg it around to the manicure shop and see if she's still there. If she isn't, find out when she left and where she was headed. A few more minutes won't make any difference either way but I must say I'm starting to feel a bit uncomfortable with all this."

Jennifer nodded and two stepped back to the reception desk.

"Mrs. Geraint, the hairdresser should be here any minute. If he arrives, please ask him to wait. And the flowers might come, too. If they do, could you just put them away in a fridge and we'll sort them out later, when we know where we're at?"

"Of course," said Mrs. Geraint. "I'm sure she'll turn up. Maybe she just stepped out to pick up a new pair of tights, and it'll have been something and nothing."

Clutching at that new straw of hope, the two girls made their way back upstairs. Moments later they were sitting in Anne's room, as Jennifer tried to fight back the increasing sense of panic that was rapidly turning to fear.

"I'm going to ring her parents' room, just to make sure, but after last night, I imagine that's the last place she would be. On the other hand, she could have dropped in to sort out her dad, I suppose," said Anne, "and it could have taken longer than she thought it would."

She placed the call, asked the question, and listened to the reply.

"Thank you, Mrs. Thompson. Yes, of course, we'll let you know right away if we hear anything."

She put the receiver down and looked at her friend.

"I take it the answer is no," said Jennifer flatly.

"Meg Wynne isn't there, but her dad isn't, either, and Mrs. Thompson doesn't know where he is. He went out a while ago."

"Probably at the off license, getting in his supply of Dutch courage," said Jennifer.

They looked at each other in silence, each girls' mounting concern mirrored in the other's face.

"Right," said Anne. "That's it. You get off to the manicure shop to see if you can find out anything and I'm ringing Emyr."

She reached for her mobile, looked to her friend for final approval, then punched in the numbers.

"Hello, it's Anne here. I'd like to speak to Emyr, please. And tell him it's urgent. Thank you."

A moment later she heard Emyr's calm voice.

"Hi, Anne. What's up?"

"Emyr, is Meg Wynne with you? She's not back from her manicure, she's not answering her door or her mobile, and no one has seen her. Do you think she could have had an accident? We're getting really worried that something's happened. The hairdresser's going to be here any minute and we can't find her. Is she with you? Please say she's with you."

A heavy silence hung between them until finally Emyr said softly, "No, she isn't here. I haven't spoken to her since last night. Hang on. I'll come over to the hotel. Should be there in about twenty minutes."

"Okay," said Anne. "We'll meet you in the bar."

She ended the call, turned to Jennifer, and told her Emyr was on his way.

"Come on, let's get downstairs. I need to think this through and I'm desperate for coffee. I really need to get my head around this."

On their way through the reception area they noticed a meticulously dressed man, with a large suitcase, sitting in the upholstered chair in front of the window. He caught their eye and waved them over.

"Hello. Are you Anne and Jennifer? I'm Alberto, the hairdresser come to do your hair. The receptionist has just told me there's a delay. Not to worry. There's plenty of time. I'll just make myself comfortable here, and you can fetch me when you're ready."

"Oh, Alberto, thank you! We aren't sure what's happening, exactly, so we'll get back to you as soon as we can. Thank you for being so cool," Jennifer said. "So sorry about all this. There's been a mix-up of some kind and we're just trying to get it sorted."

The girls left him under the watchful eye of Mrs. Geraint and Anne hurried into the lounge as Jennifer, with a hopeful wave, set off on the short walk to the Happy Hands manicure shop.

The lounge was empty and Anne chose a table just inside the entrance. A few minutes later she got up, went through to the dining room, and asked if three coffees could be delivered in about ten minutes. Sinking slowly back into her seat, she held her hands out in front of her and studied her nails. A moment later she jumped up, walked over to the window, and looked up and down the street.

As she was about to return to her seat, Mrs. Thompson, looking as drab as the baggy, camel-coloured trousers and loose beige top she was wearing, entered the lounge looking about her like a timid child who has crept fearfully downstairs after dark to see what the grown-ups are doing. Clearly very upset, she placed a hand on Anne's arm, and looked up at her.

"What on earth could be holding her up?" she asked softly, her eyes wide with alarm. "Do you think something has happened to her?"

"Course not, Mrs. Thompson," said Anne in what she hoped was a reassuringly light tone. "She'll just have gone out for a pair of tights or something like that. You'll see. She'll be back any minute."

Meg Wynne's mother, who seemed diminished in the bright light from the tall windows, nodded and then, seeming to take comfort from Anne's words, pulled herself together.

"I think I'll just walk around the town for a bit and see if I can spot her," she said. "After all, it's not a very big place, is it, and she can't have gone far."

"That's a good idea," said Anne heartily. "And we'll let you know just as soon we hear anything."

Mrs. Thompson hesitated.

"I just feel I'd rather be doing something. I'm feeling so anxious just waiting around. And I don't want to be alone in that room."

More like she doesn't want to be alone in the room when that drunken brute of a husband gets back, thought Anne. God, what a way to live.

Mrs. Thompson slipped out of the room as invisibly as she had entered it.

A few minutes later, Emyr arrived, looking mildly flustered, but in control. Anne stood up to hug him and before they could speak, a waiter arrived with a pot of coffee. As they sat down and prepared to pour it, Jennifer bounded into the room.

"You don't need to tell me, Jennifer; I can tell from the look on your face," Anne said.

Jennifer shook her head and swallowed. "I spoke to the manicurist. Meg Wynne arrived on time, had the manicure, left, and that's all there was to it," she said. "Good job I got there when I did, though. She was just closing for the afternoon." Turning to Emyr, she continued, "We're worried, Emyr. It's simply not like her to disappear like this, without saying anything to anyone. You must see that."

Emyr took a sip of coffee and gently placed the cup back on the saucer.

"Honestly, Jennifer, I think you're overreacting. She could be anywhere, doing just about anything. It hasn't been that long, has it?"

The two girls looked at each other, and then Anne put into words what each had been thinking.

"Emyr, was everything all right between the two of you last night? You didn't have a row or anything, did you? I know it's an awful thing to think, let alone ask, but do you think she could have changed her mind, and just, well, bolted? Done a runner?"

Emyr looked so startled and then, a look of such dismay flashed across his face, that Anne was almost sorry she had suggested it.

"No, honestly, everything was fine," he said. "She wasn't getting cold feet or anything like that. I'm as puzzled as you are by all this, but I think she's just been delayed somewhere and she'll be back any minute.

"So I think you two should carry on, get your hair done, and get dressed, or do whatever it is girls are supposed to do before a wedding, and we'll all just go ahead with everything and stick to the plan. What else can we do?"

He looked from one to the other.

"David's gone to sort out a problem with the buttonholes—they were supposed to have a Gruffydd ribbon on them and they didn't so he's over the road at the florist's waiting while they put that right. Shouldn't take too long."

As he stood to leave, Anne pulled him back down into his chair.

"Emyr, we haven't been in her room. I think you should get the key from the desk so we can take a look around. We didn't want to go in until you got here. We need to check her room, just in case."

"In case what?"

"Well, what if she's fallen in the bath and hurt herself? Or we can see if her clothes are missing, or if it looks as if she's coming back, or whatever. At least then we might be nearer to an answer. I'm just so confused by all this. It's starting to seem so unreal, like it's happening in a dream. Jennifer and I are concerned, and we want to do whatever needs to be done."

Emyr looked from one to the other, and then stood up again.

"Okay, let's go. We'll get the key."

They made their way to the front desk.

Mrs. Geraint looked up from her daybook and expecting what was coming, reached behind her for the key to Meg Wynne's room.

"Under the circumstances, the manager will have to accompany you. Just let me ring through to his office."

She picked up the telephone, and when the manager answered, spoke briefly.

"Mr. Burton, it's the situation I told you about. They want access to her room."

After a brief pause, she replaced the receiver, and nodded in the direction of the dining room door.

"He'll be right out. It's hotel policy that we would never give a key to a guest's room unless a manager is present. I am sure you understand. It's for your own protection, really."

The three nodded and stepped back toward the stairs as the hotel manager entered the reception area.

He clasped his hands in front of his chest and gave a nervous chuckle.

"Good morning," he said, glancing at the old-fashioned room key Mrs. Geraint handed him. "I hear you have some concerns that your friend hasn't turned up. Let's go on up and take a look, then, shall we?"

He led the way. Halfway up the stairs, the manager paused and turned to face them. His blue dress shirt, under a suit that needed pressing, was pulled tight across his stomach, anchored by protesting buttons.

"I'm sure she'll turn up. What would a wedding be without a hitch or two?"

CHAPTER SIX

As the little group reached the door of Meg Wynne's room, the manager paused. Then, at a nod from Emyr, he knocked firmly on the door, and waited for a response. When there was none, he said in a loud, firm voice, "Hello, Ms. Thompson? It's the manager here. Is everything all right? I am here with your fiancé and friends, and we'd like to come in."

After again looking to Emyr, he placed the key in the lock, turned it slowly, and opened the door. Quietly, respectfully even, he entered the room and motioned for the others to follow.

The room looked as if it had been given a good tidy up. The duvet had been drawn up, the wastepaper basket was empty, the drawers and doors were closed, and everything seemed in order. A faintly floral fragrance hung in the air.

"Could she be in the loo?" Anne whispered.

The door was open, and a quick glance revealed that Meg Wynne was not there.

"It doesn't look to me as if she left in a hurry," Emyr said. "It looks as if she just stepped out for a moment, and will be back at any minute."

"Neat and tidy, is she, then, your fiancée?" the manager asked. "Does this room look the way you'd expect her to leave it? I can check and see if the maid has been in, but it looks as if she has."

Emyr nodded.

The level of tension in the room was almost unbearable. Finally, Anne looked toward the closet and taking a deep breath, suggested they look inside.

"We need to know if her clothes are here, or if it looks as if she's gone. I'm sorry, Emyr, but we do need to know. You must see that."

His face betraying no sign of emotion, Emyr nodded. "I'll do it."

Grasping the glass doorknob, he pulled the door open, then leaned forward for a closer look as the two girls crowded in behind him.

"I think it's all here, but you look," he said as he stepped to one side.

Anne and Jennifer peered in. There was Meg's gown from last night, a business suit, a couple of jackets and blouses, three pairs of jeans and in a plastic wardrobe bag, her wedding dress. Shoe boxes lay neatly lined up on the floor along with a little pile of running gear.

"The clothes she brought with her seem to be there," said Anne thoughtfully, "and she's already moved some into the Hall. I don't know what she was wearing this morning, I don't know everything she brought with her, but it all looks okay. The thing is, though, what about the jewellery?"

She turned to the manager.

"Meg Wynne had some beautiful pieces with her. We brought a couple of boxes down ourselves last night," she said. "Do you know if others were placed with you for safekeeping?"

"We were given a few boxes," he replied, "but of

course I wouldn't know what was in them. Mrs. Geraint gave Ms. Thompson a receipt for them, and as far as I know, they're still in the safe."

The group looked at one another in silence as Emyr sank down on the edge of the bed.

"Well," he said, "she isn't here now, and I have no idea what's going on, or what to do. What time is it, anyway?"

Anne glanced at her watch. "It's getting on for one."

Emyr sighed.

"I think what we should do, all we can do, really, is carry on. We can't call it off. What if she came back only to find we'd given up on her? That would be . . ." The uncompleted sentence hung in the air.

He stood up and walked over to the dresser where Meg Wynne had left a few toiletries. He picked up her favourite perfume, gently removed the cap, and after a moment's hesitation, closed his eyes and held the bottle to his nose.

Anne and Jennifer moved at the same time toward him.

"It's okay," he said. "Go downstairs and get the hairdresser. Let's do it. We've got people driving in from England all the way to Wales, and everything's all arranged. Come on, you've got to get ready."

With one last look around, the friends filed out, leaving the manager to pull the door quietly shut behind them.

"Emyr," said Anne, turning to him when they were in the corridor, "I'm sorry, but I have to say this. I think we should ring around the hospitals. What if she's been hurt?"

Emyr looked startled.

"Maybe you're right. I'll do it when I get home," he

said as they walked on. "In the meantime, go to your rooms and I'll tell the hairdresser to go on up."

Anne and Jennifer exchanged a quick glance, and Anne spoke for both of them.

"I'm moving my gear into Jennifer's room. Tell the hairdresser to come to room two-oh-six. But give us ten minutes."

Emyr nodded, and with the manager, headed in the direction of the stairs as Anne and Jennifer returned to their rooms.

A few minutes later Anne, laden with an armful of bags and clothes, pushed her way into Jennifer's room, threw the clothes on the nearest bed, and sat down beside them.

"I'm really starting to get scared, Jenn. I'm beyond worried. It's all seeming like a bad dream now, that I can't wake up out of. It's just going on and on."

Jennifer looked thoughtfully at her.

"There's one thing I don't get," Anne went on. "Is Emyr in complete and utter denial? Why would he not call the police? They might be able to help. That's what they're here for and they're good at this kind of thing. They know what to do. We don't. Or at least I don't."

Jennifer pushed the pile of clothes out of the way and sat down beside her friend.

"I know, Anne. I feel the same. But we've got to do this, like Emyr says. I don't think we have a choice. Look, let's send down for some sandwiches, cold drinks, and fruit so at least we can have a bit of lunch. I'm not particularly hungry, but it's something we should do. It's like in those awful movies when things start to go wrong, and someone will say, 'You have to keep your strength up,' or," and Anne joined in, 'What you need is a nice cup of tea!'"

They smiled at each other, and then Anne reached for the telephone.

"I think there's something in that," she said. "Actually, I do fancy a nice cup of tea. Do us good. I'll order one for the hairdresser, too. What was his name, again?"

"Alberto," said Jennifer.

"Alberto," laughed Anne. "In real life, he's probably Benny from Birmingham and nobody took any notice of him until he went upmarket as Alberto."

The brief burst of laughter had eased their tension and a few moments later when Alberto appeared, they were in better spirits and ready for him.

"We've ordered up tea for you," Anne told him, "and lunch for all of us. I know you've been kept waiting and you must be famished. Who do you want to do first?"

"Oh, it doesn't matter to me, dear girl," he said. "What are you wearing in your hair? Any flowers, clips, bandeau, fascinator, diadem, tiaras, hats, or anything like that?

"God, no," said Anne. "Just hair, that's all. We want it just like it is, only better."

Alberto laid out his kit on a towel and went to work wetting down her blunt-cut hair, so he could style it. He was a rather burly man, with a neatly trimmed beard and long eyebrow hairs that gave him the look of a startled artist. He caught some strands of her hair between his index and middle fingers and examined them closely.

"So what's happened to your friend, then?" he asked. "Any news?"

"No," replied Jennifer. "No news. Have you ever heard of this happening before?

"Hmm, I don't think so," Alberto replied. "Not the bride just up and disappearing, although I did have a bride cancel the wedding at the last minute, once. It was terrible. One of the bridesmaids had heard from the best man, who thought it absolutely hilarious, that the groom had had it off with some tart the night before, and she decided to tell the bride all about it. Thought she would want to know. The poor woman was hysterical, as you can imagine, and said she couldn't marry the man because if he would do that on the night before they got wed, how could she trust him after they were married?"

As Alberto reached for his hair dryer, a knock on the door signalled the arrival of tea and sandwiches. While he looked around for the nearest electrical outlet, Jennifer opened the door, brought in the tray, and set it down on the dresser. With his hair dryer in one hand and styling brush in the other, he added shape and volume to Anne's hair as he continued his story.

"I've often thought about that whole scenario. Would it have happened if the groom hadn't been drunk? Did the bridesmaid do right to tell the bride? I think so. If it had been me, I would have wanted to know. Should the bride have called off the wedding? I think it took a lot of courage to do that. There's the whole issue of everything already paid for, and what people will say."

Anne and Jennifer were silent, lost in their thoughts.

"You know, I could murder for a cup of tea. Why don't we take a break now and we'll sort out Jennifer in a few minutes. Shall I be mother?"

Alberto poured the tea, handed it around, helped himself to several sandwiches, and then gingerly lowered himself into the most comfortable chair in the room.

"What happened to that bride afterward?" asked Anne.

"I don't know," said Alberto. "If she changed her mind and married the bloke later, or if she married someone else, I wasn't invited back to do her hair a second time. The really interesting thing was, she made up her mind to call it off when I was only halfway finished with her, and told me to get my hands off her head and leave her alone. So I did, and she spent the rest of the day with only half her hair done. It was the strangest thing. Made her look very wild."

"She must have been past caring," said Anne.

"Oh, she was that, all right," agreed Alberto. "At least about the hair."

Twenty minutes later Jennifer's hair was done and Alberto was packing up his things and getting ready to leave.

"Look," he said, "I'm sure your friend will turn up, but I've got other appointments booked, and I need to move on. Here's my card so just call me on my mobile if you want me to come back later to see to her. Come to think of it, I wouldn't mind a call later anyway, telling me what this is all about."

The girls thanked him and showed him out.

"Well," said Anne, "I'll leave a message for Meg Wynne downstairs with reception and on her room phone that we're waiting here for her."

She closed the door behind her, leaving Jennifer contemplating the little bowl of fruit.

CHAPTER SEVEN

Emyr drove slowly through the town before reaching the turnoff that would take him to Ty Brith. He knew that his next task on this terrible, confusing day would be to tell his father that Meg Wynne was missing, and he was absolutely dreading it.

In the final stages of pancreatic cancer, Rhys was so frail, and going downhill so rapidly, that Emyr was afraid of the effect this news would have on his much-loved father. He wondered if he should ask the doctor to be present when he told him, and then decided there wasn't time.

As he drove up the final stretch to the Hall, he pictured the candlelit scene from the night before. How happy Dad had been, he thought. Everything reminded him so much of the good old days—the women in their evening dresses, the men in black tie, the delicious food so beautifully presented, the way the dining room had been done up. It had been months since Emyr had seen Rhys looking so animated and engaged. The dinner party had done his father so much good and now, just one day later, everything seemed poised to crash and burn.

He parked his car at the back of the Hall and pushed open the door to the back passageway. The familiar slate tiles, the anoraks hanging on hooks with muddy boots lined up beneath them and a jumble of umbrellas jammed into a hideous dog-shaped stand all seemed so familiar and ordinary.

He walked into the kitchen to find Gwennie seated at the table dressed in her day uniform of grey dress with white collar and cuffs, eating a ham and tomato sandwich. His sleepy black Lab rose from her bed by the Aga, stretched, and ambled over to greet him.

"Hey, Trixxi," he said as he reached under her sporty red and white bandana to ruffle the fur on her neck. "Who's my good girl, then? No, we're not going walking. Finish your nap and then someone will take you out."

Obediently she returned to her bed, turned around in it a couple of times, and with a small sigh, flopped down, and closed her eyes.

"Where is everybody, Gwennie?" he asked.

She looked up at him.

"The boys are in the dining room just starting their lunch and Louise is seeing to your father, Mr. Emyr," she said. "He's up in his room, getting ready, I believe. By the way, Trixxi has already been out. Had a good ramble, by the looks of her. I had to pull one or two burrs off her."

"Right, Gwennie, thanks."

He opened the kitchen door and entered the long downstairs corridor that would take him to the front hall. When he reached the stairs, he put his hand on the well-worn, well-polished carved banister and swung around it as he had done countless times since he was a child. Slowly he walked up the stairs until he reached the first floor, then headed down the hall toward his father's room, located at the end of the corridor.

He knocked and then entered.

The room was not only spacious, with the high ceilings of a more gracious era, but it was a corner room, with magnificent floor-to-ceiling windows overlooking the sweep of the driveway at the front of the house on one side, and a matching set of windows giving a spectacular view of the valley on the adjoining side. The room had recently been redecorated and was masculine, functional, and restful in soft beige tones with dark brown accent pieces.

Rhys was seated in the wing chair beside his bed, wearing a comfortable dressing gown and slippers.

"Hello, Emyr," he smiled. "I've had my bath, and I'll be getting dressed soon. How are you holding up, then? All right?"

Emyr looked at his father's nurse, who was busy sorting out cuff links.

"Louise, I wonder if you'd be kind enough to leave us for a few moments," he said.

The woman nodded, set the cuff links on the dresser, and quietly left the room, closing the door behind her.

Emyr sat down on the edge of the bed, took his father's hand in his, and looked at him.

"Dad, I don't really know how to tell you this, and well, to be honest, I'm not even sure what to tell you, but something has gone wrong, and unfortunately, we don't even really know what's happened. But Meg Wynne seems to have gone missing, without saying a word to anyone. She didn't say anything to me. I haven't spoken to her since last night. She didn't call the wedding off, she's just not here. We can't find her and we don't know where she is or what's going on."

The old man sighed.

"I'm so sorry, Emyr. This must be unbearable for you. She left no note, no word, nothing?"

Emyr shook his head.

"Not with me, not with Anne or Jennifer. Nothing. She went out this morning, and now she's, well, vanished. She's just not here anymore. Nobody has seen her, nobody knows anything."

Rhys seemed to shrink inside himself, as if the news had diminished him.

"So what are you going to do?" he asked.

"Well, it's too late to call the wedding off, because people are driving in from all over the place, and we can't get in touch with them. They'll most likely go directly to the church, so what we're doing is just carrying on."

"I think that's all you can do," Rhys agreed. "By the way, have you told the rector? He needs to know."

"Oh, God, I didn't think of that," Emyr said. "I'll get David to do that. He can sort out some of the details. We'd better call her parents again, too, unless Anne or Jennifer already did that."

Rhys sat quietly for a moment, and then looked at his son.

"Have you called the hospitals? What about the police?"

Emyr shook his head.

"Dear boy, I think I'd like to lie down now. I'm not going to get dressed and go to the church. I'll stay here and you can let me know what happens. But, Emyr, I think you should call the police sooner rather than later."

He sighed and reached up to touch his son.

"This has really knocked the stuffing out of me and although I would have made the effort for her, not now. Not for this. Ask Louise to come back in now. I'm very tired and I need to lie down. You get on and do what you have to do. Forgive me."

Emyr patted his father's shoulder and nodded. He left the room to find his father's nurse, and then went in search of his reliable, trustworthy old friend.

It was rumoured that David had made a lot of money in the booming London real estate market and although he had apparently held down no real job for years, he lived very well in an understated mews house in Devonshire Place, from which he was unself-consciously building a reputation as a dedicated man about town. Celebrity-studded charity events and dinner parties or nightclubbing into the wee hours with the drunken daughters of a viscount seemed to take up more and more of his time. Impossible-to-get front row seats for opening nights and backstage passes at sold-out rock concerts were no problem for him. But amongst the people in his set, dark whispers were starting to circulate of long nights spent at exclusive gaming tables with careless wagering costing him astronomical sums.

David was in his bedroom, talking on his mobile as he mixed a whisky and soda from the drinks tray.

"How many?" he was saying. "We need three times that many. Tell them to get their fingers out and get it done." He pressed the button to end the call, set the mobile down on the windowsill, and looked up as Emyr entered.

"You all right, old son? You don't look so good. Getting nervous? Here have a drink with me, and then we'll get changed. Get you to the church on time and all that, eh?" He sipped his drink.

Unable to meet his gaze, Emyr looked around the room and then out the window at sheep grazing in the lower field.

"David, it's bad news, and it's getting worse, I'm afraid."

He told his friend that Meg Wynne was missing, and then asked him to help sort out the logistics of informing the people who needed to be told.

"You can get the numbers from the directory in the estate office downstairs. You'll have to call the rector—he might already be at the church—or leave a message with his wife. And call Meg Wynne's parents at the hotel and then check in with Anne and Jennifer. Tell them my mobile's switched on. I think they're in Anne's room now, maybe Jennifer's, I can't remember. Reception should know. Or try both. Do whatever you have to do. Oh, and for what it's worth, I tried calling Meg Wynne in London but there's no answer and her mobile isn't switched on.

"I'm going to ring the hospitals, and you'll just have to try to stay on top of everything else, David. I'm sorry to dump all this on you, but I can't think what else to do. And I can't handle all the details. And speaking of details, you might have to cancel the photographer and the disc jockey—all that. The girls will know what to do, and they'll help you. Ring them."

David gave his friend a sympathetic look and put his hand on his arm.

"I'm really sorry it's come to this, Emyr. But maybe she just decided at the last minute marrying you wasn't right for her. Maybe this is for the best."

"For the best! What the hell are you saying? How could not turning up for her own wedding possibly be 'for the best'? Best for who?" He shot a look of pure anger at his best man and then exhaled softly. "Look, I don't think anything would have prevented her from marrying me. As awful as it is, I'm starting to think that the only reason she's not here is because she can't be. I think something's happened to her."

He ran his fingers through his hair and turned to look out the window.

"If she'd just been delayed, held up somewhere, see, she would have called by now. This is serious."

He gestured to David's phone.

"Now, please, make the calls, there's a good lad."

Emyr turned to go as David reached for his mobile.

In her flat above the shop, Penny reached for her jacket. She'd planned to spend the afternoon painting, an escape she normally looked forward to, but this afternoon she felt unsettled and out of sorts. At first, she thought her sense of unease and anxiety had to do with Emma's passing but as she picked up her field painting case, her thoughts returned to that odd incident in the shop just before closing when the bridesmaid had rushed in, panting slightly, asking after Meg Wynne Thompson.

There's something not right there, she thought. Still, it's probably all been sorted by now.

She shrugged off the feeling as she let herself out of the flat, locking the door as she balanced her portable easel, folding stool, and painting case filled with brushes, papers, and paints.

To supplement her income, she sold watercolour landscapes in the small art gallery above the village tea shop. Views of Llanelen, nearby Gwyther Castle, Bodnant Gardens, and neighbouring towns were always popular with tourists and, in the summer, she had trouble keeping up with the demand.

She had lived on her own for a long time. There had been boyfriends along the way, a serious involvement even, but no permanent man in her life. She sometimes felt a deep sadness about that, thinking about all she had missed and how much easier her life might have been if she had not had to rely so much on herself. But she had had a difficult, complicated childhood in Nova Scotia, in and out of foster homes, and found affection hard to give and harder to receive, although she certainly tried to be kind and considerate in a genuine, sincere way. Several of her boyfriends had wondered vaguely why she always seemed to sell herself short, and why she had apparently settled for so little. But her life was what she had made it, and by not asking for or expecting very much from anyone, she hadn't been given very much. Still, at some point she had recognized that when she was on her own, she was in pretty decent company.

Everything she had, she had earned herself. With no encouragement or support from anyone, she had determined early on that what she needed above all else was an education and she had put herself through Mount Allison University, earning a bachelor's degree in fine arts. The summer after she graduated she worked endless hours in a downtown bar, earned enough money for a plane ticket to Paris, and set off to see the magnificent collections in the great art houses and museums of Europe. It was a life-changing experience and she knew by the end of that summer that she would not be returning to Canada.

She felt she belonged in Britain, telling herself that she would recognize her home when she found it, and it had almost happened that way. The reality was that Llanelen had seduced her. The true beauty of the valley, Penny had come to realize over the years, lay in its ever-changing timelessness. It had been what it was for centuries, and yet, somehow, depending on the season, the weather and even the time of day, it was constantly renewing itself. She had never tired of it or taken it for granted.

But if the magnificent, constantly changing views had attracted and held her, it was the welcoming warmth of the Welsh people she had come to love.

She had been sketching and painting in the area for so long that a few years ago, when her greatest challenge became finding fresh ways to look at familiar scenes, she had started the Stretch and Sketch club and invited other local artists, with varying degrees of expertise and enthusiasm, to join. The members rambled and painted together and turned to one another for support and suggestions.

"Have you been up to Ffridd Uchaf," one artist would ask another. "The leaves are phenomenal in the pasture at the moment. You should try to get up there before the rain brings them down."

The group invited a guest speaker to join them every other month or so at a breakfast meeting held in the small meeting room of the Red Dragon Hotel. A favourite speaker had been a botanist from nearby Bodnant Gardens who described in great detail the secret lives of plants. Another time, a representative from an artists' supply company who recognized a target-rich audience when he saw one, had cheerfully driven a few miles out of his way to demonstrate the benefits of his company's new and improved lines of papers and paints.

As she trudged along, the day's crowded thoughts gradually fell away, leaving her mind free to focus on the painting to come and as she entered the woods, with its sun-dappled canopy of leaves, she felt energized and refreshed by the soft squelching of leaves underfoot and the summery sound of birdsong. Before long, she reached a clearing with a view of the river and in the distance, a neighbouring village. She paused for a moment to take in the boundless blue of the sky, embellished with a smattering of fluffy clouds. She unpacked her gear, set up her stool, unfolded her easel, and put up a piece of rough watercolour paper. The afternoon sun slanted down the valley and as the subtleties of light and shadow changed from minute to minute, she gazed at the scenery through her homemade viewfinder. After choosing a small group of grazing sheep as her focal point, she began a quick sketch of the sheep and the trees and hills that surrounded them.

She enjoyed the feeling that painting outdoors, or en plein air, always brought—that she was where she belonged, doing what she was meant to be doing. She reached down and swirled her sable brush in a little jar of water, and then opened her travelling palette case. She eyed the cobalt blue, and once more looked up at the sky. Within minutes she was lost in her work, the whispering brushstrokes gradually laying down the view in front of her.

By three-thirty, Emyr, David, and Robbie Llewellyn were dressed and ready to leave for the church. They made their way downstairs and through the house, past Gwennie who stood at the entrance to the kitchen. When they reached the parking lot at the back of the house, they all turned toward David's BMW.

"I think we should take the Range Rover, Emyr," David said, gesturing at the Hall's utility vehicle. "I'm having a bit of trouble with mine; I think the alternator's going. We'll be better off in yours. Don't want mine giving up the ghost in the middle of the High Street."

Emyr and Robbie stopped.

"Okay, David, but the Rover isn't as clean as it should have been. There's a lot of mud and spatter on it. Still, does it matter?"

"Well, look, Emyr, let's do it this way. We'll take the

Rover, but I'll drive." He motioned to Robbie. "Hop in the back."

When everyone was settled, David put the car in gear and they set off down the long driveway on their silent journey to the church.

A short time later they pulled up in front of St. Elen's, the beautiful stone church that had been given pride of place several centuries earlier in its majestic setting beside the river. The group made their way along the path leading to the church where a small group of wedding guests had gathered. The pastel blues, pinks, greens, lilacs, and ivories of the women's elaborate hats and coat dresses contrasted with the sturdy stone of the church's façade, lending an air of festivity and lightness.

Emyr and his groomsmen passed quickly into the church, with a few nods here and there, and walked to the vestry where the rector had said he would be waiting for them.

"Ah, Emyr," said Rev. Evans as he stretched out his hand. "I am so sorry to hear there has been a problem with Meg Wynne. I do hope she's all right. We must try to think how we can handle this for the best, to give as much dignity as we can to the occasion. I take it you have still not heard from her?"

"No," said Emyr, "nothing. We've rung the hospitals but nobody has seen her."

"Right, well then," said the rector. "Then here's what I suggest we do."

By four o'clock, as gentle organ music provided a soothing backdrop, the congregation was seated, amid the usual rustling, whispering, throat clearing, glancing about to see who had been invited and who had not, and smiling and gesturing at old friends.

Emyr and David took their places at the front of the church, and stared ahead.

Silence fell as Robbie appeared at the back of the church with Mrs. Thompson on his arm. She was dressed in a floor-length beige dress with a detailed floral pattern embroidered across the bodice. Her matching hat, with broad brim and spiky leaves bobbing off it, could not hide her puffy, red eyes or look of bewilderment. The guests watched as the two made their way slowly down the aisle, followed by Mr. Thompson, red faced and sweating.

As they realized what they were seeing, guests turned to each other and a low murmur filled the church. Why wouldn't the father of the bride be walking down the aisle with his daughter? Something must be very wrong. After seeing Mrs. Thompson into her pew, and watching as her husband awkwardly took his place beside her, Robbie returned to the rear of the church to watch and wait.

The sanctuary, with its whitewashed walls, carved rood screen, choir stalls, and dark roof beams had been tastefully decorated in an understated way; there were no bows on the pews or strategically placed flower arrangements. The only floral pieces were two enormous baskets of pink peonies, in perfect proportion for the size of the room, which had been set at the front of the church on either side of the altar.

The rector stepped in front of the congregation, and held up his hand. As the late-afternoon sun filtered through the stained-glass window, scattering a kaleidoscope of colours across his snowy surplice, the music stopped and a heavy, ominous silence settled over the assembled guests.

"*Prynhawn da,*" he greeted the congregation in Welsh. "Good afternoon.

"Ladies and gentlemen, I am afraid I have an important announcement to make."

An immediate hush, lightly laced with a frisson of excitement at such an unusual beginning to a wedding, swept over the crowd.

"It seems that our bride, Meg Wynne Thompson is missing, and . . ."

The wedding guests turned to one another with varying degrees of shock, confusion, or mild misplaced amusement on their faces and began whispering.

The rector, looking as stern as members of his regular Sunday morning congregation had ever seen him, again held up his hand and looked sternly from one side of the room to the other.

". . . and as I have never been in this position before, I am not sure exactly how best to proceed. But I think we should all sit quietly here, and please remember exactly where you are, for about twenty minutes to give the bride time to arrive if there has been a delay or she has been held up for some reason we haven't been told about. At the end of that time, I will speak to you again."

As Rev. Evans sat down in his chair at the front of the church, the organ recital resumed and the minutes ticked by with unbearable slowness as somber organ music filled the church.

After what seemed an eternity, the jarring, anachronistic sound of a ringing mobile snapped everyone back to reality. All eyes turned to Emyr as he quickly left his pew, ducked behind the screen, and then emerged a few moments later and whispered something to the rector who then gave a tiny shake of his head.

Rev. Evans again stood before the congregation, his eyes dark with concern. He looked at his wife for reassurance, and when she gave him a slight nod of encouragement, he began to speak.

"I have to tell you now that as we have received no word of Meg Wynne, we are going to consider the wedding, on this day, to be postponed. As it is getting on for teatime, and many of you have come a long way, we are suggesting that you make your way to the Red Dragon Hotel where a meal has been prepared for you.

"So now, I would ask that we leave the church in a quiet, orderly fashion, starting with those in the back rows. The families will leave last."

The shocked stillness that had settled over the congregation was broken only by the heart-wrenching sound of sobbing coming from the front row. Meg Wynne's father, unused to performing small gestures of comfort but seeming to recognize that something was expected of him, put a stiff, reluctant arm around his weeping wife's shoulder.

CHAPTER EIGHT

At four-thirty, Anne stood up, smoothed the front of her bridesmaid's dress, and walked slowly and resolutely toward the closet.

"Whatever it is, Jenn, it's over and I'm getting changed out of this bloody dress."

"Me, too," Jennifer replied. "I doubt I'll be wearing this dress again. Can you think of any reason why you would wear yours?"

Anne shook her head as she stepped lightly out of her frock, leaving a slippery puddle of pale pink silk in the middle of the floor.

Jennifer picked it up, folded it carefully, and set it on the bed. A moment later, hers had joined it.

"We'll keep them together and take them to a charity shop, yeah?" she said. "They'll be more use as a set. Maybe they'll bring someone else better luck, someone who doesn't know their story. I wonder if we even need to get them dry-cleaned. After all, we never even got to leave the room in them. Pity, that. They were really lovely dresses."

After a long day of intense pent-up frustration and mounting fear, the tears finally came, suddenly and in abundance. She reached for some tissues, sat on the bed, and wept silently for her lost friend. As Anne started toward her, arms outstretched, the telephone rang.

"Hello? Yes?" Anne said. After a moment of listening silence, while keeping an anxious eye on her distraught friend, she replied firmly, "Yes, David, I see. Right. Well, what else could you do, really? Yes, I'll tell Jenn and we'll ring you later. Thanks for letting us know. Bye."

She replaced the telephone and sat down beside Jennifer.

"That was David. The rector's made the announcement. He and Emyr have left the church and are on their way to Ty Brith to be with Emyr's father. Apparently he's taking all this very hard. Well, he would do, wouldn't he? So the people from the wedding have been sent over here for their meal, David's called off the photographer and the deejay, and he's asking us if we can sort things out here, keep an eye on everything, whatever that means. And oh yes, they've finally called the police.

"It's getting on now for five, so we'll need to keep all the rooms until tomorrow anyway. Also, the police could arrive at any time, and I expect they'll want to talk to us, and see what we know, which isn't much.

"This isn't nearly over, Jenn. In fact, I think something really bad must have happened, so we'll have to hang together on this."

She paused to give her friend time to collect herself, but the tears kept coming.

"Well, you have a good cry, and when you're feeling a little better, we'll decide what to do next. Are you hungry? Do you think we should go downstairs and show ourselves at the reception, or whatever it would be called?"

Jennifer started to wail.

"No, probably not," Anne answered her own question. "There will be too many people asking questions. Why don't you rest up for a few minutes? Me, I need a proper drink and God knows I deserve it. I'll be back in about twenty minutes."

She closed the door behind her, then opened it again and popped her head back into the room.

"You know, Jenn, I've just thought that if the police are going to be arriving here at any minute, we might as well get ready for them. The first thing they'll ask is, 'When did you notice she was missing?' Personally, I think they'll wonder why they weren't called in sooner. Right, I'm off. See you later or join me in the bar if you feel like coming downstairs."

As she made her way down the carpeted stairs to the ground floor, the soft sound of murmured conversation rose to greet her. She wondered if she should look in at the small group of disoriented wedding guests that had gathered for a subdued meal in the hotel's ground-floor reception room. Deciding against it, she strode purposefully to the lounge and ordered a large vodka and tonic. Taking it to an empty table near the window, she sat down and took a long, grateful sip. It had been an endless, emotionally draining day and she hoped she would never have to go through anything like it again. As she was about to take her second sip, she was hit by the flash of understanding and insight of a sudden idea when she realized that as of tomorrow, things were going to get much worse.

When she returned to the room Jennifer was feeling a little better. She had stopped crying and was in the bathroom trying to repair her red, blotchy face.

"Now the way I see it, Jenn," said Anne, "we need to call Emyr immediately and get him ready for the time he's about to spend in the media spotlight. We need to designate a spokesperson, and put together a media plan. And we need to do it tonight, before the police get here."

The call to the police had been logged in at the small North Wales police station in Llanelen and then passed on to Llandudno. Missing persons cases are always taken seriously, and given the circumstances of this one, the sergeant who took the call gave it a high priority. The case was passed on to a senior officer, who summoned his sergeant, and together they set off for the Red Dragon Hotel in Llanelen.

"Now this case is a bit unusual," Detective Chief Inspector Gareth Davies told his sergeant as she drove along the narrow country road trying not to scrape the high hedges or low stone fences that seemed to be about two inches from their unmarked car. "Normally, the husband would be the next of kin, but in this case, because they weren't actually married, we'll have to start with the parents and see what they can tell us. We'll ask them to sign the release form in case we need to distribute photographs."

The detective chief inspector was tall, in his midfifties, with a handsome head of grey hair neatly but not fussily trimmed. His face had a kindly, understanding look about it, which made him seem approachable, congenial even, but prime suspects in the past had learned the hard way that he was not the collegial fellow he seemed. His love of cycling kept him fit and his love of gardening meant he had something in common with just about everybody. His companion, Detective Sergeant Bethan Morgan, was considerably younger, and blessed with a head of dark curls and a ready smile which gave her a fresh, uncomplicated look. She was keen to get on in her career and radiated the kind of enthusiasm that her superiors found both endearing and mildly alarming.

Half an hour later they pulled up at the hotel, entered the lobby, and asked at the reception desk for the Thompsons' room.

Their knock was answered by a distraught, worn-out woman.

"Yes?" she asked anxiously.

"Hello. I'm Detective Chief Inspector Gareth Davies and this is Detective Sergeant Bethan Morgan. We're following up on a report of a missing person, Meg Wynne Thompson, and we'd like to talk to you. You are her parents? Good. May we come in?"

Mrs. Thompson stood to one side as the police officers entered.

"Please," she said, "I'm so glad you're here. If you can find a place to sit, do."

Accompanied by the sound of a toilet flushing, her husband emerged from the en suite lavatory to find the two officers standing near the window, their eyes scanning the room. Thompson was a big man, exuding bluster and resentment mixed in with the sour smell of last night's drink. Decades of hard drinking and smoking showed in every line on his face.

"We don't know anything about this," he almost shouted at the officers. "We barely know her anymore. She's got a mind of her own and what she's done, we don't know. She could be anywhere. We only know what the bloody bridesmaids tell us and that's not very much. They're the ones you should be talking to."

"Right, well, let me just ask a few questions, so we can see where we are," Davies said coolly. "Let's start at the beginning. When was the last time you saw your daughter?"

"That would have been last night at the dinner," Mrs. Thompson said. "The Gruffydd family had a lovely dinner at the Hall, because Emyr's father isn't very well, you see. The wedding party with all the young people were there and the families."

"The police don't care about all that," Mr. Thompson told his wife angrily. "Just let me answer the questions and they'll soon be done with us."

As he finished speaking his wife shrank back into herself. She looked down at the hands clasped in her lap, and was silent. Morgan looked at her thoughtfully.

"Can you think of any reason why your daughter might have suddenly decided not to go forward with the wedding?" she asked.

Mrs. Thompson looked at her husband, and seemed about to say something, then, thinking better of it, went back to the quiet contemplation of her hands.

"No, I can't," said Mr. Thompson. "She knew she was on to a bloody good thing."

"Can you think of any place where she might have gone?" continued Morgan. "Did she come here in a car? Is it still here or is it gone, do you know?"

Thompson glared at them.

"Look, I've just told you that we don't really know our daughter anymore. She's been on her own, living in London for some time. We live in Durham and we don't keep in touch. She can't be bothered with us. As I said, she's a very independent woman, knows her own mind, and to be honest, is much closer to her friends than she is to us. So you'd be better off talking to them, because we don't know anything. We're as surprised by all this as anyone else."

When he finished speaking, Morgan stepped toward Mrs. Thompson and raised her arm to pat her on the shoulder.

Mrs. Thompson's hands flew up to cover her haggard face in a gesture that was startling and revealing.

Slowly she lowered her hands as Morgan gently touched her.

"Mrs. Thompson," she said, "we'll do everything we can to bring your daughter back. Sometimes people turn up again after a day or two and wonder what all the fuss was about."

Grateful for this small gesture of kindness and reassurance, Mrs. Thompson looked up at her with tear-filled eyes.

"Thank you," she whispered, and then added quietly, "she drove here with the girls, Anne and Jennifer. I think the three of them came in Jennifer's car."

Davies turned to face Mr. Thompson.

"Sir, there are certain formalities we have to go through, and one of them is to ask you, as the missing person's next of kin, to sign this form. This will give us the authorization to release photos of her, if we feel this kind of campaign would help find her. Would you be willing to sign this?"

"I guess so," snarled Mr. Thompson. "Do I have a choice?"

As he signed the document, Morgan asked Mrs. Thompson if she had any recent photos of her daughter.

"Oh you can get all that from her friends," Mr. Thompson told her. "In fact, you'd be best off getting everything you need from them.

"Anyway, we're off home tomorrow. I've got to get back to work and there's nothing to hang about here for. She'll turn up when she does."

"Let's hope so, sir. Oh, and by the way, what kind of work is it you do?"

A few minutes later, having learned from Mrs. Thompson where they could find the bridesmaids, the two officers were back in the hotel hallway. Morgan was barely able to contain herself.

"Men like that make me sick! The bastard! It's too bad we didn't learn anything."

"On the contrary, Sergeant, we learned a great deal," Davies told her.

"Really sir? What did I miss?"

"Oh, you didn't miss it. You just haven't put it together. We learned that Thompson's a vicious, controlling bully who manages his family by intimidation. And experience has taught me that everything else we uncover here, no matter where this case leads us, will follow on from that. And it could very well lead us back to him.

"Now then, I'd like you to get on to Durham and see if they've got anything on him. With a drinking problem like he's got, I'd be surprised if he hasn't had a run in or two with the law."

A few minutes later they had reached the bridesmaids' room and were quickly invited in. While both women were subdued, Jennifer seemed the more distraught. Davies got right to the point.

"I understand you two were the bridesmaids. Who's Anne and who's Jennifer?" he asked.

"I'm Anne."

Davies nodded at her.

"Right. Well, we're very sorry to disturb you in your room, but we thought it would be better if we could talk in private. I have some questions I need to ask you and DS Morgan here will take a few notes."

He looked from one to the other.

"Can you tell me when and where you last saw Ms. Thompson?"

"We haven't seen her since last night, just before we

all went to bed," Anne replied and went on to describe the events of the day as clearly as she could—who they had spoken to, up and down the stairs, in and out of rooms, phone messages left, and hopes raised and dashed.

"And did you check with this manicure woman to see if Meg Wynne kept her appointment?" asked DS Morgan.

"Yes," said Anne. "Jennifer went around there, and she said Meg Wynne kept her appointment, everything went fine, and then she left."

"Well, since that's the last place we know she was, we'll start there," DS Morgan said, "if you can tell us where we can find her. Now from your knowledge of your friend, would you say this is something she would be likely to do?"

"Not turn up at her own wedding? Absolutely not!" said Jennifer, "and that's what we've been saying all day. This is so out of character and that's why we're really worried. What do you think could have happened?"

DS Morgan looked to her superior and then, choosing her words carefully, tried to be realistic but reassuring.

"It's still very early in our investigation, so it's too soon to say. But at this point, we're treating it as a missing persons case. We know this Meg Wynne had enough money that if, for some reason, she wanted to disappear, she was certainly in a position to do that. We're keeping an open mind. You'd be surprised how often the people turn up. We'll also have a ring around the local hospitals. Sometimes people are hurt or injured and it's days before they can be identified."

She paused.

"However, if, for some reason she has chosen to disappear, remember that people always run from something or to something. Give that some thought. See if you can come up with anything."

The two police officers got up to leave.

"There's something else we'd like to know," said Morgan. "Tell me about the arrangements here. Who was staying at the hotel?"

"Well, we each had our own rooms, that is Jennifer, Meg Wynne, and I," said Anne.

"And Meg Wynne's parents have a room here, too," added Jennifer.

"Yes, that's right," said Anne. "I just moved my stuff in here today because Jennifer and I wanted to be together, but we've kept all the rooms until tomorrow."

"And Miss Thompson's room? Did you go in there at all today?"

"Yes, we got the manager to let us in earlier, when Emyr arrived."

"Did you disturb anything or was anything out of place when you went in?"

"No, the room had been made up and everything seemed to be there. She has some jewellery in the hotel safe. When we got in last night from the party she took her hair clip and earrings and put them in their boxes, and we took those down ourselves and asked that they be put in the safe. But there may be pieces in her room that we don't know about."

"Well, that'll do for now," Davies said. "Here's my card. Call me if you think of anything else, no matter how trivial or silly it might seem to you. Let me decide what's important."

"There is one thing we wanted to say to you," Anne said.

The two police officers looked expectantly at the girls.

"It's just that we work in PR, so we know the value

of publicity. If there's anything we can do to help get the word out that Meg Wynne is missing, we're only too glad to help. I expect your press office will be taking this up, and they'll probably want this."

Jennifer held out a photo of Meg Wynne.

Davies took it from her and held it to one side so Morgan could see.

The photograph showed an elegant woman seated in a period chair with delicate armrests. Her full-length, pale aquamarine dress shimmered under the photographer's lights but it was to the large diamond on her left hand, as it rested gently on her right forearm, that the viewer's eyes were drawn. Meg Wynne gazed serenely at the camera, the smallest of smiles at the corner of her mouth. She appeared to be in a grandly decorated room, with a large tapestry behind her.

"It's her engagement photo," Jennifer said. "She looked especially beautiful there, we thought. Her father-in-law loves that photo."

"And where was this taken?" asked Davies.

"At the Hall, at Christmas. She brought the photo back with her when she returned in the New Year."

Davies nodded as Morgan snapped her notebook shut.

"Right, then, you'll be around if we need you again, will you?" Morgan asked. The girls nodded and the police officers thanked them and left.

In the hallway, Morgan stopped and looked at the photo again.

"What is it?" Davies asked.

Morgan shook her head.

"I thought you had to be a member of the royal family to get your picture taken looking like that. She must really be something."

*   *   *

Anne and Jennifer began to tidy up their room. "Jenn, I want to get out of here. I think we should ring the Hall and see if we can go over there. If they haven't had dinner yet, maybe we can wangle an invitation and if not, maybe Emyr and David would like to go out someplace quiet, to get away from all this."

As they made their way to Meg Wynne's room, where the manager was waiting to let them in, Morgan wrapped up a phone call and turned to her boss.

"That was Durham Constabulary, sir. Thompson's known to them. Got form and lots of it. Mostly bar brawls and domestics going back a long way."

After thanking the manager for letting them in, they began their preliminary examination of the missing bride's room.

"This is an odd case," said Morgan as she gently rummaged through the cosmetics bag on top of the dresser. "It doesn't feel right. There isn't enough evidence to classify it as other than a missing person, but there's something very wrong, and I can't help but think that we should be treating this room as we would a crime scene. Get the scene-of-crime officers in to document and photograph everything."

"You might be right, Sergeant, but for now she's just missing." He looked around the room. "Still, we don't want anyone coming in here. I'll have a word with the manager, and we'll seal this room. Nothing in, nothing out. We'll give it a really good going over in the morning."

Morgan moved away from the dresser, toward the closet.

"Sir, I wonder if I should have a closer look at her dress. It might be helpful later if we knew exactly what was here. We should also have it out just to check and make sure there's nothing behind it in the closet, or that nothing's fallen down, don't you think? Something we've overlooked."

Davies gave her a conspiratorial smile.

"All right, Bethan. Go on, then. Purely for the investigation, you understand," he said, shaking his head lightly.

"Of course, sir!"

Morgan removed the garment, encased in its heavy transparent plastic bag, from the closet and laid it tenderly on the bed. As she slowly pulled the zipper down, the gown was revealed as a masterpiece of contemporary dress design.

She looked at the label, and gasped.

"Oh my God, it's by Suzanne Glenton. I've read about these, but never dreamed I would actually get to see one. Look at the elegance of it."

In the palest of ivory, with a beaded bodice, it was a strapless confection worthy of a princess.

Morgan gave a little shudder and looked up at her boss. The excitement of being so close to something so utterly beautiful had been replaced by a chilling thought.

"I can tell you one thing for sure. Seeing this dress makes me think that Meg Wynne did not choose to miss her wedding. What woman would pass up the opportunity to wear this dress, I ask you?"

Davies's eyes narrowed slightly and he nodded.

"And there's something else," Morgan continued, gazing down at the dress. "We need to determine what jewellery she had, and where it is now. We have to make sure all the important stuff's accounted for."

Davies looked at his watch and nodded again.

"Good work. Well, leave the dress on the bed, and let's get the tape and seal this room. I'll leave word for the manager that no one is to enter until we come back in the morning. Of course, there's still a chance, I suppose, that she could come back.

"Still, we should brief the press office, and get that side of things moving. And before you leave Llanelen, could you ask uniform to let us know where the CCTV cameras are and get the tapes to us in the morning?"

With one last look at the dress, Morgan turned to go.

"Would you like to get a coffee before the drive home?" Davies asked.

"No, better not, thanks, sir," Morgan replied. "It's getting on and I've still got lots to do. I'd really been looking forward to an early night," she added wistfully.

Davies accepted this, and the two made their way down the stairs and out of the hotel. He hated going home to his empty house in Llandudno. But then, he hadn't much liked going home to it when his wife had lived there, either.

CHAPTER NINE

Of course, Llanelen being the kind of village where everybody knows everybody and nothing ever happens, word spread like wildfire that something *had* happened at the Gruffydd-Thompson wedding. And Evelyn Lloyd, the former postmistress who prided herself on keeping well abreast of village affairs, had been thrilled to have a front-row seat at what would surely turn out to be one of the most sensational turn of events ever to take place in the town. Well, not exactly a front-row seat, but she had been right there in the third row on the groom's side of the church when the rector made that stunning announcement that the bride had gone missing.

Practically trembling with excitement, she was already going over in her mind how she would recount the details of the day, from her own personal vantage point, and with whom she would share them. It was at times like these that she dearly missed the late Mr. Lloyd, who had always been there with a lovely cup of tea in the morning, a willing spirit, and outstanding listening skills.

As the wedding guests carefully picked their way along the river walk to the Red Dragon Hotel for the refreshments that had been laid on for them, Mrs. Lloyd was considering whom she should call first and one name came to mind, for several reasons.

Her niece, Morwyn Lloyd, would want to know everything Mrs. Lloyd could possibly tell her, not only because she was a former girlfriend of the bridegroom, but because she worked as a feature writer on the *Daily Post*. There had been some discussion among the paper's senior editors whether or not the wedding should be covered as a news event. In the end, it was decided that the days of newspaper reporters and photographers attending society weddings were long gone unless the bride or groom happened to have serious social standing, such as being a drug-addicted model, an up-and-coming actor with a scandal brewing, or a junior royal. So readers of the Monday edition would see only a brief write-up and a formal photograph of the newly married couple.

Now of course, everything had changed and Mrs. Lloyd knew that Morwyn would want her to get as much information as she could from her fellow guests while they were doing their best to get through their tea.

The hotel had been booked months earlier to cater the wedding reception dinner: Welsh roast beef with duchesse potatoes and a medley of fresh vegetables, followed by a lemon sorbet, white chocolate mousse wedding cake, with an impeccable selection of fine wines and Veuve Clicquot Rosé. All that would now likely never be served, with so many guests arriving early, peckish, but with nothing to celebrate.

The kitchen was in turmoil, but under the head chef's direction the staff had managed to put together platters of fresh-cut sandwiches, small cakes and biscuits, carrots and celery, along with tea, coffee, and cold drinks. The refreshments were really for the benefit of the out-of-towners, who had made long journeys that day, and then, with the unexpected turn of events, would have been left wondering what to do next and where to go for their dinners.

As she loaded up her plate with sandwiches, Mrs. Lloyd looked around the hotel's special event room, which did duty for dances, wedding receptions, and large meetings. She saw a few familiar village faces along with some well-dressed young people she did not know. She thought it unfortunate but understandable that there was no one from the wedding party or either family. The rector wasn't there, but his wife, Bronwyn, was doing her best to help everyone feel a little more at ease. The atmosphere was subdued and awkward. No one knew quite what to do or say, and yet, because they were all dressed in their wedding finery, there was no mistaking the reason they were there. Most of the women, including Mrs. Lloyd, had removed their hats.

With some uncertainty, unusual for her, she made her way over to Bronwyn Evans.

"I'm sure I speak for all of us, Bronwyn, when I say how unfortunate all this is," she began. "But I think your husband did a splendid job of holding everything together at the church. It must have been very difficult for him. Gone home, then, has he?"

"No, Mrs. Lloyd," Bronwyn replied stiffly. "He's gone up to the Hall to see if he can be of any comfort to Rhys. This is going to be difficult for him."

Sensitivity not being her strong suit, Mrs. Lloyd pressed on.

"Yes, I see that it is. It really is too bad. What on earth could have happened, do you suppose?"

Bronwyn looked levelly at her and drawing herself up, prepared to deliver, what was for her, a blistering riposte.

"Really, Mrs. Lloyd, I have no idea. I know as much

or as little as you do. Now, if you'll excuse me, I must just pass these sandwiches around."

As she watched the rector's wife move gracefully from one person to another, offering a sandwich here and a reassuring smile there, Mrs. Lloyd reached her decision. There didn't seem to be much more to be learned here, so she would just finish up her sandwiches, perhaps take one or two for later, and make her way home to telephone Morwyn.

As Saturday evening drew on, the village braced itself for a Llanelen Saturday night. The Leek and Lily was unusually crowded and everyone had an opinion on what had happened.

At the Hall, Anne, Jennifer, David, and Emyr were discussing how to answer questions about Meg Wynne's disappearance. Reporters were bound to hear about it and then ring up asking invasive, insensitive questions. Although he always had business to attend to in London, David had agreed to stay until mid-week to act as the family's spokesman and to provide support for Emyr. As a group, with Anne taking the lead, they drafted a statement that David would read to the media when they began clamouring for information or comments.

Rhys had taken the news of Meg Wynne's disappearance very badly, and he seemed to have gone downhill over the course of the evening.

"The pain waits for me," he had told Emyr. "When it has stopped, even for a little while, I know it is still there, watching and waiting."

In the peace of his bedroom, Rhys lay back on his pillows. His once robust body was now wasted and frail, his skin sallow and pale.

"I am so very sorry, Emyr," he said. "About Meg Wynne."

"I know you are, Dad," Emyr said. "Now get some rest. I'll see you later."

"Be sure to come and tell me if there's news," replied his father, as Louise, his nurse, arrived with fresh bedding and Rhys's prescribed medication.

Emyr made his way downstairs just as the telephone began ringing.

Oh God, he thought. It's starting.

It was. The first reporter to call was Morwyn Lloyd and as agreed, David Williams took the call.

"Yes, I can confirm that Meg Wynne Thompson did not arrive for her wedding as planned, and that the police are treating this as a missing persons case," he said, reading from the statement Jennifer and Anne had prepared for him.

"Both families are distraught and praying for her safe return."

When Morwyn pressed him for more details, he told her that as far as he knew Meg Wynne had kept an appointment in the morning, and no one seemed to know what had happened to her after that. If anyone had seen her, or could provide any information on her whereabouts, it was hoped they would come forward and contact the North Wales police who were looking into her disappearance.

"And one more thing, Mr. Williams. Do you have a recent photograph of Ms. Thompson I could have? I would be happy to come up to the Hall and get it within the hour."

Arrangements were made for Morwyn to collect a copy of Meg Wynne's engagement photograph, and then the little group decided they should get something to eat. They opted to stay in, and settled for a simple meal of Gwennie's lentil soup from the freezer followed by a cheese omelette that the girls whipped up and fresh, crusty bread, all accompanied by a crisp white wine. But nobody was very hungry and most of it went uneaten.

Gathered around the kitchen table, they tried to reassure one another between the long silences broken only by the occasional snuffling and whining from Trixxi who went from one to the other, touching her nose on their knees to offer comfort but always returning to Emyr's side.

Finally, emotionally shattered from the long day, they decided to call it a night. Under the last rays of the setting sun, Jennifer and Anne drove slowly back to the hotel, leaving the Hall to settle into the coming darkness of sleep.

"She's out there somewhere," Anne said softly. "She's out there. And we haven't got a clue where she is."

Back at the Red Dragon Hotel, Meg Wynne's mother was asking the same question.

"What could have happened to her? Where can she be? Why would she disappear like that?"

"For the last time, woman," shouted her husband. "I don't know. She's got money and lots of it by all accounts. She can go anywhere she goddamned well chooses. And look at the bother she's caused. The bloody police all over the place, with their questions and mucky looks."

CHAPTER TEN

Penny was surprised when her telephone rang at eight on Sunday morning. She was even more surprised that her early morning caller was a police officer asking if she and another officer could come around immediately to ask her a few questions.

Although most people would have asked what it was about, Penny just agreed to meet with them and said she would wait for them downstairs in the shop.

A few minutes later Morgan and Davies were on her doorstep.

It was a lovely morning, the start of a perfect June day, with a fresh, light breeze gently stirring the tree-tops under a cloudless blue sky.

"Would you like to talk in the shop or do you want to go up to the flat?" Penny asked. "I must tell you I'm a little nervous. Should I offer you a cup of tea or coffee? I don't often get visits from the police, so it's a bit . . . well, you know."

Davies smiled reassuringly at her, taking in her red hair and trim figure.

"Actually, I do know. Well, first things first, I'm Detective Chief Inspector Gareth Davies and this is Detective Sergeant Bethan Morgan, and thank you, no, we'll not trouble you for a drink. We're fine."

Morgan smiled encouragingly at Penny.

"And let me begin by apologizing for troubling you at this hour, but we need to get an early start today. If you're planning to get to church, we'll try not to keep you," he added.

Penny led the way into the shop.

"This will do nicely," Davies said, as he and Morgan sat in the two clients' chairs and Penny pulled up a seat to face them. "I expect you know why we're here."

Penny looked blankly at him, her face clouded and troubled. "No," she said, "absolutely not. I've not got the faintest idea why you're here."

The two officers looked at each another and Davies took the lead.

"Well, we're investigating a missing persons report. Meg Wynne Thompson has gone missing."

"But she can't be," Penny exclaimed. "She just got married yesterday. What on earth could have happened to her?"

"That's what we're trying to find out," said Morgan, "and as far as our investigation goes, you're ground zero."

"Sorry, I'm not taking this in," Penny said, looking from one to the other. "I'm not following you."

"We're not doing a very good job of explaining this," Davies said. "Let's go back to the beginning.

"According to the information we have, Meg Wynne Thompson came to your shop yesterday morning for a manicure."

"That's right," Penny said. "She did. It was nine o'clock, the first appointment of the day. She was right on time, which I liked."

"Good," said Davies. "Right, well, she came here for a manicure, and so far, we haven't been able to trace her movements after that, so you'll understand now why we're here. At this point, we believe you were the last person to have seen her."

Penny struggled to make sense of what she was hearing.

"I'm staggered. Are you saying that after she left my shop she just disappeared?" She sat back as Davies gave her a bit more time to think about what she had just been told.

"And she didn't show up for her wedding?" Penny asked.

"That is correct."

"Oh, poor Emyr. That's terrible, just terrible."

"So now, Miss Brannigan, is it? I need to know everything that happened here yesterday. Start at the beginning if you don't mind, and walk me through it. Don't leave anything out. The sergeant here will take notes."

Penny walked over to the small work desk against the far wall, and picked up a burgundy appointment book and small metal box.

She returned to Davies and opened the book to show him the page for Saturday.

"Here she is," Penny said, pointing to an entry. "She was here at nine for a manicure. It was uneventful, ordinary."

Morgan was writing frantically while Davies, paying close attention, leaned slightly forward, maintaining eye contact.

"What was she wearing?"

"Hmm. Let me think." Penny paused for a moment and looked away.

"She had on a kind of pink plaid boxy jacket with fringe, just along here," Penny said, running her hands down an imaginary lapel. "Blue jeans, I think, and some kind of strappy sandals. Fancy shoes like the other two girls were wearing when they were here on Friday.

People were saying how totally inappropriate those shoes were for the country. Just silly, really."

"What did you talk about?" Morgan asked.

"Not much, actually. The usual client chitchat. She didn't seem to want to talk. She did say, though, that she had chosen peonies for her flowers and it wouldn't be long before everyone would want them. She said she'd even designed a special peony fragrance for herself. She seemed very sure of herself, very confident with her choices."

"Did she seem troubled, or upset, or anything like that?"

"No, she didn't. But come to think of it, she didn't seem very nervous or excited, either, the way most brides are on their wedding day. Not that I see that many of them."

"Really? I would have thought wedding parties would be a natural for a business like yours," Davies said.

"Oh they are. I just don't get to see them on their wedding day. Bridal parties are usually done the day before. There's too much to do on the day, and the manicure takes up too much time, and then your nails are a bit tacky and you can't get on with things. So I was rather surprised when Meg Wynne made the appointment for yesterday, not Friday. The other girls came in on Friday. Anne and the other one."

"Jennifer."

"That's it. They seemed like nice girls. Very supportive of their friend. So that was all there was to the manicure. Wait a minute! Yes, right, one of the bridesmaids, I can't remember which one it was, came by yesterday, around lunchtime, asking if Meg Wynne had been here and did I know where she went afterwards. I did wonder about that at the time and then I thought no more about it."

She thumped her forehead lightly with the heel of her hand.

"Of course. I should have realized then that there was a problem, but I never would have dreamed that she wouldn't turn up for her wedding. That's the last thing you'd expect."

Davies continued to look at Penny, while Morgan stole a glance at her watch.

"Right, well, you've been very helpful and we appreciate that," he said. "Just a couple more questions. How long did the manicure take and did she say where she was going after she left you?"

"It took about forty-five minutes, a bit longer, maybe. And no, she didn't say where she was going. I just assumed she would be going back to the hotel or somewhere for hair and makeup and all the rest of it."

Morgan folded up her notebook and looked expectantly at her boss.

"One more thing. I wonder if you can tell us what you were doing yesterday."

Penny gave him a puzzled look.

"Me? I had a full morning in the shop until about lunchtime, and then I walked up to Ffridd Uchaf to go sketching. I like to work with the afternoon light, see. When I got back, I tidied everything up. I have to do the accounts on Saturday, if I'm to have any hope of staying on top of them. Then I had an early supper and read a chapter or two of the new Maeve Binchy. I watched a bit of television, and then went to bed. I don't lead a very exciting life, I'm afraid. Very dull and predictable it is, to be honest." A moment later she added, "Why would you even ask that? You surely don't think I had anything to do with this, do you? I didn't even know the woman, for goodness sake."

"I was wondering why you hadn't heard about the wedding, that's all, and obviously it was because you were away from the town."

After a few moments of silence, Penny followed up with something that had just occurred to her.

"I guess it will be on the news," she said.

"Oh, it's got all the ingredients," Morgan agreed. "This story'll be all over the news today. You may get some calls from reporters, once they figure out you were one of the last people to see Meg Wynne Thompson."

"I hope not," Penny said, looking from one to the other. "I don't like the sound of that. What should I say if a reporter calls?"

"Just confirm she was here," Morgan said. "They shouldn't bother you for any more than a day or two. Everything blows over quickly, and they move on to the next thing."

The two police officers stood up.

"What's in the box?" Davies asked, looking at the box Penny had brought over with the appointment book.

"It's the box I keep client cards in," Penny said. "I write down the date of each client visit, and what colour of polish she chose."

"Is that really necessary?" Davies asked.

"It is," Penny said. "I used to get customers coming in and they'd say, 'I didn't like the last polish as much as the one I had the time before that,' and they'd expect me to remember what that was, so I started keeping notes on what polish they have, and then it's all very simple. So I have a note here that tells me what Meg Wynne had. I could also tell you what the bridesmaids had, if you need to know that."

"I think that's one detail too many," smiled Davies,

"but you never know. Here's my card," he added, handing one to Penny. "Call me if you remember anything else you think we should know, even if you think it's not important. Don't hesitate to call."

A few minutes later the officers were setting off to walk the short distance to the Red Dragon Hotel where the manager was expecting them.

"What did you think, sir?"

"I thought she was genuine and uncomplicated. She told us what she knew and that's it and all about it."

For now, thought Morgan.

When the police officers were gone, Penny went upstairs to her flat and put the kettle on. Maybe they didn't want a coffee, she thought, but I certainly do. While she waited for the water to boil she wandered into her bedroom and riffled through her closet. Although she hadn't planned on going to church that morning, the police visit had got her thinking and she didn't want to be on her own. Anyway, there might be news. She reached into the closet and pulled out a navy blue shirtwaist dress with hunting scenes on it that she had bought at a charity shop in Llandudno. That'll do, she thought.

At Ty Brith, Rhys Gruffydd's condition had worsened overnight and the doctor had been called. After spending a few minutes with her patient, she talked quietly with Emyr outside his father's room.

"He is in decline, I'm sorry to say, and I don't think the end will be too long in coming. Not today, not tomorrow, but soon. He will likely be comatose at the end, so my advice would be that if you have anything left unsaid, or if there's anything you want to ask him, now's the time. We'll continue to keep him comfortable, but that's really all that's left for us to do. Is there anything you want to ask me?"

Emyr shook his head.

"You go back in," the doctor told him. "I'll show myself out."

Emyr quietly opened the door to his father's room and made his way to the bedside chair. He sat down and took his father's hand.

"Dad, it's me," he said gently. Rhys turned his head toward the sound of his son's voice, opened his eyes, and gazed lovingly at his only child in the peaceful glow of the muted sunshine that filtered through the beige blinds.

"Ah, Emyr," he said softly. "I can guess what she told you and I have come to accept it. Don't worry about me. I am just so sorry to have to be adding to your troubles with everything else you have to worry about."

"Dad, you mustn't think that," Emyr said.

"Emyr, there's something I wanted to say to you about Meg Wynne. I know some people don't like her, they think she's arrogant and above herself, but she reminded me in a lot of ways of your mother."

"Oh, Dad, please don't."

"I have to, Emyr. I need to say these things, and I want you to hear me out."

Rhys paused for a few moments.

"Water, please."

Emyr held the glass to his father's lips. Rhys took a delicate sip through the bent straw and nodded. Emyr replaced the glass on the bedside table and then sat down.

"I'm not stupid," Rhys continued. "I know exactly what kind of woman Meg Wynne is. I understood her because I'd seen it all before. And what's more, I believe I know what she would have become, once she realized that no one was going to hurt her anymore, and that she was safe with you. She needs you. And you need her. She's a very smart, strong woman.

"In the end, once she'd learned to trust, she would have come to love you, truly love you, and I think you two would have had a wonderful life together. Like your mother and I did."

The effort of speaking had tired him, and Rhys sank deeper into his bed and himself. He picked at the duvet covering his sunken chest.

"I'm going to rest now. I don't think I'll be getting up again. Not today, anyway."

The day before, the area outside the church doors had been crowded with wedding guests in their finery, but today it was the usual Sunday morning crowd, and then some. Morning service had attracted quite a few lapsed churchgoers, all hoping to hear the latest news on the missing bride. They filed into the cool interior of the church, took their seats, and as the rustling stopped and whispered chatter died down, the rector took his place in front of them and morning service began.

"Bore da," he said. "Good morning. Let us pray."

At the nearby Red Dragon Hotel, Davies and Morgan were in hotel manager John Burton's office, watching him open the safe.

"Yes," he said. "Here we are," as he looked at the entries in an old-fashioned leather-bound book and then peered into the depths of an equally old-fashioned wall-mounted safe. "Everything's in order. She, that is Meg Wynne Thompson, left two items with me and here they are."

"One small box, green, embossed CYM in a gold oval with gold dragon," he read.

"One wooden presentation box with a small gold-coloured pentagon with a 'CG' on the top."

The manager set them down on his desk, within easy reach of the police officers, stepped back, and folding his hands together, chuckled nervously and waited.

Morgan picked up the first box, and opened it.

Inside was a plain gold man's wedding band.

"That'll be Welsh gold," said the manager, peering at it. "They say pure Welsh gold is now the most valuable of all the precious metals."

"The royal family's wedding rings are made from Welsh gold, aren't they?" asked Morgan.

"Indeed they are," said Burton. "It's become very rare since the Clogau mine closed down. Supply and demand, don't you know."

Clogau rose gold, the rarest and most expensive in the world, was discovered in 1854 at the Clogau St. David's mine near Dolgellau in Snowdonia. By 1998, the gold seam had become too thin to work, and the mining operation was closed, leaving only the reserves.

Morgan snapped the lid shut and set the box down on the desk.

Letting out a small sigh, she picked up the other one, and opened it.

A smile lit up her face as she showed the box to the two men.

"You'll appreciate this, Mr. Burton," she said, pleased with her little joke.

Nestled inside was a Welsh dragon brooch, its fiery red-gold wings gleaming against the white satin lining.

"Well, everything seems to be in order here, then," said Davies. "And this is all you had?"

"Let me just make sure," said the manager, looking again at the register. "No, wait. There should be two more. Two others were brought in after these ones. They were listed in her name, but she didn't entrust them to us herself."

He reached into the safe and withdrew the two boxes that Anne and Jennifer had given to the night clerk late Friday night.

The men watched as Morgan examined the chandelier drop earrings and diamond hair clip. It was difficult to tell what she was thinking, but Davies knew she had to be feeling something like envy and longing.

Silently she handed the boxes back to Burton, who replaced them in the safe.

He hesitated for a moment, and then, leaning forward with his hands braced on the desk, looked at Davies.

"I hope I'm not being insensitive here," he said, "but I was wondering about the rooms and how long they would be needed. And also, what if Ms. Thompson doesn't come back? How long should I keep the jewellery boxes? Who should I give them to? Should I give them to her parents, or her fiancé? It's a bit difficult to know what to do for the best, and I wondered if you would be kind enough to explain to me what our position is here at the hotel?"

Davies scratched the back of his neck and thought for a moment.

"Yes, I do understand that all this is a bit tricky for you. Let's talk about the rooms first. I expect the bridesmaids and her parents will be leaving today, as planned, and as for her room, we are going to go through it again this morning, and then we'll release it to you, and the contents to her parents."

Burton, listening carefully, nodded.

"This jewellery now, is a bit different," Davies continued. "Why don't we hold it for you? We'll take it off your hands and give you a receipt for it, and that way, if there's any disagreement over it later, that won't be your problem."

Burton nodded gratefully.

"Of course, what we hope will happen is she'll turn up within a day or two in London or somewhere, and then we'll make sure everything is returned to her."

With a relieved smile, Burton turned away again to remove the boxes from the safe once more.

"All right then?" said Davies. "Very good. Thank you so much for all your help. If you would put those boxes in a bag—any old bag will do—the sergeant here will give you a receipt for them and we'll pick them up on our way out. When we're finished upstairs, we'll take the tape down, and let you know on the way out that we've finished with the room.

"Oh, and here's my card. Call me if you think of anything else, no matter how trivial or unimportant it might seem to you."

Davies and Morgan made their way upstairs to Meg Wynne's room, checked that the tape across the door had not been disturbed, and then peeled it away.

Everything was as they had left it the evening before, but now, in the bright sunlight of a beautiful June morning, the room felt stale, closed in, and lifeless.

"Let's see what we can find," Davies said. "Handbag, credit cards, money, address book, diary, passport, receipts, anything and everything like that. I'll start over here, including the closet," he said, pointing toward the window side of the room. "You do over there, the dresser, and bathroom."

They worked their way around the room for about twenty minutes without speaking. There was the occasional sound of a drawer opening and closing, clothes hangers being pushed along the rail, bedclothes being turned over, and one or two cracks of protest from Davies's knees as he bent down and stood up again.

Morgan held the curtains back to check the windowsill and then, opening the drawer in the nightstand, glanced in. She leaned closer, then withdrew something and called out to her boss.

"Why on earth would she be reading this?" she asked, holding a slim volume entitled *Street Drugs*. "I would have thought something from the *Shopaholics* series would have been more in her line."

Davies glanced over and then held out his hand. She crossed over to him and handed over the book. He thumbed through it, shook his head, and gave it back to his sergeant.

"Go through it carefully, see if any pages are marked and make a note of it. You're right, it does seem strange."

A few minutes later Davies crossed his arms and looked around the room.

"Right," Davies instructed. "That's it. We've done all we can. We'll notify the manager that we're finished and he can let her parents take her things. If they want them."

He glanced at his watch and then gestured at Morgan to get ready to leave.

"Our bulletin should be on the noon news. Let's hope it gets results. And now, let's follow up with surveillance tapes of the street that might show which way she went. We're looking for, say, nine A.M. and later. We'll leave no stone unturned."

They stepped out into the hall and just as Davies was about to close the door, Morgan stuck her foot in front of it to keep it open.

"I'll be right back," she said over her shoulder as she headed back into the room.

A few moments later, she returned, holding up a scrap of yellow paper.

"It looks as if she was writing something, changed her mind, and then tore it up. A first draft of a letter, maybe. This little piece was hiding under the waste-paper basket. Probably fell out when it was emptied. It was you saying that about no stone unturned that made me realize I should have looked under the bin."

She smiled up at him.

"Good work," said Davies. "Now I wonder. What do you suppose it can tell us?"

CHAPTER ELEVEN

As Rev. Evans began his sermon that morning, Penny's thoughts began to drift, and she decided to spend the afternoon sketching. When church was finally over, she returned home to pack up a bread roll, some cheese, an apple, and a bottle of water, change into comfortable walking clothes, and collect her pencils and notebooks. A few minutes later, she was crossing the town's landmark three-arched bridge, and heading off in the direction of Gwyther Castle, where she knew she could find solitude and serenity in the newly restored formal gardens and enjoyment in the nostalgia of the way things used to be a century or two ago.

As she walked along the road she passed fields where sheep grazed contentedly. A few lifted their heads from their grassy task to watch her go by, and then returned to their munching. Her thoughts turned to Emma, and how deeply she missed her. She felt resentful that this messy and unexpected business with the runaway bride, or whatever she should be called, was distracting her, and other townsfolk, from mourning Emma with the dignity and respect she deserved. Penny wanted to be able to remember her friend in an uncomplicated way, for the lovely, cultured woman she was, and not have her memory tied in to all the disruption and unhappiness that this Meg Wynne person was causing.

She was also struggling with guilt and blaming herself that Emma had died alone. I've spent so many nights in that cottage, she thought. If only I'd spent that night there, that one night, I might have been able to do something. She could find no comfort in any of it.

In the hills above the town, seated in front of a small waterfall, she sketched in a distracted, perfunctory kind of way. Unhappy with what she had done, and unhappy with herself, she finally decided to pack it in. She returned home in the mid-afternoon, hungry and somewhat tired in a bored, restless way to find a telephone message waiting for her. Morwyn Lloyd of the *Daily Post* would like to speak to her and would she please ring her back.

Not until I've had a warm bath and maybe an early supper, my girl, thought Penny as the tub began to fill and a shepherd's pie warmed in the oven.

An hour later, she called Morwyn and answered her questions honestly and openly, as that young police sergeant had suggested she should, without volunteering or guessing at anything.

Throughout the evening she tried to watch television, but found herself wandering around the small flat, picking up a book and putting it down again after rereading three paragraphs, straightening out and dusting things that didn't need seeing to, poking around in the fridge and just generally feeling thoroughly miserable.

Eventually, it was time for bed and she was grateful to crawl into its welcoming warmth.

While Penny had been in the Welsh woods trying to concentrate long enough to produce a decent sketch, Morgan started looking through the videotapes the local constable had produced. The national bank on the Market Square had a surveillance camera trained on the outdoor cash point, and although it was positioned to capture the image of anyone using the automatic money dispenser, it incidentally videotaped everyone who passed along that busy street.

The bank manager had handed over the tape for Saturday, midnight to noon, explaining that the tapes were changed twice a day, held for a fortnight, and then recorded over. He didn't know of any other surveillance cameras covering that part of the town, although he thought the garage owner had had one installed after an attempted robbery there a year or so ago.

"The major crime aspect of big city life hasn't reached us, yet, thank God," he said, "but all branches of this bank throughout the country have been fitted with them. We are a bank, after all, and people expect us to have them. Nobody takes any notice."

In a corner of the large, windowless briefing room, where the television and VCR stand had been parked in a corner, Morgan sat down with a cup of coffee. The grainy black-and-white film showed the usual Saturday morning activities of any High Street in Britain—a well-dressed woman stopping for a quick greeting with a friend, a couple of teenage girls withdrawing a few pounds to buy a new lipstick at the chemist, and traffic moving slowly around the town.

Finally, just before nine, she saw a woman who fitted Penny Brannigan's description of Meg Wynne Thompson round the corner into the square, pass by the bank, and disappear from view heading in the direction of the nail salon.

It was not possible to see her face, but Morgan was sure it had to be Meg Wynne.

Now, she thought, I need to see if she comes back

this way. She fast-forwarded to a quarter to ten and watched the tape. About six minutes later, the figure appeared again, headed back the way she had come.

Excited, Morgan reached for her mobile and phoned Davies.

"That's good that you've spotted her," Davies said, "now we've got something to go on. So you'll need to interview the shopkeepers along the route, put up some flyers, see if you can find any townsfolk who saw her, and all the rest of it."

Just before two the next afternoon villagers entering St. Elen's for the funeral of Emma Teasdale looked at each other in amazement and smiled. Coming from the open door was the lilting, unmistakable sound of harp music.

"How wonderful, utterly wonderful," said Mrs. Lloyd to the woman beside her.

As they took their places to the sounds of Debussy's "Clair de Lune," many took comfort in the music. Centuries before, the area had been home to some of Wales's finest harpists and harp makers and this gentle tribute to a woman who had placed such a high value on music was appreciated by the villagers as appropriate beyond words.

"I think I know who was behind this," whispered Mrs. Lloyd, nudging her neighbour.

The music continued for several more minutes while everyone settled into their seats and then Rev. Evans took his place to begin the service, exchanging a grateful, conspiratorial smile with his wife.

"Good afternoon. *Pnawn da*," he began. "We are gathered here today to commemorate the life of our departed sister, Emma Teasdale, and we will begin by remembering the immortal words, 'I am the resurrection and the life, says the Lord. Those who believe in me, even though they die, will live, and everyone who lives and believes in me will never die.' "

About forty-five minutes later, when the final hymn had been sung and the benediction spoken, the doors of the church opened, and the coffin was carried solemnly to a quiet corner of the churchyard where a grave had been prepared to receive it. A small procession followed, led by the rector whose white surplice fluttered softly in the breeze.

Surrounded by the friends who had admired, respected, and even loved her in life, the coffin of Emma Teasdale was gently lowered into the ground.

Standing at the foot of the grave, reading from his *LLyfr Gweddi Gyffredin* or *Book of Common Prayer,* Rev. Evans continued with the solemn service.

"We therefore commit her body to the ground; earth to earth, ashes to ashes, dust to dust; in the sure and certain hope of the resurrection to eternal life."

One by one a few mourners, including Penny, came forward and scattered handfuls of earth on the coffin. After a final few moments of silent good-byes, they turned away and made their way slowly from the churchyard to the hotel where a modest tea awaited them. As she turned away from the gravesite, with one last look over her shoulder, Penny thought the service had been exactly what Emma would have wanted, and that she would have been deeply touched by the harp music. But as she made her way out of the cemetery, past generations of tombstones rising out of the newly mown grass, she was aware of an idea trying to form in the back of her mind that something had not been quite right.

As she tried to bring it to the surface, Mrs. Lloyd,

dressed in her best black suit that she wore only to funerals, caught her up.

"Well, Penny," she asked, "what did you think of the service? I think Emma would have loved it, especially the music. I wonder who the harp player is. I don't think she's anyone we know, is she?"

Penny let go of her thoughts, and turned to Mrs. Lloyd.

"The music was wonderful," she agreed. "Very moving and so appropriate."

As they reached the steps of the hotel, Mrs. Lloyd moved on to the topic that was never far from her mind.

"There was a slap-up tea laid on for us on Saturday after the wedding," she said. "Or nonwedding, I guess it was. Really a very nice effort, though, all things considered. I hope this one will be as good. Do you think they'll have those nice little empire biscuits I like so much?" she asked eagerly.

Penny shook her head.

When the last of the mourners had left the churchyard, two men in overalls made their way to the grave and in a practiced, unemotional way began to fill in the grave. And as the sparkling Conwy River flowed endlessly, silently by, Emma Teasdale was laid to rest.

CHAPTER TWELVE

Everyone who attended the funeral was glad to get to the Red Dragon for a cup of tea and a sandwich, although for those who had been there just two days earlier after the wedding that never was, it was all uncomfortably déjà vu.

Penny, who hadn't been at the wedding, had no such feelings and was anxious to talk to Bronwyn Evans about the music.

"Bronwyn, was it you who arranged for the harpist?" she asked.

"Yes, Penny, I cannot tell a lie. It was. Did you like it?"

"Oh, it was magnificent—absolutely perfect! It made me cry when I thought how much Emma would have loved it. You know how much she loved music, and to think that you did that for her. She would have been so honoured," said Penny. "Oh look at me! I'm getting all soppy at just the thought of it!"

Bronwyn laughed lightly, put her arm around Penny, and said, "I really should have consulted you, Penny, but I wasn't sure that Victoria would be able to make it. Look, why don't you come and tell her yourself how much you enjoyed her music."

She steered Penny toward a woman in a lavender silk

dress who was standing alone looking about her with uncertainty.

"Victoria, I'd like you to meet Penny Brannigan," Bronwyn said, smiling at her. "Penny wanted to tell you herself how much she enjoyed your music. Penny, this is Victoria Hopkirk." She smiled at both of them as if she had just found one solution to two problems. "I'd better see to the coffee, so I'll just leave you two to get acquainted."

The two women smiled shyly at each other. They were about the same age, but Victoria was slightly taller, with a somewhat serious, anxious look about her. Her blond hair was pulled back and held at the nape of her neck with a large black bow that matched black leather court shoes that looked expensive, and well cared for.

Penny held out her hand, which Victoria shook warmly.

"Yes," said Penny. "I did enjoy the music, but more than that I want to tell you how much your playing would have meant to my friend, Emma. She loved beautiful music."

"Thank you, Penny," said Victoria. "I'm often asked to play at weddings, but not at funerals, and yet, if you think about it, a harp at a funeral would seem to be a natural thing." She started to smile, and then hesitated.

"I'm curious to know how you came to be here," said Penny. "I mean, how did Bronwyn ever find you?"

Victoria's large brown eyes clouded for a moment.

"It's a long story, but I'm staying for a bit with my cousin, who happens to be an old friend of Bronwyn's," said Victoria. "I've been coming to this area all my life, and I know it pretty well, so when I needed a change of scenery, I came here."

The two women chatted for a few more moments and then decided to get a cup of coffee from the refreshments table. Penny looked around the room and suggested that they sit on the chairs that had been arranged along one wall, underneath the windows overlooking the square.

"Bronwyn told me that you and Emma Teasdale were very close friends," said Victoria when they were seated, their knees turned toward each other. "She was very dear to you, and I'm so sorry for your loss."

Penny smiled at her and then looked down at her coffee cup.

"Thank you," she said simply and after a few moments added, "she was a wonderful woman, Emma was. Very accomplished and generous. I do miss her. Something strange has been happening here that I really wish I could discuss with Emma. Have you heard about the missing bride? Apparently she was last seen in my manicure shop. There's just something about—"

She broke off and looked up as Alwynne Gwilt from the Stretch and Sketch group approached.

"Penny, sorry to interrupt, but I have to get back to the museum and wondered if I could have just a quick word with you. I've got some photos I'd like you to look at, if you don't mind. Took them up on the high pastures, and just not sure which point of view to use for my painting. I like the one with the sheep, but the other one, the one with the dog taken from higher up, is rather good, too. Would it be breaking the rules, do you think, if I blended the two views, as it were? Do you think the two focal points would work?"

She peered anxiously at Penny.

"I'd be so grateful if you would just take a look at them and let me know what you think. No hurry." She handed the packet of photos over to Penny, who tucked them in her bag and then introduced Alywnne to Victoria.

"Well, I'll leave you to it," said Alwynne. "Must go. Have to get back to the office. We're working a new exhibit for fall. Photos taken during World War Two. So sorry about Emma, Penny, but it was a lovely service."

Penny and Victoria watched her leave and then sat together in companionable silence as the room began to empty.

"Have you ever noticed that when one person leaves, it seems to give everyone else permission to go, too?" Penny asked. "Funny, that.

"Anyway, if you're going to be around a bit," she said, handing over a business card, "why don't you give me a call and perhaps we can meet up for a coffee or lunch."

"I'd love to," Victoria said. "Actually, I might come around for a manicure. Haven't had one in ages."

After saying good-bye to acquaintances, accepting a few condolences, and thanking Bronwyn again, Penny made her way out of the hotel and headed for home.

On the way she stopped into the Spar to pick up a few things for dinner, along with the local newspaper.

A few minutes later she let herself into the shop, checked her telephone for messages, jotted down a couple of telephone numbers, and then made her way upstairs.

She put the food in the fridge and poured herself a glass of water, went to her desk, telephoned the clients who had left messages, and took their bookings.

She then turned to the paper, whose front-page story, written by Morwyn Lloyd, was all about Llanelen's missing bride. After glancing at the engagement photo of Meg Wynne Thompson, Penny began reading the article, wondering if she had been mentioned.

POLICE SEEK MISSING BRIDE shouted the headline.

Police are seeking the public's assistance in locating Meg Wynne Thompson, who mysteriously disappeared on the morning of her wedding to Emyr Gruffydd, only son of local landowner Rhys Gruffydd.

"We have absolutely no idea where she is or what could have happened to her," said Gruffydd's friend and best man, David Williams. "We are asking anyone who has seen her to please come forward."

Ms. Thompson was last seen on Saturday morning having a manicure at the Happy Hands salon, Station Road, owned by Penny Brannigan.

"It was straightforward, really," said Ms. Brannigan. "I did her nails, and she left the shop about ten A.M. I assumed she would be going back to the hotel to complete her preparations for the wedding."

Thinking that Morwyn had done a good job quoting her accurately, Penny's eyes drifted back to the photo. She looked at it closely, looked away, and then, pressing her fingers over her mouth, scrutinized it. She took off her reading glasses and held the paper closer to her face. Finally satisfied, she folded up the paper and set it on the table.

She sat back, folded her arms, and thought for a few moments, and then got up and grabbed her handbag off the counter. She scrabbled about inside until she found what she was looking for, and then picking up the telephone, carefully dialled the number on the card she now held in her hand.

Then, she took one last glance at the newspaper.

"Oh, hello, it's Penny Brannigan here. I did the manicure on Saturday morning for Meg Wynne Thompson, the missing bride."

"Yes, Miss Brannigan. How can we help you?"

"Well, it's just that the officer, the chief inspector, Mr. Davies, gave me his card and asked me to call him if I thought of anything else."

"And have you?" asked Morgan. "Thought of anything else?"

"Well, no, not really, that's not it exactly," said Penny. "But I'd like to know if that woman whose photo is in the paper today, Meg Wynne Thompson, is that really her photo?"

"Yes," said Morgan, "that's the photo we were provided with. That's her. Why do you ask?"

"Well, it's just that I'm pretty sure that the woman in that photo is not the woman who came to me on Saturday morning for a manicure. If that's the real Meg Wynne Thompson, then the woman I saw was not."

CHAPTER THIRTEEN

Morgan was silent for a moment while she considered what she had just heard.

"Now, Miss Brannigan, please, let me make sure I understand this correctly. You're saying that you don't think the woman who came to you on Saturday morning was Meg Wynne Thompson?"

"That's right," said Penny. "They look a lot alike, same kind of haircut, same build, maybe, but there's something different about the face, around the mouth. And there's another reason why I don't think it was the same woman."

Morgan listened without speaking and then moved to end the call.

"Right. Well, thank you for this, we'll be in touch. Are you at home now if we need to see you tonight?"

"Yes, I'll be here for the rest of the evening. But I've had a difficult day, and if it could wait . . ."

Morgan rang off, knocked on Davies's door, and burst in at his shouted, "Come in!"

With his jacket off and shirtsleeves rolled up Davies looked every inch the busy detective. His office was painted a pale, institutional green, with a window covered in dusty blinds that overlooked the car park. On top of two file cabinets behind his desk stood several limp houseplants that he was nursing back to health. There were no family photos on his desk but a couple of plaques on the wall spoke to his community involvement and dedication to duty.

He peered at Morgan over his glasses.

"Yes, Bethan, what is it?"

"I've had that manicure woman on the phone, Penny Brannigan. She has some interesting information for us. She kept your card, apparently."

"I'm astonished," said Davies.

"That she has information?"

"No, that she kept my card and actually rang us. How many cards do you think I give out in a year? Five hundred? And the minute I'm out the door, they're in the bin. Nobody ever keeps them and nobody ever calls back. I wonder why I bother.

"But never mind. What did she want?"

"Well, sir, if she's right, the case has just gone in a different direction. According to Brannigan, we've got a ringer here. She says the woman who came to her for a manicure on Saturday morning couldn't have been Meg Wynne Thompson. Or at least the woman she saw is not the same woman whose picture was in the *Post* today."

Davies held his pen at both ends and looked levelly at his sergeant.

"Could she be wrong? After all, that was a formal kind of photograph. She would have been wearing fancy makeup . . . maybe had her hair done differently."

Morgan nodded. "Right, but she said there was something else, and it really rang true for me. She said in the photo Meg Wynne's hands are resting in her lap. She said she could be wrong about the face but she does know hands, and those aren't the nails she worked on that morning. And she spent almost an hour looking at them. Everybody's hands are different, she said, and so are their nails."

Davies gazed thoughtfully at her, and then rose slowly from his seat.

"Is she in? We'd better get around there and interview her again.

"If she's right, there are all kinds of implications. Everything we've done so far has been misplaced because we've got a whole new timeline here. Meg Wynne could have gone missing at least an hour earlier than we thought she did. And then who the hell is the woman in the surveillance video? What's her connection with all this? See if you can get them to enlarge and enhance an image from the video so we've got something to show her. That Penny woman."

The two set off for Llanelen where Penny, tired and emotionally drained from the funeral, was reluctantly ready to talk to them.

"I've been down to the shop and picked up the client card I wrote that morning. It's really all I have. Of course, I thought I was writing it for Meg Wynne, but whoever she was, that other woman, here's the card."

Penny gave them the small card with the details of the service she had provided to the woman she had thought was Meg Wynne Thompson on Saturday morning.

Davies turned it over slowly, and then looked at Penny.

"I'm sorry, Miss Brannigan, but we're going to have to ask you to go over everything that happened once again. But before we do that, would you please take a look at this photo and see if you think this is the woman who came to your shop on Saturday morning? Take your time."

He handed Penny a photo lifted from the grainy surveillance video. She looked at it carefully, and then nodded.

"It's a bit difficult to tell about the face, but the clothes are exactly right. I would say that's her."

Half an hour later, after having heard Penny tell her story again, the two police officers left.

"She was remarkably true to the first version, her story didn't change at all. Not in any detail," remarked Morgan as they made their way to their car.

"I wish all our witnesses were so good," agreed Davies.

"But it looks as if we've got something much worse on our hands now than a simple disappearance. I think she's right, that there was another woman. And that means, well, I don't have to spell it out for you, do I?"

Finally alone, Penny sat down on her sofa, put her feet up, leaned back, and closed her eyes. Her body was tired, but her mind was not.

She needed to reflect on the events of the day, starting with the funeral and the beautiful music in the church. She smiled as she recalled it. There was no doubt Victoria was very talented and Penny wondered if she had made a CD. What would that be like, Penny wondered, listening to a CD of harp music in the evening, say. Would it be peaceful and comforting or just terribly depressing?

As her thoughts turned to Victoria, she was glad they had met and looked forward to getting to know her better. Maybe she would stay in the area for a bit longer.

With that, Penny felt tears welling up. Her friendship with Emma, as unlikely as it might have seemed to others, had been dear to her. She found it hard to accept that the clever, dedicated teacher whom she had known as a caring friend was gone. And while she was giving herself over to long-forgotten emotions that felt strange and uncomfortable, she finally recognized them for what they were. She was grieving.

The funeral, though, had been lovely and exactly as Emma would have wished it.

But as she thought about it, Penny realized again that something about it hadn't been quite right. Something she couldn't put her finger on had been out of place. Shaking her head, she told herself to leave it alone, and whatever it was, it would come to her when she least expected it. Or maybe it wasn't anything important, just one of those niggling details that don't seem right at the time, and are forgotten the next day in the business of everyday life.

For Morgan and Davies, the disappearance of Meg Wynne would take up a great deal of their time over the next few days as they checked bank account and credit card activity, and re-interviewed everyone who had been connected with the wedding. Their search took them to London where they searched her flat, talked to her colleagues at the design firm, and interviewed her neighbours.

They came up empty.

"I think we've reached that point in the investigation," observed Morgan, "when we need a really good break. I hope something turns up soon."

Meg Wynne, it seemed, had simply vanished.

CHAPTER FOURTEEN

She hadn't vanished off the pages of the *Daily Post,* though. Morwyn Lloyd was writing a new story almost every day, based on material given to her by the police, who were trying to keep the story alive in the hopes that some small detail would jog someone's memory and lead to the break they so desperately needed.

NEW TWIST IN MYSTERY OF THE MISSING BRIDE-TO-BE

Police are seeking a woman who apparently posed as missing bride-to-be Meg Wynne Thompson shortly before her disappearance on Saturday.

Detective Sergeant Bethan Morgan from North Wales police said that there is widespread concern for Ms. Thompson, who has not been seen since Saturday morning. At first, detectives believed she had had a manicure at the Happy Hands salon on Station Road, but now think the woman who had the manicure was someone else who, for unknown reasons, was posing as the bride.

"If anyone knows who this mystery woman is, we would ask them to come forward," she said. "We believe this woman might be able to help us find Ms. Thompson and return her safely to her family.

"We certainly are hopeful but as time goes on we become more and more concerned about her well-being."

Ms. Thompson had been scheduled to marry Emyr Gruffydd, son of local landowner and businessman Rhys Gruffydd, on Saturday afternoon. For unknown reasons, she did not appear at the church, and has been the subject of a widespread police missing persons inquiry.

Over the next few days, however, the story gradually fell off the front page and a photo no longer appeared with it.

Llanelen life was settling back into its cosy routine, until a chance remark by Mrs. Lloyd changed everything.

On Thursday afternoon she arrived for her usual manicure carrying a large bag from Marks & Spencer.

"Oh, Penny," she said as she carefully set her bag down beside the appointment-book table. "This has been such a dreadful week and I don't mind saying I hope I never see one like it again."

"Very true," agreed Penny as Mrs. Lloyd settled herself at the manicure table and Penny prepared her warm soaking liquid.

"Of course, for you, dear, Emma's funeral would have been very upsetting. I know you two were very close, as would only be natural, seeing as how you were both incomers, so to speak.

"Not that we ever thought of you that way, of course," she added as an afterthought.

Penny smiled at Mrs. Lloyd. Honestly, the woman was impossible, but still, you had to like her. Most of the time.

"The whole wedding experience was very upsetting for me, I can tell you," Mrs. Lloyd went on. "I was right there as it all unfolded. I saw everything. I can't tell you how simply shocked everyone was when the bride didn't turn up. No one knew where to look or what to do. I must say, though, that Bronwyn handled everything beautifully. She really is the most gracious woman and such an asset to her husband. Yes, that Thomas Evans chose very well when he chose her. He certainly knew what he was doing."

Mrs. Lloyd was off and running. Penny nodded agreement every now and then, murmured an occasional "Mm hmm," and went on with her work, through the shaping and filing of her client's nails and the application of the base coat.

"What colour will you be having today?" asked Penny. "How about Chocolate Moose from the Canadian collection? You like that one."

"That will do very nicely, thank you, Penny."

As Penny began applying the first coat of polish, Mrs. Lloyd was off again.

"As you know, Penny, I've always prided myself on being well turned out. There's nothing quite sets a professional woman apart like a smart suit, I always say. And I do like the way they've brought out suits for more formal wear. I had a very fetching one for the wedding, if I do say so myself, but I was very disappointed in my hat. In fact, it's over there in the Marks and Sparks bag; I'm taking the bus this afternoon up to Llandudno to return it. They're very good about taking things back, I find, Marks and Spencer. But of course, I am one of their best customers; I've worn nothing but their clothes for years. Or perhaps I should say they dress me! I believe that is the fashion parlance. I find they do a good line for all ages."

Penny started work on Mrs. Lloyd's other hand.

"No, the hat wasn't quite right, I'm afraid. Oh, the colour matched my suit all right, I made sure of that and there was nothing actually wrong with the hat itself, it just didn't suit me."

Mrs. Lloyd paused for a moment, held her hands at arm's length, and gave them a critical look.

"Yes, I think that colour will work very well with the dress I'll be wearing to the bridge game tonight.

"While these are drying, Penny, just go and fetch me my hat out of the bag, and I'll show you what I mean."

Penny sighed inwardly, but knowing the importance of humouring the client, did as she was asked, and handed the large turquoise hat, with its wide brim, tall crown, and masses of netting, feathers, and bobbing wispy bits to her customer. Mrs. Lloyd carried it carefully over to the wall-mounted mirror and placed it on her head.

With a broad, upward sweep of her hand, she gestured at the hat.

"There now, Penny, do you see what I mean? I don't think the hairdresser did anything different, but for some reason I can't get the hat to go on properly. It's sitting up way too high!"

Tilting her head this way and that to get a better look at the hat, Mrs. Lloyd caught sight of Penny, standing behind her, reflected in the mirror. She was shocked by what she saw.

Penny's normally pale, freckled face was a mask of puzzled intensity as she struggled to process what she had just heard. Her eyes widened, and then her face turned ashen as if all the blood had drained from it. She couldn't speak and tried desperately to swallow.

"Good heavens, Penny! Whatever is the matter with you, girl? It's only a hat from Marks and Spencer—there's no need to take on like that. What's the matter with you? You look as if you've had a terrible shock! Are you all right? Are you ill? Should I call somebody?"

Penny shook her head and sat down on the small chair beside the appointment-book table. She was trembling slightly and used the edge of the table to steady herself.

"No, Mrs. Lloyd," she said in a low voice. "I'm all right, but I need a drink of water. I'll be right back."

Penny disappeared into the preparation room while Mrs. Lloyd took off her hat and replaced it in the bag.

If she didn't like it that much, she thought, I'd better get it out of her sight before she returns. She could hear water running in the small supply room, and a moment later Penny returned, looking somewhat more composed, but not herself.

"Mrs. Lloyd, I'm terribly sorry, and I know you aren't going to be pleased with me, but I'm afraid I can't do your second coat just now. Something you said has really upset me, and I need to sort it out. Well, not so much upset as made me realize something. I'm very sorry, but I have to ask you to leave. Please forgive me. Look, come back tomorrow morning, and I'll finish your nails for you and there won't be any charge to you for this manicure."

"Well, really, Penny, this is a bit much, I must say," said Mrs. Lloyd, as Penny scrambled to collect her bags and hand them to her. "Will you not at least tell me what I said that's made you take on like this? I can't think what I said that could have upset you. Is it something personal?"

"No, no, Mrs. Lloyd, it's not personal, it's just something else," replied Penny. "I hardly know what I'm doing just now, but I have to make a very important telephone call. I'm so sorry, but I need to be on my own."

Mrs. Lloyd took her handbag and Marks & Spencer bag from Penny and made her way out of the shop and into the street. As she glanced behind her, she saw Penny turning the shop sign to CLOSED and then switching the lights off.

Making her way across the square, Mrs. Lloyd decided to return home to make a phone call of her own.

"It was simply the most astonishing thing, Morwyn," she was telling her niece a few minutes later. "And in mid-manicure, too! One minute we were going along fine and the next minute I was being rushed out the door. 'Here's your turquoise hat and what's your hurry?' she might as well have said. I didn't know what to make of it. I can tell you, if it had been anyone else except Penny I wouldn't be setting foot in her shop again anytime soon. But obviously something's upset her deeply or she wouldn't have reacted like that. I've never seen anyone so flustered. And all because of a hat! A hat! Honestly."

"Tell me again, Aunt, exactly what you said that set her off," Morwyn said. "Word for word and don't leave anything out."

Penny, meanwhile, after shutting the shop door, returned to the small chair beside the telephone table.

A few minutes later she rose, made her way resolutely upstairs to her flat, and picked up the telephone in one hand as she reached for Davies's business card with the other.

She picked up the receiver and after a moment's hesitation, set it down again.

What if he thinks I'm an hysterical idiot, she thought. She looked at the phone for a few more moments, picked it up again, and quickly entered in the numbers.

"It's me again, Sergeant Morgan," she said when the call was answered. "Penny Brannigan in Llanelen. Something terrible has occurred to me, and I need to talk to you about it."

Morgan listened and then thanked Penny and rang off. She knocked on Davies's door and entered.

"I've just had Penny Brannigan on the phone again, sir. She's asked if we can go around and see her. She doesn't want to go into it on the phone. She sounds very upset."

Davies looked at her.

"What's she upset about?"

"She thinks she might know where Meg Wynne Thompson is. Or, I should say, where her body is."

CHAPTER FIFTEEN

Penny was standing on the pavement outside her shop when the police officers arrived.

"Let's go upstairs," she said as they made their way through the shop. "I don't want to talk here. Follow me."

She led them upstairs to the flat and into the small sitting room. With a brief gesture at the sofa, Penny sat down in the matching armchair.

"I'm very sorry if I seem upset, but I am," she began. "I've had something of a shocking idea and I felt I needed to tell you about it. I may be wrong. I hope I am. But I don't think so."

"What is it Miss Brannigan? Please tell us what's happened," said Morgan.

"Whatever it is, it's obviously affected you," said Davies gently. "Look, let's have Sergeant Morgan get the kettle on, and we'll take a few moments before you start."

He gestured with his head toward the kitchen and Morgan rose obediently and went to organize a cup of tea.

"Would it be easier to tell just me, Miss Brannigan, or do you want to wait for Sergeant Morgan to return?" he asked.

Penny nodded.

"You want to wait?"

Penny nodded again.

"That's fine. Miss Brannigan, did you want us here because you didn't want to be on your own just at the minute?"

Again, a nod. Penny could barely bring herself to look at him, but when she did, she was encouraged by the concern in his eyes.

A few moments later Morgan returned with three mugs of tea, a carton of milk, and the sugar bowl.

"How do you take your tea, Miss Brannigan?"

Penny indicated the milk, and accepted the mug Morgan handed her. She took a sip, and then put the mug on the table between them.

Davies leaned back and then nodded at Morgan, who took out her notebook.

"Right," he said. "In your own time, Miss Brannigan. You think you know where Meg Wynne Thompson is. Please tell us."

Penny looked at him, took a deep breath.

"Look, there's no easy way to say this, so I'm just going to say it. I think her body's underneath Emma Teasdale's coffin."

In the stunned silence that followed, Davies, who had been about to take a sip of tea, paused with his mug halfway to his lips as if he had been flash frozen.

He recovered himself quickly, set his mug down on the table, and took charge of the conversation. "Who is Emma Teasdale, please?"

"She was buried on Monday afternoon. She was my friend and I miss her very much."

Penny's eyes filled with tears and Morgan handed her a tissue.

"I have to ask you," said Davies, leaning forward

with his hands clasped together between his knees, "why would you even think such a thing?"

"Since the funeral, I've had this awful feeling that something wasn't right, but I couldn't put my finger on it. I kept telling myself it was probably nothing, the way you do, but the feeling wouldn't go away. I was going to ask Bronwyn Evans or some of the others who were there if they noticed anything wrong, but I kept telling myself not to be so silly, that it was just all in my head. And then today, when Mrs. Lloyd came into the shop, she was going on and on about her hat, how it wasn't right, and then she put it on. And then she said, and I'll never forget this, she said, 'It's sitting up way too high,' and I realized that was the problem at Emma's graveside. You know how you gather around the grave at the end and you toss earth on top of the coffin as the rector says the 'Dust to dust, ashes to ashes' bit?"

The police officers nodded.

"Well, that's what wasn't right. The coffin was too high. It was too close to us when we threw the earth on it. And now, I think the reason it's too high is because there's something underneath it."

Again, there was a heavy silence as the two police officers took in what they had just heard. The sound of their breathing seemed amplified in the stillness.

Finally, Davies spoke.

"We need to be very careful with this, Miss Brannigan. I know you loved your friend, and you would not be telling us this unless you were quite certain of it. But is there any chance you might be mistaken? Because there's only one way for us to find if you're right and that is not something we would ever do without very good cause."

"I know," Penny said. "But I believe that's what

happened and I thought it was my duty to tell you. What you decide to do with this information is obviously up to you."

She made a little impatient, fluttering gesture with her hands and looked from one to the other.

"But do you know that feeling you get sometimes when you've misplaced something, and you've looked absolutely everywhere for it? And then you step back for a moment, think about it, and suddenly, with absolute certainty, you know exactly where it is? And you go straight there and you look in the pocket of that jacket you haven't worn for ages and sure enough, there it is. What you lost. That's how I feel about this. I feel absolutely certain that if you look there, you'll find her. Meg Wynne Thompson."

She sat back, distressed and exhausted. The late-afternoon sun filtered through the curtains lighting the flowers on her desk, the art books on her shelves, and the watercolours on the walls. Morgan, drawn out of the moment, looked around and wondered admiringly how anyone could live such a clutter-free life.

"Miss Brannigan, do you have anyone you could call who might come and stay with you for a little while? Is there anyone you'd like us to get?" Davies asked. "Normally, I'd suggest that the WPC here stay with you, but in light of what you've just said, I'm going to need her back at the station."

Penny met his gaze.

"Well, since Emma died, I don't really have a very close friend, and everyone who might be able to come over is probably at work."

She sat there for a moment.

"There's Bronwyn, of course."

A moment later, she added, "Wait, there is someone, actually, but I don't have her phone number. She's called

Victoria Hopkirk, and Bronwyn Evans, the wife of our rector, knows where to find her. She seemed a sensible, kind woman. I don't know her very well, but I quite liked her. Could we ask her?"

Davies nodded at Morgan, who excused herself to make the arrangements.

"The thing is, though, Miss Brannigan, we're going to have to ask you to keep this to yourself for the moment," said Davies.

He smiled at her and she was surprised by how reassured she felt.

He stood up and took a few steps to take a closer look at one of the paintings.

"Is this yours?" he asked, turning around to look at her.

She nodded.

"Very nice. I like landscapes. I like when things look the way they're supposed to look."

"That'll be the policeman in you."

This time, she smiled and he nodded.

Morgan returned a few moments later.

"It's done, sir. Mrs. Hopkirk said she'd be happy to keep Miss Brannigan company. She should be here in about twenty minutes."

Morgan looked at Penny.

"I told her you weren't feeling well, that you'd had a bit of a shock. She was concerned but seemed rather pleased that you asked for her. I got the feeling that she quite likes you, too."

"Good," said Davies as he sat down again. "Well, that's that, then."

While Morgan tidied away the tea things, Davies and Penny went over the funeral scene again in greater detail and when Victoria arrived, the two officers took their leave.

"What's going to happen now, sir?" asked Morgan when they were in the car. "Do you think she's credible?"

"She very well may be," Davies said cautiously, "because she's an artist and what's been bothering her, I think, is that from an artistic point of view, the perspective at the gravesite was wrong. But still, she could be mistaken, and I'd feel more comfortable if we had another point of view. If somebody else noticed something amiss, I'd feel better about moving forward with this. What we need is corroboration.

"And who has the best view of the coffin at a committal service?" he asked slyly. "And who's probably seen more of them than anybody else?"

Morgan grinned, turned the car around, and reached for her mobile.

"Good one, sir! Interesting, isn't it, that I only had to press redial?" she said as she handed her phone over to her supervisor in the passenger seat.

"Ah, good afternoon again, Mrs. Evans," said Davies. "This is DCI Davies here. I wonder, do you think we might pop in for a word with your husband?"

A few minutes later they were shown into the rector's comfortable, if somewhat shabby study. What the small, book-lined room lacked in style, it more than made up for with the beautiful view of the rectory garden leading down to the River Conwy and the hills beyond.

Noticing Morgan detaching from business for a moment to admire the view, Rev. Evans smiled at her.

"I often look out that window for inspiration," he said to her. "And every time I do I understand what the psalmist meant when he wrote, 'I will lift up mine eyes unto the hills from whence cometh my help.' Well, I say psalmist, but it was David, actually."

Bringing herself back to the business at hand, Morgan nodded.

"We're sorry to disturb you, Rev. Evans," she began.

"No need to apologize," he replied. "I wish I could tell you I was giving some deep and profound thought to Sunday morning's sermon, but you've actually caught me napping. Please, have a seat."

He gestured at two chairs on the other side of his desk and looked intently at his visitors.

"What can I do for you?" he asked.

"We'd like to talk to you about the funeral of Emma Teasdale, especially the committal part of the service," Morgan said.

"Oh, yes?"

"Did you happen to notice anything odd or unusual when you were at the gravesite? Was there anything about the scene that struck you as unusual or out of place?"

The rector sat back in his chair, put his hands in a prayer position, and gently touched the ends of his fingers to his mouth.

"Odd or unusual. Hmm, let me think."

A few moments later, he leaned forward.

"Well, now that you mention it, there was one thing. Something about the coffin seemed different. I did notice that, and in fact, I think I mentioned something about it to Bronwyn that night."

"Can you tell me what that was, Rev. Evans?"

"It was just a little thing, but I noticed that I could read the name and dates on the brass coffin-plate quite clearly. I can't see as well as I used to, and now the plates are a little blurry, so I thought, Oh, that's very good. They've started making the letters larger so us over fifties can read them better. But then I said to Bronwyn that night, 'Why would us over fifties, or anybody else for that matter, ever need to read the coffin-plate?'

"So that seemed rather unusual, but I thought no more about it."

Trying to contain her excitement, Morgan glanced at her supervisor and asked her last question.

"Can you tell me the name of the undertaker who would have arranged for the plate?"

"Certainly," said the rector. "It was Philip, just across the square. Philip Wightman. Wightman and Sons."

Morgan sat back as Davies took over.

"Rector, we are going across the street for a word with Mr. Wightman, but we need you to stay awake. I expect we'll be back to finish this conversation in about fifteen minutes. Is that all right with you?"

Rev. Evans sighed.

"Certainly, it is. Quite all right. I guess now I really will have to make a start on that sermon. If it puts me to sleep, that doesn't bode well for my poor parishioners, does it?"

Morgan and Davies smiled at his gentle joke, and took their leave.

A few minutes later the shop bell tinkled as they entered the premises of Philip Wightman.

Slipping on his jacket as he emerged from the back room, Philip took the measure of his visitors and extended his hand.

"Hello," he said. "I'm Philip Wightman. May I help you?"

Davies and Morgan showed their warrant cards and got right to the point.

"We'd like to know about the brass nameplate you used for Emma Teasdale's coffin," said Morgan. "Was there anything different about it?"

"Different?" asked Philip. "No, it's not different from any other nameplate we would use. Why do you ask?"

"We're following a line of investigation and the nameplate may be important," Davies said. "What can you tell us about it?"

"I don't do the engraving myself, that's outsourced, as they say, but I do affix the plate to the coffin. I need to make sure everything is spelled correctly, see."

"And this one was no different from any other nameplate you might have used in the past little while?"

"No. The font changed in the 1970s—it used to be more of an italic script—but this plate was like any other I would use."

"And the type was no larger?"

"No."

"Thank you, Mr. Wightman, that'll be all. We appreciate your time this afternoon."

The jingling shop door safely shut behind them, Morgan and Davies looked at each other with a mixture of anticipation, excitement, and dread.

"So if the type wasn't any larger, that must mean . . ." Morgan started to say.

". . . that the coffin was closer to him, giving him the impression the words were larger," Davies finished. "He thought he saw what he expected to see, that is, the coffin at its usual depth, so his brain explained the nameplate by suggesting the typeface was larger."

He sighed.

"Start the paperwork, Morgan," Davies ordered. "You won't see this very often, maybe once or twice in your career, but we need to get on to the Home Office with a request for an exhumation. Normally, when you call for an exhumation it's because you need to examine what's inside the coffin. We're not going to open the coffin, but because we'll be disturbing human remains, to be on the safe side, we're going to do the paperwork and put in a formal request. That way, it's all aboveboard. No complaints later.

"I'll double back and let the rector know and then drop around before I go and talk to Miss Brannigan myself.

"Oh, and one more thing, Morgan. The next time she calls, put her straight through to me. I'm starting to really like the way that woman thinks."

CHAPTER SIXTEEN

"Oh, dear God!"

The rector's face was a study in heart-wrenching distress underwritten by amazement. "I cannot believe that such a thing could be possible. Oh, who would do such a wicked thing?"

As the implications for his church began to dawn on him, his face hardened slightly, his shoulders squared imperceptibly, and he readied himself for the challenge that lay ahead.

"Well, you'd better tell me what to expect so I can be prepared for whatever you plan to do," he said, placing his hands on the desk in front of him. "And whatever you need me to do," he added.

"We're putting the paperwork in place now," Davies told him, "and we expect the Home Office will give it priority and treat it as urgent. We should get the approval later tonight, and we're mobilizing equipment now. My sergeant has your number, but just to be on the safe side, you'd better let me have it, too, and one of us will ring you as soon as we hear anything."

The two men stood, and Davies offered his hand, which the rector accepted and shook. With a business-like nod, which he hoped would be seen as reassuring, Davies left. As the door closed behind him, the rector sank back into his chair with a worried, puzzled look on his face.

And now back to our manicure lady, thought Davies as he made his way through the centre of town to the small side street where her shop and flat were located.

Penny met him at the door.

"You seem a bit better, now," he said to her on the way upstairs. "Feeling a little more settled?"

"I am, thanks. I'm glad Victoria was able to be here, but I wish I could tell her what's the matter."

"We can fill her in now," Davies said. "I've come to let you know what's happening."

He entered the small living room where Victoria was sitting at one end of the sofa. She looked startled and started to rise when he entered, but he gestured to her to stay seated.

"Victoria, this is Detective Chief Inspector Davies. He's come to tell us something," Penny said.

"Hello," Davies said to her and then, turning to Penny, added, "I wanted to bring you up to date. Do you think we could sit down?" Without waiting for a reply, he moved a plaid cushion out of the way and lowered himself into the wing chair as Penny sat down beside Victoria. The two of them leaned forward and looked at him expectantly.

Davies cleared his throat and then looked at Penny.

"We are going ahead with an exhumation order, and if we get the approval later this evening, as I think we will, we intend to move quickly.

"I'll leave you now. You can tell Mrs. Hopkirk what you know but I ask that the two of you keep it to yourselves for the time being. Word will be out soon enough, I imagine."

"How soon?" asked Penny. "When will you do this?"

"We'll go at first light tomorrow."

"That soon?"

"That soon. It's always better to get this sort of thing over and done with as quickly as possible before the rumour machine can really take hold. As it is, too many people will probably know about it."

Leaving a stunned Penny to sort out a mystified Victoria, Davies made his way back down the stairs and out into the street. He reached for his mobile to call Morgan to come and get him. If Penny Brannigan was right, and he was now starting to think that she was, they would need to have a quick dinner and prepare themselves for a long, busy night.

A few hours later the fax machine in the North Wales headquarters churned out the document they had been waiting for.

"Right, Bethan, you're going to have to work flat out for the next couple of hours. I need you to organize the press office, arrange for the videographer and still photographer, the crime scene people—everybody. The earth moving equipment is ordered?"

At Morgan's nod, he gave her a friendly pat on the shoulder.

"Well, then, I'll leave it with you. I need to notify the superintendent and the other senior officers. Get everything ready tonight and then pick me up at four-thirty. We'll aim to start at first light or just before.

"Oh, and don't forget," he added, "we'll need a few rolls of yellow tape to establish the perimeter area."

Sometime in the night, Penny was awakened by the gentle sound of rain pattering on the leaves of the trees outside her window. As she lay there listening, wrapped in melancholy, she thought of the whole sorry business that would unfold in the coming day, and felt a small tear trickle down her cheek. The rain was making everything seem unbearably sad. She turned over and looked at the clock—4:22. She doubted she would be able to get back to sleep but it was too early to get up, and besides, she didn't want to disturb Victoria who had settled in for the night on the sofa. She would have to wait it out in the silence of the predawn darkness, with her fears and memories to keep her company.

As she lay there, her thoughts turned to Emma and how much she missed her quiet, undemanding companionship. Philip Wightman had been right; they had been a lot alike, especially in the way they took great pleasure in the simplest things. They had read the same kinds of books, mostly biographies and mysteries borrowed from the local library but sometimes bought secondhand from the village bookstore; treated themselves on special occasions to afternoon tea with scones, strawberry jam, and clotted cream in the village tea shop; and regularly taken long rambling walks in the beautiful countryside that framed the town while they discussed what kind of dog they'd choose to have trotting along beside them—if they were to get a dog, that is.

They always had a jigsaw puzzle on the go in the front room of Emma's cottage that they pieced together on lazy Sunday afternoons, gin and tonic in hand, as the warm sun filtered through the mullioned windows, casting dappled grey shadows that shifted and swayed in time with the gentle rustling of the apple tree in the front garden. Penny remembered fondly how her friend used to hide the lid of the puzzle box so she, Penny, would have to put it together without knowing what the final image was meant to look like. But Emma was predictable in her choice of puzzles and Penny knew that eventually they would have assembled a lighthouse with threatening waves crashing around it in the moonlight, an exuberant garden filled with blowsy roses in every imaginable colour, or some idealized Scottish castle perched high on a hill. But once, after Penny had complained she was getting a bit bored with all the chocolate-box landscapes, a picture of a smiling Queen Mother in a hat dripping with lilacs had emerged.

"Now then, Miss Smarty Pants," Emma had teased. "I knew the flowers on her hat would mislead you! It didn't turn out to be what you thought it was, did it?"

As Penny was drifting back to sleep a small convoy was winding its way along the dark, damp road leading to Llanelen. The vehicles' headlights gave off an eerie, diffused yellow light revealing mist clinging to black trees. And as the rain let up just before sunrise the vehicles came to a stop beside the church and cut their engines.

Moving silently in the muted greyness that signals the coming dawn, a practiced, proficient team of experts went about their tasks. Conversation was kept to the minimum and when they needed to speak to one another, they spoke in soft voices.

Their arrival, however, had been noticed.

"Someone's coming, sir," said Morgan in a low voice, pointing to a figure emerging from the darkness.

"That'll be the rector; he said he wanted to be here and I'd expect him to be," replied Davies.

"Good morning," said Rev. Evans as he broke through the mist. He looked as if he had dressed in a hurry and Davies doubted if he'd slept much that night. "I thought it would be appropriate for me to be here for Emma—to provide a spiritual presence, no matter the outcome.

And my wife will have coffee for your team whenever you're ready for it. Just knock on the door and let her know."

"That's very good of you, Rector," replied Davies. "We're going to press on, now, but I'm sure the coffee will be most welcome in an hour or so. We've put up the barrier tape, so if you wouldn't mind standing just over there," he said, pointing in the direction of a small stand of trees at the edge of the tenting which had been erected to protect the site, "we'll try to do this with the least amount of disruption possible. I think everything's in position now."

He gestured to the officer standing nearest the earth mover and, as the first notes of birdsong announced the beginning of the dawn chorus, the sound of heavy equipment starting up filled the air. The machine worked viciously, swiftly and efficiently. The grave was opened and lifting equipment placed under the coffin. With large clots of mud clinging to its sides, the coffin containing the mortal remains of Emma Teasdale was slowly lifted out of the earth and gently swung to one side where it was lowered to the ground and covered with a tarpaulin. The grave gave off a dank smell of dark, forbidden earth mixed with rotting leaves.

Standing at the top of the empty grave, Davies motioned to the lighting expert to switch on the overhead set of tungsten lights. Suddenly, the scene was lit with the bright white glare of lights that shone with ferocious intensity into the grave.

Davies nodded again and the videographer and still photographer took their places, ready to record everything as it happened.

"Ready, sir!" said a scene-of-crime expert as he lowered a small ladder into the grave. He scrambled down, stepped off the second to last rung with a soft thud, and began working carefully and systematically in one corner of the grave. The tension grew as he brushed aside the damp dirt and placed it in a small bucket which was then lifted to the top and piled to one side.

A few minutes later, he gave a shout.

"I've found something, sir. Look, it's a shoe."

He held it up for those above him to see.

"It's a strappy, black sandal type."

He handed it up to Morgan, who took it in her gloved hand and examined it before placing it in a plastic evidence bag.

She nodded at Davies.

"It's a Chanel sling back. It could very well belong to Meg Wynne. If the shoe fits, sir—"

She was interrupted by another shout from below.

"There's definitely something here."

They leaned over the side and looked where the officer was pointing. There, emerging from the rich, dark Welsh soil, was a human foot.

"Female, by the looks of it, sir. The toes are painted."

CHAPTER SEVENTEEN

"Sergeant, ring the coroner. She'll have been half expecting the call."

Davies then ducked his head and turned away. Morgan, making no effort to conceal her excitement, leaned over for a better look.

The officers continued with their work and a few minutes later the body was revealed. She was lying on her side, fully clothed, with her arms above her head.

"She looks as if she had been thrown or rolled over the side," Morgan commented to Davies. "She isn't displayed or laid out. She's floppy. She was dumped."

Davies glanced at the photographer and videographer to make sure they were capturing everything.

A few moments later came another shout. "I think we've got her handbag, sir!"

"Let's have it," Morgan called down.

She pulled on a pair of latex gloves, reached down for the small black bag, and turned it over to look at the logo. Kate Spade.

"For everyday," Morgan muttered. She unzipped the bag and looked at the contents. A lipstick, a mobile telephone, a small change purse, and a leather billfold bulging with plastic cards. She pulled out the first one, a platinum American Express card, and showed it to Davies. He looked at the name and nodded.

"Make the calls, Sergeant," he ordered, "but I want the important elements done in person, not by phone. Ask the Durham force to go to her parents' home to tell them that we've found a body answering their daughter's description so they can prepare themselves, pending a formal identification. This could be national news within hours, and best they hear it from us. We'll ask Emyr Gruffydd if he'd be willing to identify the body. Otherwise we'll have to wait until the father can get here.

"We're also going to need dental records; you'll probably need to get those from London. We've had the wrong woman once before in this case, and we need to be absolutely sure."

Morgan nodded and took a few steps back from the grave.

The police officers continued processing the scene. Soon a plastic bag containing a mobile phone was handed up.

Morgan shot Davies a puzzled look.

"I've already got her mobile," she said. "It was in her handbag." "You'll need to trace both of them," Davies told her. "She could have had two. Some people do, but I can't think why. I've only got the one and I hate it."

Several minutes later the activity in the grave stopped and the officer looked up.

"I think that's everything that's here, sir," he said. "Shall we prepare to move the body?"

Davies looked around.

"Not yet. The coroner needs to take a look first," he said. "She should be on her way by now. Where the hell is she?"

He looked around. Beyond the churchyard and across

the river he could now make out the town's three-arched bridge; the coming lightness had imperceptibly pushed aside the heavy darkness of night. Lighter shades of grey touched the trees around the graveyard and soon the first faint blushes of dawn would signal that a new day had begun.

Davies looked down at the officer standing in the grave.

"Make absolutely sure you get everything there is to be had out of this grave," he said. "We've only got one chance to do this. And make sure everything you do get is processed properly—fibres, fingerprints, the lot."

A few minutes ticked by, and Davies remembered the rector's offer of coffee. Now's the time, he thought, and asked one of the officers to knock on the door of the rectory and let Mrs. Evans know they were ready for it.

"And be sure to thank her," he added testily.

As the officers were standing under the trees drinking their coffee, the coroner arrived, suited up, and climbed into the grave.

Davies watched as she knelt beside the body and gently examined it.

About ten minutes later she was standing beside him explaining her preliminary findings as the officers prepared the body for removal.

"Be careful," Davies called down to them. "Don't drop or lose anything. Sorry," he said, turning back to the coroner.

"As I was saying, there are several heavy blows to the back of the head just here," she said, almost touching the back of her own head with a gloved hand, "with what looks like some kind of flat, blunt instrument. There are also ligature marks around her neck, so on top of the head wounds, she was strangled. Can't tell you with what, yet, but whatever it was, it wasn't left in place on the victim."

She picked up her bag and prepared to leave.

"We'll have more for you after the autopsy, but I would say the body's been dead for about a week. As for manner of death, do I need to tell you? But for the record, it's clearly a homicide."

Two hours later the shrouded body was on its way to the morgue in Bangor for identification and autopsy, the coffin of Emma Teasdale had been returned to the earth, and the team had dispersed to begin writing their reports and processing still photos and videos. Davies was on his way to pay a call.

"I came to give you the results myself," he said to an anxious Penny, "and to thank you. We did find a body exactly where you thought we would, and although we're waiting on final and formal identification, we're pretty sure it will turn out to be that of Meg Wynne Thompson. So thank you for coming forward with what was really only a hunch or a bit of intuition. If it hadn't been for you, we probably never would have found her. And I'm sure that's exactly what the killer was counting on."

He stopped for a moment, and seemed unsure whether to continue.

"I hate that word, 'closure,' I have no idea what it means, but people always use it in circumstances like this, and say, 'Oh, well, at least now her parents can have closure,' so for what that's worth, I'm sure her parents will be grateful to have a body they can bury. I've seen other parents, and believe me, it's far worse not knowing what happened to your child."

Penny looked up at him with her lips set in a firm line and nodded.

"Would you like a cup of tea or coffee?" she asked. "Victoria was just about to put the kettle on, weren't you?"

"I was," she said as she left the room. "Really, I was."

"How long is she going to stop with you?" Davies asked. "Just out of curiosity. I thought she was just coming over to sit with you for an hour or so."

"We're not sure, but we're enjoying each other's company, and I'm in no hurry for her to leave and she's in no hurry to get back to her cousin, so I expect she'll stop with me for another day or two," Penny replied.

Davies nodded thoughtfully.

"Look," he said, "I think if you don't mind I won't have that coffee now. We've got a lot on just at the minute and I need to get back to the station." He hesitated, looked over Penny's shoulder, and finally managed to bring his eyes back to hers.

"I wondered if I might take a rain check. On the coffee. Another time when we're not so . . . when things aren't . . ."

"Yes, of course," said Penny. "When everything is more . . ."

She smiled at him, tentatively at first, but then openly and comfortably.

"I really want to thank you for taking the time to come by and tell me yourself. Maybe when you know more, you'll—"

She was interrupted by Victoria returning with the coffee tray.

"Victoria, the chief inspector won't be staying for coffee after all," said Penny, as Davies stood up. "He's got rather a lot on today, and he's decided to leave."

"Right," said Victoria. "Well, another time, perhaps."

"Yes," said Davies. "I'll see myself out." He nodded

at the two women and then made his way to the door at the top of the stairs.

Victoria watched as Penny's eyes followed his progress.

When the door had closed behind him she looked thoughtfully at her new friend.

"This is so awful, I know, Penny, but you have to admit it's also terribly exciting. You're at the centre of a murder investigation! Now why don't I pour our coffee and then we can go over everything that happened that morning? Maybe you'll remember something else that could help the police!"

Penny sighed, closed her eyes, and leaned her head back on the chair.

"You know, Victoria, we were up really early for this today and I'm suddenly totally knackered. I didn't sleep much last night, as you can imagine, and I think I'll go back to bed for an hour or so before it's time to open the shop. I really can't deal with any more of this right now."

Victoria looked aghast.

"Oh, how stupid of me! Of course, you must be exhausted. I should have thought. What a moron I am!"

Penny smiled at her.

"Don't be so hard on yourself and don't talk about yourself like that. Your brain might be listening! We'll definitely have this little chat, though, because I do want to go over everything very carefully and try to remember as much as I can. I might have missed something, but I can't think what. Maybe it'll come to me. Or maybe that's really all I do know."

She yawned as she stood up and nodding at the coffee tray, suggested Victoria put some in a flask to keep warm and she'd have it in an hour or so.

"Penny, how about this?" said Victoria. "What if you go back to bed and get a bit more sleep and I'll open up the shop? I can't do your appointments, but I can call everyone and re-book, and take messages, tidy up a bit, make sure everything's in good order, and be all ready for you. You could come down for lunch, and you'd probably feel much better for the morning off."

Penny gave her a grateful look and agreed.

"That would be absolutely wonderful, Victoria! Thank you. I'd love to get my head down."

A few minutes later she had undressed, slipped under the covers, and was fast asleep.

Victoria puttered about in the shop until late morning, and then went out to buy a new magazine for the waiting area and some salad for lunch. In the shops, there was only one topic on everybody's lips and she thought how the pubs would be buzzing that night.

As Victoria stood in the short queue at the supermarket, Morgan and Davies were on their way to Ty Brith. Of all the aspects of her job, Morgan found giving people bad news the most difficult, and what they had to tell the bridegroom was the worst possible news of all.

A few moments later they had been shown into a small sitting room on the ground floor and asked to wait.

They could hear voices coming from upstairs and soon the sound of hurried footsteps coming down the stairs. Emyr entered, his face a study in apprehension mixed with a dash of hope. As he looked at them his expression changed to fear.

"Hello," he said, struggling to maintain his polite composure. "You've come with news and from the looks on your faces, it isn't good."

Davies nodded at his sergeant.

"Mr. Gruffydd, I'm afraid we do have bad news,"

Morgan began. "Earlier this morning we recovered the body of a woman and, pending formal identification, we have reason to believe it's that of your missing fiancée, Meg Wynne Thompson. We have come to suggest that you prepare yourself for the worst. And I am sorry to have to tell you this, sir, but the indications are that she met with foul play."

Emyr sank into the nearest chair and looked at them.

"But who? How? Where did you find her? Where was she? Had she gone back to London?"

"Mr. Gruffydd, I'm sure you must have a lot of questions, but we can't answer all of them yet. What I can tell you is that the body of a young woman answering her description was discovered this morning buried in the local cemetery."

"But that's incredible . . . how could that have happened? It doesn't seem possible!"

"Well, it did happen, and that's what we have to work on. Of course, this means we have a different kind of investigation on our hands now, and I'm sure you'll give us your full cooperation. In fact, it would be very helpful to the investigation if you would agree to look at the body, with a view to identifying it."

"Yes, of course. Absolutely. That goes without saying," said Emyr. His face collapsed as he tried to deal with his emotions, and then, as the chilling reality struck home, he was blindsided by what to do about his father.

"Oh, God! What am I going to tell my father? He's so near the end now, should I tell him or not? This will break his heart. Which would be better for him—to die knowing, or not knowing?"

The two police officers looked at each other and then Morgan leaned forward.

"Why don't you ring the doctor and see what he has to say?"

"She," said Emyr distractedly. "The doctor's a she. And she'll be coming out later to look in on him."

"Oh, right, well, I'd ask her what to do, if I were you. She'll know what to do for the best."

The two police officers got up to go, leaving Emyr with his head in his hands.

"Just one more thing, Mr. Gruffydd," said Davies. "We'll need to re-interview members of the wedding party and get their fingerprints. We have their names and contact numbers, but we will need to speak to you again on a more formal basis, just to start clearing things up and eliminating people. I'm sorry, but I'm sure you understand there are certain procedures we have to follow."

Emyr looked up at them, nodded slowly, and started to rise. "No, we'll see ourselves out," said Davies. "Stay where you are. And please know that we are very sorry we had to bring you this bad news."

As the officers made their way through the main hall, they caught a glimpse of a woman they took to be Rhys Gruffydd's nurse, making her way toward them. As she approached, she seemed startled to see them but recovered her composure quickly. About the same age as Morgan, she wore her fair hair pulled back in a pony-tail with two long pieces at the front hanging down on each side of her eyes. They were long enough to get in the way, but not long enough to stay tucked behind her ears. She was wearing a light purple tunic with match-ing trousers.

"I'm looking for Mr. Gruffydd," she said. "His father needs him. Now."

"In there," Morgan said, gesturing toward the sitting room.

Moments later, the nurse emerged and started quickly up the stairs, followed by Emyr.

"It's my dad," he said as he turned to look back at the officers. "He's taken a turn for the worse."

As the officers made their way to the car, Davies turned to his sergeant.

"What is it with these girls today?" he asked grumpily. "Why do they all wear their hair hanging in their eyes like that? And why do they all have to look the same? Down at the station there must be ten of them, they're all the same age, they all wear the same clothes, talk the same, and I swear I can't tell them apart."

CHAPTER EIGHTEEN

The next morning, the rector replaced the telephone receiver and walked down the narrow hall to the kitchen where his wife was just starting to think about what to make for lunch and, after poking around in the refrigerator, was leaning toward quiche and salad.

Bronwyn closed the refrigerator door and turned to face her husband as he entered the room. Sensing something was wrong, she gave him the quizzical look that he immediately understood in the way long-married couples do.

"That was Emyr. His father's life is drawing peacefully toward its close."

"Peacefully toward its close? Why would you be talking like that?"

"I read it somewhere. It was said about a king, George V, I think. I've always liked the simplicity and dignity of it." He shrugged, and added, "Oh, all right. I've probably always been looking for an excuse to use it." He straightened his shoulders and moved closer to her.

"The doctor's on her way, Emyr said, and I've been summoned to the Hall. I know I'm going there to attend to Rhys, but I can't help but wonder how Emyr will possibly cope with all this. His burden of grief has to be overwhelming, what with his fiancée and now his father. It seems like too much to ask someone to deal with that. I'll do what I can, but it won't be enough."

His wife nodded sympathetically.

"I'll have your lunch waiting for you when you get back," she said in her practical way. "You'll probably want a little something now to tide you over."

"Good idea," her husband replied. He put his arm around her waist and pulled her gently toward him.

"You know, Bronwyn, I don't tell you this nearly often enough, but I have been so blessed all these years, having you as my wife. I love you dearly and I'm grateful for every day we've had together."

Bronwyn smiled at him and then, knowing he had to be feeling somewhat awkward because he, like most Welshmen of his generation, did not often put his feelings on display, put her arms around his waist and rested her cheek on his chest. Tenderly, he placed his hand on her head.

"Get away with you, Thomas," she laughed into his tie. "You're just trying to get around me because you're angling for a biscuit."

"And that's another thing I like about you," he replied, kissing her hair. "How well you know me, my dear girl. I wouldn't say no."

A few minutes later, looking unusually solemn, he was on his way to the Hall.

At the Llanelen police station, Davies put the phone down. Morgan looked over at him across the small office and waited.

"That was the pathologist with the preliminary examination results. As the coroner told us, there were at least four strong blows to the head, at the back. Not enough to kill her, maybe, but certainly enough to bring her down. Apparently she put up a fierce fight—gave it everything she had. She died of strangulation. The killer used something like a stout cord with a very small braiding pattern on it. There were other, smaller injuries, like bruises on her arms."

Morgan straightened the keyboard on the desk in front of her and then looked at her superior.

"And were there any signs of, well, anything of a sexual nature?" she asked, somewhat primly.

Davies shook his head. "No, thank God." He looked out the window for a moment and then back at his sergeant.

"All this would have been so much easier if we'd known from the beginning what we were dealing with. We lost so much time during the first crucial hours when we thought she was just a runaway bride. Someone was very clever. In terms of distracting and delaying, it certainly worked against us."

Morgan nodded and started gathering up her files that were strewn across the borrowed desk. When she was feeling overwhelmed or unsure, Davies had noticed, she tidied up her desk. He wondered if she thought clearing her workspace would free her up somehow for the tasks to come, or if she just found comfort in it. A bit of both, perhaps.

"All right, Bethan, here we go. We'll get the full report and autopsy photos soon. We're going to need an incident room, so you'll have to find out if there's a space here in Llanelen we can use. I don't think there should be a problem with that."

Oh very handy, she thought. Somebody might not have a problem with spending more time in Llanelen.

"We can start with the undertaker and the grave diggers—anyone who had any connection to the burial or gravesite. You're also going to have to organize the fingerprints from the wedding party, go over the times again, check everybody's story. Durham can get the parents' prints and the Met can do the bridesmaids."

He stood up and walked over to the coat stand beside the door and picked a lightweight windcheater off it.

"I've learned over the years that the answers are usually in the files, it's just that we're not reading them right. You might start with that," he said as he slipped on his jacket and fiddled with the zipper. "But it can wait until morning. We've had a very long few days and we've got more coming up. I'm going home to get a few hours of sleep and I suggest you do the same. There's going to be overtime this weekend, I'm afraid."

And then, with a casual, "See you later," he was gone.

Morgan looked after him for a few moments with a mildly puzzled look on her face and then returned to the straightened stack of files on her desk. A few minutes later she was deeply engrossed and making a few cross-references as she referred back to her notes.

The room was quiet and warm, but she could make out the gentle buzz of voices in the hallway as officers made their purposeful way through the building. Engines started up in the car park as station life went on around her.

It would help if I knew what I was looking for, she thought. I'll start with a timeline.

As she flipped through her notebook to find what she had written hours and days ago, she was surprised to see Davies enter the room.

Looking mildly sheepish, he walked over to the desk where he had been sitting and picked up a set of keys.

"Won't get far without these, will I?" he said as he lightly tossed them in the air.

"We've all done that, sir," she said with a wan smile.

As the smile faded, a thoughtful, slightly worried look replaced it. "Um, and I'm sorry, sir, but I wonder if you could just give me a bit of direction here. Tell me again exactly what I'm meant to be looking for."

Davies stopped and looked at her. The edges of his mouth slackened and his eyes narrowed slightly.

"You're looking for someone who wasn't where he was supposed to be. Or who was somewhere he had no reason to be. And who then went on to have a very dark and busy night."

Morgan nodded and switched on the computer as her boss left. This time he did not return.

Penny, meanwhile, was feeling better for the extra sleep that Davies was now pursuing, and quietly enjoying the deferred mug of coffee in her small sitting room as Victoria filled her in on the morning's events.

"The talk in the shops was nothing but the body," she said. "Well, it would be, wouldn't it? But I've been thinking, Penny," she said, leaning forward to make her point, "that you probably know more than you think you do. We could solve this. I know we could."

Penny sat back in her chair and laughed.

"What, you mean like those dotty middle-aged amateur lady sleuths that you see in books? Tramping all over the evidence, touching things they shouldn't, putting themselves in harm's way, and just generally annoying the police?"

"That's exactly it!" said Victoria as they both laughed.

"Don't be ridiculous!" said Penny. "Oh go on, then. When do we start? Or more to the point, how do we start? What should we do first? I'm new at this."

Victoria looked at her blankly and the two broke into gales of laughter.

"I guess we haven't got the sleuthing thing down,

yet," said Penny a few moments later. "But it'll come to us, I'm sure. Although I think this would definitely be more in Mrs. Lloyd's line!"

And then, realizing how much better she felt, added, "What's for lunch, by the way? I'm starving."

And then, in that instant, she started forward as she remembered the shop.

"It's okay," Victoria reassured her. "Your first customer isn't until three. You'll be working until seven tonight, though."

Victoria nodded at her.

"Perhaps you should consider having regular evening hours. The ladies loved the idea and it would bring in women who have to work during the day."

Penny looked at her thoughtfully.

"You're probably right. I've been thinking about making some changes. But for now, let's have lunch. And while we're doing that, I think I know where we need to start. We need to find out who that woman was who took Meg Wynne's manicure. She's involved in this. She has to know something. Maybe a lot."

Victoria thought this over for a moment.

"Unless, of course, somebody was using her and she didn't know what she was part of. Maybe somebody told her it was a wedding prank. But you're right. Let's cherchez la femme."

"Right," said Penny, "That's what we'll do. But first, let's cherchez my lunch. And after that, let's get you sorted out."

"Sorted out?" asked Victoria.

"Well, if you want to stay on a bit longer—and you're welcome to—I thought it might be a good idea if we cleared out the box room and put you in there. We can even paint it and make it really nice. Decorate it up a bit. What do you think?"

Victoria smiled gratefully at her.

"That would be wonderful. My cousin has been very kind, but she does have three teenagers, and it gets a bit noisy. Also, my being there meant one of the kids had to give up her bed, and really I was just in the way. And I'm in no hurry to get back to London. In fact, I've been thinking I'd quite like to relocate here. In many ways, London's for the young." After a moment, she added, "In any event, it's not for me anymore."

"Well, that's settled, then," said Penny. "But while we're having lunch, and before we get to the main mystery, why don't you tell me what you're really doing here?"

"Oh, that's easy," said Victoria. "I'm getting over a bad divorce. There's a fair bit of money tied up in London real estate and I can't move on with my life until it's all settled."

"A bad divorce," mused Penny. "When you think about it, is there any other kind?"

Victoria shrugged.

"The scary thing is, it's not easy starting over at my age." Her eyes gave Penny a quick once-over and she smiled. "Our age."

She thought for a moment, and then, making her decision, plunged in.

"I guess I'm a bit age sensitive because my husband left me for a younger woman, an American he met on a flight to New York. I can't tell you how awful that made me feel."

She covered her eyes with her hands for a moment and then continued.

"He had a good head for business and we did all right. More than all right, really. Beautiful home, wonderful vacations. It was all so perfect and then suddenly, it was over."

"And you had no idea it was coming?" asked Penny gently.

"Looking back, of course there were signs but I suppose I was in denial. I didn't really acknowledge that anything was wrong until it began to dawn on me that I couldn't do anything right. Things that never bothered him before suddenly seemed to make him so upset and angry. Finally I realized that it wasn't even about me, anymore."

She sighed. "And then he left and well, here I am."

"You've got your wonderful harp playing," Penny said. "Tell me about that."

The mention of music lifted Victoria's mood instantly.

"I had a good business going there in London. Performed at upmarket events—embassy parties, fancy weddings, corporate do's—that sort of thing. Even Clarence House a couple of times for the prince of Wales, I'll have you know!

"But once I turned fifty most of the bookings dried up. I think they wanted someone younger to decorate the room, along with the music, if you see what I mean."

"Well, we certainly don't have any ageism here in Llanelen," declared Penny. "If we did, we'd all be out of jobs. I'm sure once word gets around you'll find yourself as busy as you want to be."

CHAPTER NINETEEN

On Saturday morning came the news that Rhys Gruff-ydd had died in his sleep. While the news was expected, his passing was met with sadness; he had been well liked and respected throughout the region, and people said he would be remembered as a fair employer who had done much over the years to help the poor. But as preparations began for his funeral, folks wondered how his son could possibly handle the deaths of the two persons dearest to him. It was nothing short of tragic for Emyr, they said, that his father and his fiancée had died so closely together.

But of course, it was the way his fiancée had died that held their attention, although not much was known about the details.

As Penny and Victoria set up shop for the day's business, they eagerly discussed what they now considered their case.

"I've got an idea," said Victoria. "I'll sit in the chair where la femme we're cherchez-ing sat, you sit where you sat, and we'll go over everything just like it happened that morning. Maybe something will come to you. After all, this is where it all started."

"Oh, good one," said Penny as she dashed across the room and sat down on her stool. "Here," she said, flapping her hand at the client's chair across from her, "sit down. We've only got a few minutes."

"Right," said Victoria a few moments later, offering up her hand. "Here we are, then. You're you and I'm the mystery woman. What happened next?"

Penny took up Victoria's hand and looked at it critically.

"Well, it was the usual manicure, and we talked about the wedding, because there's me thinking she's the bride. Well, I wouldn't have any reason to think otherwise, would I?" She put Victoria's hand on the table and sat back and looked at her.

"But now that I think about it," Penny said, wagging a finger, "she was very sure of herself, very confident. You wouldn't have thought for a minute she was getting married that day, because usually brides are fluttery and nervous, if you know what I mean. In a state of heightened excitement. Can barely control themselves."

Victoria nodded but said nothing, leaving Penny to follow silently where her train of thought was taking her. After a few moments Penny got up, slowly walked over to her supply cupboard, took a few items out, and returned to the table with three cotton balls in a small silver-coloured bowl and a bottle of nail varnish remover. She shook some varnish remover onto a cotton ball, picked up Victoria's hand, and started removing the polish.

"Sorry," she said. "Can't help myself." She wiped away at another nail and then set Victoria's hand down and looked at her friend.

"But this one," she went on thoughtfully, "this woman was businesslike. Professional. Well, yes, confident. That's just the best word for it."

She picked up the hand again, looked at all the nails, wagged her head left and right, set the hand down, and reached for the other one. Her face clouded over as she struggled to capture a fleeting thought.

"What is it?" Victoria said softly.

"It's something she said that struck me at the time as being a bit, oh, I don't know, not over the top but indicative of how self-important she was, how full of herself. She said something like she wasn't having roses at her wedding. No, she was going for peonies and lily of the valley. Peonies, she said, would be the next big thing and she'd even designed a peony-based fragrance for herself . . . it almost made me laugh until I thought she might just be right. I've always thought peonies hugely underrated, as flowers go, not that I know that much about them but they're beautiful to paint."

Suddenly, a knock on the shop door snapped them back to the reality that Penny's working day was about to begin.

"Oh God, it's the first client, and we aren't really ready yet," yelped Penny. "You let her in, while I just finish up here."

"You'd better give me the bottle of nail varnish remover, then," said Victoria. "I've got one hand on and one hand off."

"Oh, right. Well, we'll take care of that at lunchtime. We've got to finish this conversation. I think it's going somewhere, but I'm not sure where. The reenactment really helped bring it all back. It's too bad we have to stop now."

"Morning, sir. Feeling better?"

Davies gave his sergeant a small, tight smile, nodded in acknowledgement, and made his way to his desk.

"Anything come in overnight that we need to look at?" he asked as he placed his morning cup of coffee on his desk and sat down heavily.

"There's this, sir," she said, offering him a large white envelope marked CONFIDENTIAL in large red letters. "It's the autopsy report and photos. The strangulation and head bashing you know about."

He nodded.

"But they found something else. Embedded in her upper right arm they found a needle from a syringe. It was broken off and twisted at an angle as if she'd wrenched her arm away from the person who was doing the injecting, like this." She twisted around quickly to her left. "The toxicology tests are still in the works. They might pick up traces of something on the needle."

They looked at each other and Morgan put into words what they were both starting to think.

"So, am I right in thinking that he tried to kill her *three* ways? Blows to the head, strangulation, and some kind of weird lethal injection? It doesn't make sense. Does it? What kind of person would do that?"

Davies winced.

"It doesn't seem to make sense, but that's what our job is. We have to find the sense in it."

After a moment's silence Morgan continued.

"And there's one other weird thing. They found a small piece of curved, red plastic, about two inches long, all tangled up in her hair, at the wound site. They can't guess what it is or where it came from, but from the look of it," she pulled a photo from the envelope and placed it on his desk, "it might be a handle of some sort. See how it's curved? What do you think?"

Davies peered at the photo and shrugged.

"Oh, and forensics called. They've been through everything found in the grave including the two mobiles. One belonged to Meg Wynne, the other belonged to a—" She paused while she flipped over a couple of pages in her notebook. "To a Simon Redfern. Reported stolen or lost last month in Putney, apparently."

Davies gave a small snort of disbelief.

"Putney!"

"Yes, sir, it's located in the London borough of Wandsworth."

"I know where Putney is, Bethan, I'm just staggered that something like that would turn up in our case. And who's this Simon Redfern when he's at home? How does he figure into all this?"

"Well, that's just it, sir. He's an eleven-year-old boy. His mum reckons the phone was nicked off him at the playground, or fell out of his coat on the bus or something like that."

Davies put his chin in his hand and shook his head.

"Is it just me being old fashioned or is it normal for an eleven-year-old to have a mobile phone?"

Morgan snickered.

"With respect, sir, it's you being old fashioned. Kids much younger than eleven have them. Come to that, everybody has one."

Davies shook his head. Everybody already knew his views on mobile telephones, so there was no point in going into it.

"Anyway," continued Morgan, "we know that one mobile belonged to Meg Wynne and the other one has two unidentified sets of fingerprints on it. Adult prints, not young Simon's."

"Well, look into it. Have they traced the calls on them yet? And we still need to interview the staff at the Hall."

Morgan continued riffling through her notebook.

"About the second phone. I wondered if maybe a grave digger could have dropped it in. Might have found it or picked it up secondhand somewhere. I'll ask them when I speak to them if they can shed some light."

"It's possible, I suppose."

Davies set down his coffee mug and cleared his throat.

"Bethan. Sergeant."

"Sir?"

"I'm going out for a bit. You carry on here."

"Anywhere nice, sir?"

"Nowhere special. Llanelen."

"Ah, right."

"Yes, I'm going to have another word with her, you know, Ms. Brannigan."

"That would be Penny Brannigan, would it sir?" asked Morgan.

"Don't be cheeky, Sergeant."

"No, sir. But if you don't mind my saying, sir, you might want to get a haircut before you go."

Davies patted the back of his neck.

"Really?"

"Well, yes, sir, she is in the grooming business after all, and well, women notice these things."

"I'm due for one anyway, I guess," he said as he prepared to leave. "Right, well, I'll ring you later, let you know how I got on."

Morgan watched him go and once he was safely out of the room, smiled to herself. She shook her head gently and her dark curls shone in the morning sun.

This is going to be good, she thought. He just doesn't know it yet.

As lunchtime approached, Penny turned to Victoria and suggested that she pick up some salad and sandwiches from the local supermarket.

"I'll just finish up here with Mrs. Lloyd, and then we can go upstairs, make some tea, and continue where we left off this morning," Penny said.

A moment later Victoria caught her drift.

"Oh, right. Right. I'll be back in a few minutes."

She was just pulling the door shut behind her as Davies made his way down Station Road. He watched her turn right and set off in the opposite direction before he approached the door to Penny's shop. Peering in, he watched as she took a bottle of polish from the third row and showed it to her customer. When the customer nodded, Penny sat down and began to apply the varnish.

"Don't look now, dear, but I think you have a peeping Tom," said Mrs. Lloyd, who had returned to have her nails redone after her regular manicure had ended so abruptly with what she was now referring to as "that unfortunate business over my hat."

"There's someone watching you through the door." Penny turned to look, and seeing who it was, smiled and waved at him to come in.

CHAPTER TWENTY

"Good morning, Chief Inspector," said Penny as Davies cautiously pushed open the door. "Do come in. This is Mrs. Lloyd, one of my regular clients. Mrs. Lloyd, this is Detective Chief Inspector Davies. He's leading the Meg Wynne Thompson investigation."

Mrs. Lloyd gave the police officer a careful once-over and then nodded pleasantly. "Ah, Inspector," she said. "Very clever of you to find me here, especially as this isn't my regular day, is it, Penny dear? No, I was wondering why you hadn't been to see me before this, but never mind that, you're here now. What would you like to know?"

Mrs. Lloyd sat back expectantly while Davies collected himself and Penny tried to hide her amusement. Slowly he approached the table where she was sitting.

"What exactly do you have to tell me?" he asked.

"Well, I would have thought you'd be around to take a statement," Mrs. Lloyd said. "You and that lady officer of yours. I know you've been talking to people, and I was there and saw everything, and yet you haven't spoken to me yet."

"You were?" Davies asked incredulously. "What did you see, exactly?"

"Yes," said Mrs. Lloyd impatiently. "I was in the church when they made the announcement that the bride was missing. I was almost in the front pew so not much got past me."

"It never does," said Penny, looking intently at Mrs. Lloyd's nails.

"Well, that's very true," agreed Mrs. Lloyd with a modest degree of smug satisfaction. "I was the postmistress here for many years, and as you probably know, Inspector, in the post office we're trained to be observant. In an important position like that, you hear and see just about everything. Of course, discretion comes into it, too, but you learn to tell the difference between what's important and what's not."

"Rather like police work, perhaps?" suggested Penny, smothering a smile.

"Exactly!" exclaimed Mrs. Lloyd.

"Now, then, Inspector, shall I start at the beginning and tell you everything that happened that morning? Why don't you pull one of those chairs over here and sit beside me?"

Fifteen minutes later, Mrs. Lloyd was wrapping up her version of events as Penny was applying the top coat to her nails.

"And so, that was just about it, Inspector. The rector made the announcement and we all made our way across to the hotel for some refreshments. It was all such a pity. And such a waste, too. The church had never looked more beautiful. It seemed like there were stands of lovely flowers everywhere. Pink, they were, and very blowsy and fragrant. Peonies, I think they were but where anyone would get peonies now, I don't know. They've been over for weeks." Penny started and dropped her brush, leaving a little puddle of clear fluid on the work surface which she quickly wiped away with a cotton ball.

Mrs. Lloyd took no notice, but Davies's shoulders hunched forward slightly.

"Sorry," said Penny, recovering. "I think that you're done now, Mrs. Lloyd. Just sit there for a moment while they dry."

But Mrs. Lloyd was now deep into her recollections of the wedding that wasn't.

"I wonder in a situation like that what happened to the flowers? They weren't in the church on Sunday, were they? Were they donated to a local hospital or hospice do you think?"

She looked from one to the other.

"Or maybe to one of the old folks homes. Yes, that's probably where they went. Someplace where they could do a bit of good."

She blew on her nails.

"And, my goodness, what about all that lovely food? Went home with the hotel staff, I shouldn't wonder. Well, as I said, what a shameful waste it all was. Not that it was the poor girl's fault, of course, as things turned out, but I did ask myself at the time if it wasn't simply a matter of cold feet. Although with a catch like Emyr, that would be hard to fathom, wouldn't it?" She looked brightly at the two of them, and then, as she always did, held out her hands at arm's length for inspection.

"Very nice, Penny, as usual. What colour did you say that is?"

"Melon of Troy."

"Melon of Troy!" chuckled Mrs. Lloyd. "I never! Well, as you say, Penny, we're done, so I'll be on my way. Lovely to meet you, Inspector. If you need to speak to me again, I'm sure you know where to find me."

Penny gathered up Mrs. Lloyd's bags, handed them to her, and thanked her as she made her way to the door, where Davies was waiting to open it.

"Thank you, Inspector. I wouldn't want anything to happen to my new nails, would I! Melon of Troy!"

As the door swung slowly shut, Penny joined him and turned the sign to CLOSED. Turning around she faced Davies and smiled up at him.

"Victoria's just gone to get us some things for lunch but I'm sure there'll be enough for you, if you want to join us. I was going to go upstairs to make some tea," she said.

Davies hesitated, glanced down at her, and then peered through the glass window in the door.

"Actually, I had dropped in on the off chance that you might be free for lunch," he said. "I'd like to go over your statement again, just in case you've remembered anything else. Sometimes it helps to talk about things in a neutral environment. I think it's possible that you know more than you think you know. So far, you're our most important witness. And I did want to ask you about something, and that's . . ." He stopped as Penny leaned slightly closer to him and craned her neck to watch as Victoria turned the corner, a shopping bag in each hand.

"Excuse me," she said, reaching past Davies to open the door. "I've just got to let Victoria in. But do, please, join us for lunch. It's no bother, and we'd like you to."

"Well, if you're sure," he said, as a breathless Victoria pushed her way past them.

"Oh, God, my arms are breaking," she moaned. "There were a few items on sale so I got in some extras so we can have them on hand." Setting the bags down, she smiled at Davies.

"Hello, there, what brings you here? Joining us for lunch, are you?"

Davies looked at the two women, and smiled.

"I guess I am. Thank you."

Upstairs in the flat, crowded around the small table with cups of tea, sandwiches, salad, cheese, and biscuits, Davies looked at Penny.

"Mrs. Lloyd said something that seemed to startle you. Why was that?" he asked.

"Mm," said Penny, as she put her egg-and-cress sandwich on her plate. "It was the strangest thing. Just this morning Victoria and I were going back over the events of the Saturday morning when that woman, the bridal impostor whoever she was, came for a manicure and I remembered that she had said something about having peonies at her wedding, so when Mrs. Lloyd mentioned that there *had* been peonies at the wedding, it made me wonder."

Victoria looked at her admiringly.

"Penny, you're brilliant! Don't you see? It means that whoever killed Meg Wynne must have known what flowers she had chosen. It was an inside job!"

She looked triumphantly from one to the other.

Penny smiled back at her, and then frowned slightly.

"I'd be curious to know, though, more about Meg Wynne's background." She glanced at Davies. "You know what hotbeds for gossip villages are. There are rumours going around that she wasn't on the best terms with her father, that he drank too much, and had a violent temper."

"Oh, yes," said Davies, nodding. "We're looking into him. He's in the frame."

And then, silently signalling that the subject of the murder was closed, he reached for another sandwich.

* * *

"I'll just stay here and tidy up," said Victoria, as Penny and the policeman stood up from the table. "I want another cup of tea, anyway. You two carry on."

Davies and Penny made their way downstairs and into the salon.

"By the way," said Penny as they stood in front of the door, "what was it you wanted to ask me?"

"Sorry?"

"When you first got here, you said there was something you wanted to ask me. I wondered what it was."

"Do you know, it's gone right out of my head. Can't have been that important, I guess. If I remember what it is, I'll ring you."

Penny fiddled with her watch strap.

"I was just thinking," she said, "that perhaps Victoria and I could ask around and see what we can find out—"

Davies interrupted her. "No, don't go there," he said sternly. "I know you feel you're involved in this case, and you've been very helpful. But the last thing we need now is a couple of amateur detectives—you and your chum upstairs. We're the police, we've got resources, and we know what we're doing."

As Penny raised her eyebrows, he smiled.

"Well, most of the time, anyway. But, see, don't try to work this one. Leave it to us, and if you do think of anything else, just let me know, and we'll look into it."

He reached into his inside pocket.

"Here's my card," he said, handing it to her.

"I've still got the other one you gave me," said Penny stiffly. "I don't need that one, thank you very much."

Davies reached for the door and started to leave. He turned back to her and gently touched her shoulder.

"Remember what I said. We don't know who it was yet, but we do know he's dangerous. And thanks for the lunch. My turn next time."

When he was gone, Penny did a little dusting, put some instruments in the sterilizer, and then went to rinse her soaking basins. When she stepped away from the sink, Victoria was standing there watching her.

"What did he say?" she asked.

"He warned us off. Said we're not to go poking around. Too dangerous. Probably thinks we're just a couple of silly women. Mr. 'We Know What We're Doing' policeman," she said indignantly.

Victoria thought this over for a moment.

"Do you like him?" she asked.

"Do I like him? Where did that come from?" exclaimed Penny. "Like him? I guess. Why do you ask?"

"Because he fancies you."

Penny laughed. "No, he doesn't! He just wants to know what I know."

"Yes, he does," said Victoria. "I've seen the way he softens when he looks at you. And he looks at you more than he has to. He likes watching you. I don't think he's quite realized it yet, though."

"Hmm," said Penny. "I don't know what to say to that. It's been so long since anybody's fancied me, that I don't really know if the one or two hormones I've got left would be up to that kind of excitement."

They both laughed, and then she looked thoughtfully at Victoria.

"But I've been thinking some more about this case, and I've had an idea. We can't go to wherever it is that Meg Wynne's parents are, and we can't go to London where the bridesmaids are, but we can go to Ty Brith. We need to get into the Hall so we can snoop around and see what we can find out."

"And just how are you going to do that?" asked Victoria.

"Oh, no," said Penny. "Not me. I've got no reason to go to the Hall. But you do. And as reasons go, it's heavenly."

Victoria groaned. "Well, just don't keep harping on about it."

They looked at each other and laughed, leaning into each other, the way friends do.

CHAPTER TWENTY-ONE

On Monday morning, Victoria drove slowly up the winding road leading to Ty Brith which had been situated perfectly to give spectacular views of the Conwy Valley. As her car climbed higher, she took in the breathtaking vista of the wide view stretching all the way to the rugged peaks of Snowdonia. The endless fields, shimmering in the freshness of their summer greenery, contrasted spectacularly with the brilliant blue of the cloudless sky. In all seasons, whether lit from above by bright sunlight on a summer's day, nestled under a thin, patchy blanket of snow, or aflame in autumn foliage, the valley always looked postcard beautiful. But best of all was early spring, when gardens filled with shocking yellow daffodils signalled the arrival of warmer weather and longer days.

The Hall had been built of Welsh stone in the mid-1800s as the country retreat of a titled English land-owning family. Much loved and much used, it had stayed in the family until the 1930s when its age began to catch up with it, and rather than undertake the extensive repairs and refurbishing required, the family reluctantly decided it would have to be sold. But with the Second World War looming, no buyers came forward, and as the war years dragged on, the Hall was pressed into service as a convalescent home for wounded Welsh soldiers.

Having made a fortune during the war from its haulage interests, the Gruffydd family had bought the rundown Hall at auction and modernized it to include the best of mid-twentieth-century refinements, including central heating, en suite bathrooms, and a large, bright kitchen. It had retained, however, its shabby chic feel, complete with lots of chintz, the occasional wet dog, and the unmistakable smell of beeswax on the days when Gwennie rode her bicycle up from the village to give everything a good going over with her duster.

The small pastures on either side of the road leading to the Hall were dotted with sheep, and as her car approached, they stopped their grazing, lifted their heads, and looked at her with mild curiosity. Bits of their fleece that had snagged on the metal fence fluttered softly in the breeze. She smiled at them, envying their woolly contentment, and drove on.

When she reached the Hall, she decided to drive around to the back of the large house, and use the tradesmen's entrance. She parked her car and walked across to the back door, her heels tapping on the flagstones. She lifted the heavy brass knocker, which was shaped like a dolphin, and rapped twice.

A few moments later she heard footsteps and the door opened to reveal a small woman with a pointed nose and small, dark, meerkat eyes. She was wearing an apron and carrying a bright pink feather duster.

Ah, thought Victoria, this must be Gwennie.

"Yes?" the woman asked pleasantly.

"Good morning," said Victoria, giving her the benefit of a broad smile. "I wondered if I could have a word with Mr. Gruffydd?"

"Sorry, he isn't here at the moment," she said sharply.

"Do you expect him back soon?" asked Victoria.

"Well, now, that's hard to say," said the woman cautiously. "Depends on who you are, and what you want with him, doesn't it?"

"Of course," said Victoria. "So sorry, I'm Victoria Hopkirk and I'm a harpist and I wondered if he would like me to play at his father's funeral. Bronwyn Evans suggested I might call around and offer my services It would be—"

"Oh, yes, of course," said the woman. "I'm Gwennie. I do for him. Well, that is I used to do for his father, and now, I guess, I do for him, although there's been so much bother lately nothing's settled. You'd better come in, then. I was afraid you might be one of those reporter ladies and I know he doesn't want to talk to any of that lot just at the minute."

"No, of course he doesn't," said Victoria soothingly as they made their way down the short passage to the kitchen.

"He's just out walking Trixxi," said Gwennie. "Oh that reminds me, I'd better get her biscuit ready. She always looks in her bowl for her biscuit when she comes back from her walk and is very hurt when there isn't one." Gwennie opened a cupboard door, took a dog biscuit from the box, and placed it in the stainless steel dog bowl on the floor.

"Right. Well, have a seat," she said, gesturing at the table. "I was just thinking about a cup of tea, and I'm sure you'd like one, so I'll just get the kettle on, shall I?"

As Gwennie turned to fill the kettle, Victoria took in her surroundings.

The large, airy kitchen had been cleverly and tastefully modernized to retain its old-fashioned look and feel, but to incorporate all modern conveniences. Cream-coloured floor-to-ceiling cupboards, with open shelving decoratively displaying plates, cookbooks, and plants, took up two walls. A built-in recess housed an Aga cooker, in front of which, on the shining hardwood floor, sat a large, open Victorian gardener's basket filled with the last of the asparagus and the first of the green beans that had been harvested that morning from the Hall's kitchen garden. A few feet away from the basket was a rumpled dog bed.

The generous counter space was clear of clutter. From her seat at the well-scrubbed harvest table in the centre of the room, Victoria could see past a pottery bowl filled with bright yellow lemons into a long, carpeted hall that stretched toward the front of the house. Behind her were two large windows with a view onto the car park and the wooded grounds beyond. The room was filled with a warm, spicy fragrance that reminded her of Christmas baking.

As Gwennie puttered about, Victoria went over the discussion she and Penny had had the night before over their cups of bedtime cocoa.

"Mrs. Lloyd says that Gwennie knows everything that goes on in that house," Penny had said. "Make sure you get as much information about the wedding party as you can. Oh, and she's absolutely mad about the dog, apparently, so you might want to play that up a bit to get things started. And take things slowly. Try to find a reason to come back, once you've established yourself as someone they can trust."

Gwennie set the tea things on the table, along with a plate of freshly-baked ginger snaps.

"I can see you're fond of dogs, Gwennie," Victoria said. "Not everyone would be sure to have a biscuit waiting when a dog comes in from a walk."

"Very fond," Gwennie replied. "That's to say I like pretty much all dogs, except of course the bitey ones.

But Trixxi, now, I've come to love her, truly I have. Course I can't keep a dog myself because I live with my sister and her husband and she's that house proud she wouldn't hear of keeping any kind of pet, not so much as a gerbil, so I enjoy Trixxi's company when I'm here. And I don't mind telling you, I've been putting in long hours of late."

She offered Victoria a warm ginger snap and took one for herself.

Victoria murmured sympathetically.

"Tell me, then, Mrs. Hopkirk, what brings you to these parts?" asked Gwennie.

"Well, I've been visiting family in the area. I used to spend lots of time in this village when I was growing up and I've always loved being here. I find the scenery so, oh I don't know, serene yet inspiring."

"Oh, it is that," agreed Gwennie. "Although lately, of course," she said darkly, "we've been too busy to take much notice of it."

"Yes, you have certainly had your share of troubles and sadness here, haven't you, and that's why I wanted to offer my services to Mr. Gruffydd," said Victoria.

Gwennie munched thoughtfully on her biscuit and with a tiny hand gently brushed a crumb off her small bosom.

"Yes, he's certainly in need of support," she said. "He's all on his own now in this great big house, poor lamb. I did think maybe that Louise might stay on for a bit, but after Mr. Gruffydd died, she couldn't get on her way fast enough. Made me wonder, that did."

"Really, Gwennie?" asked Victoria innocently. "What did it make you wonder about?"

"Well, I know to those who do private-duty nursing, looking after sick and dying folks is just a job, but it seemed so callous the way she was packing her bag before he was even . . ." Her voice trailed off and she was silent for a moment. Brightening at her next thought, she perked up and continued.

"Was it you, then, who played at Emma Teasdale's send off?" she asked. "I did hear that your playing was absolutely splendid. Just lovely, folks said. I'm sure young Mr. Emyr will be very glad to talk to you."

She cocked her head in the direction of the windows.

"That sounds like them now."

They heard the back door open, and the sound of a dog's toenails scratching on the slate floor, accompanied by the unmistakable jingling of dog tags.

"Oh, who's my darling girl?" laughed Gwennie as an excited Trixxi bounded into the room, tail wagging vigorously from side to side, as she rushed past them to get to her bowl and scoop up her treat.

Emyr followed her into the kitchen, a green ball in one hand and Trixxi's leather lead in the other. He dropped them in a basket on the floor and looked questioningly at Victoria. His face was troubled and dark. Whether this was due to apprehension or grief, Victoria couldn't tell.

"Ah, Mr. Emyr," said Gwennie. "This is Victoria Hopkirk come to talk to you about playing the harp at your father's funeral."

Victoria stood up and held her hand out to Emyr.

"I'm so sorry for your losses," she said. "I'd be happy to perform at your father's funeral, if you would like me to. Mourners often find the sound of a harp relaxing and comforting."

Emyr looked at her, his dark blue eyes cold and unreadable.

"That's very good of you," he said politely, "but we've completed all the arrangements." His eyes slid toward Gwennie, who pinched her lips together, nodded slightly, and looked at her shoes.

"Mr. Emyr, if I may, there is something wonderfully soothing about that kind of music." Gathering her courage to look up, Gwennie met his eyes and added firmly, "I think your father would have loved it and after all, the rector's wife herself did suggest it."

Emyr relaxed slightly and gave Victoria a superficial smile that came nowhere near his eyes.

"I'm sorry, I didn't mean to sound ungracious. Well, thank you then, that would be lovely," he said. "Very kind of you. What would the next step be?"

"I suggest two songs, the first as the guests are arriving, and the second toward the end of the service. I can pick the songs for you, if you wish. I can easily find something appropriate or we can discuss it. Did your father have a favourite song, or is there something that reminds you of him?"

When he didn't answer right away, she added, "Maybe you'd like to think about it and I could call back tomorrow."

"That would be fine, thank you. If I'm not here, I'll leave a note or a message with Gwennie." As he turned to go, Gwennie put her hand on his arm.

"You've had a couple of calls, Mr. Emyr. David Williams called from London to say he'd be arriving tonight and that he isn't sure yet if Anne and Jennifer will be coming but he thinks they will."

"Thanks, Gwennie."

"May I get you a cup of tea?" she asked him. "Are you hungry? Would you like anything?"

He shook his head.

"No, thank you, Gwennie. I think I'll just get on with things. I'll be in the office if anybody needs me."

He nodded at the two women. "Right then," he said, and after thanking Victoria again, was gone.

Gwennie looked at Victoria, and smiled.

"How about you, then? Another cuppa?"

"Yes, please," said Victoria. "And just to be sure, Gwennie, when is the funeral, exactly?

"Wednesday at two. And Mr. Rhys's favourite song, by the way, was 'The Way You Look Tonight.' His wife, that's Mr. Emyr's mother, was a great beauty, and I think that's why he admired Miss Thompson. That, and he must have seen something in her that apparently no one else did."

They continued to chat and Victoria finally got what she came for: a natural break in the conversation when she could ask her question seamlessly and logically.

"It must have been very busy here the morning of the wedding. How on earth did you keep track of where everybody was?"

Gwennie settled back in her chair, crossed her legs, and picked up her teacup.

"I couldn't," she said. "There was just that much going on. They were having all kinds of fun, the boys were. Someone even tied a red handkerchief on Trixxi and very fetching she looked."

At the sound of her name Trixxi turned toward Gwennie, and two pairs of dark brown eyes filled with adoration.

CHAPTER TWENTY-TWO

"Tell me again," said Penny as she arranged a new duvet on the small wrought-iron bed in the box room while Victoria set up a lamp on the bedside table.

They had decided to do up the small, windowless room in white and now, with a few strategic splashes of accent colour, it looked just like something you might see in an American style magazine, they were telling themselves. It could easily pass for a guest bedroom in a Cape Cod summer house. All it lacked was an ocean view.

"The first thing that happened was Emyr came in with the dog and we talked about the funeral arrangements. He seemed very unsure but Gwennie kind of talked him into it. And then she said something like, 'David Williams called from London to say he'd be arriving tonight and that he didn't know if Anne and Jennifer will be coming but thought they would.' I wasn't sure what it meant, but figured you'd know. And, really, that's about the only thing that happened, apart from the dog bolting in and getting a biscuit. She so loves that dog.

"Oh, and Mr. Gruffydd's funeral's on Wednesday at two, but you would have got that from the paper."

Penny glanced at her, nodded, and went into the

kitchen. She returned a few minutes later with a neat beige file folder and sat down on the bed while Victoria pulled up a chair they had brought up from the salon and faced her.

Opening the file, Penny sifted through a small pile of newspaper cuttings and held one up.

"Here he is. David Williams. From London and best man for Emyr Gruffydd. He acted as the family's spokesman when Meg Wynne went missing. Anne and Jennifer were the bridesmaids."

She put the cutting back in the file and looked at Victoria thoughtfully.

"David Williams. Emyr Gruffydd. And what's the other one's name?"

"Robbie Llewellyn."

"Right. I wish Emma were here. She would have known all three of them as children, and she'd have some good insight into the men they are now. 'Give me the boy and I'll show you the man,' she used to say. She used to be able to predict what would become of the kids she taught and most of the time, she was right. Leopards and spots that don't change."

They sat in silence for a few moments while Penny shrugged off her memories and returned to the present.

"I haven't seen anything in the paper yet about the funeral arrangements for Meg Wynne. I wonder what will happen there. Would she be returned to her parents, do you think, or stay here with Emyr?"

Victoria looked blank.

"Anyway, I'll be playing at the funeral so I'll keep my ears open," she said. You're not going, are you?"

Penny shook her head.

"I've got clients and besides, I didn't know the man. But by all accounts he was well liked and there'll probably be a big turnout. You'll get to see your new friend Gwennie again. She'll be there for sure."

"Well," said Victoria, "if I'm in the right place at the right time, I might hear or see something useful. You know how it is. Once we turn fifty we become invisible, so no one will be paying any attention to me."

Penny thought about this for a moment, and setting the file on the bed beside her, looked at her friend.

"And what did Gwennie say about what was going on the morning of the wedding? I expect she could have seen or heard just about anything and nobody would take any notice of her. She's just Gwennie. Always there."

"She said everything was all topsy-turvy. There was just so much happening. She could hear the boys, as she calls them, making plans over breakfast when she went to the dining room to see if they needed fresh coffee. This one had to get a haircut, that one had to pick up the buttonholes, another one was going into the office, everybody was making a trip into town in this car or that one . . . the Land Rover needed petrol . . . they were just all over the place.

"Of course, all she really cared about was that the darling dog's routine not be upset. And she said one of the boys, she doesn't know who, took her for a nice long walk. But she'd like to get her hands on whichever one it was because apparently he lost Trixxi's lead and now they have to use the old leather one that nobody likes, least of all Trixxi, until they can replace it. And with all the dreadful things that have been happening in that family in the last couple of weeks, replacing a dog lead isn't a high priority. Oh, and the dog was wearing a red handkerchief and looked very cute. And that's about it, really."

She thought for a moment.

"You know, this sleuthing business isn't as easy as it looks. It's hard to remember everything and it's even harder to know what's important and what's not. How can you tell?"

She sighed. "Oh wait. There was something else. She said the nurse who had been looking after Emyr's father left the house in a big hurry after he died. Said it looked as if she couldn't get out of there fast enough. What should we make of that?"

Penny gave her head a light scratch, turned to look at the blank wall about three feet from the end of the bed, and then looked at Victoria.

"I don't know. It's all really confusing. Let's go over what we've got so far and what we know for sure. Whoever did this was executing a carefully thought-through plan. This was premeditated. Meg Wynne and the other woman were switched just before nine, letting everyone think Meg Wynne was still out and about and being seen. But she wasn't. And it had to have been done by someone who knew she had the appointment, and made sure the impostor was briefed, dressed right, and ready to go. And whoever did it knew the details of the wedding arrangements, right down to the flowers.

"And Meg Wynne had to have been buried Sunday night because that's when the grave was opened and by Monday it had been filled in."

"And they couldn't have buried the body in daylight— too many people could have seen them," added Victoria. "And it was *them*. This had to be a two-person job. A man and a woman."

"Exactly," agreed Penny. "I wonder. What if they kidnapped Meg Wynne and it all went wrong before they could even ask for the money? Maybe she struggled too much. They say that most kidnapping victims are dead within the first twenty-four hours. So she must have been held somewhere or else her body was hidden somewhere. But where? And more importantly, by whom? And why?"

"Maybe it wasn't about money, although there was lots of it available," responded Victoria. "The Gruffydd family could have raised any amount they needed to. No, maybe somebody hated her enough to want her dead."

"Or feared her enough to need her dead," said Penny. "From the way the bridesmaids were talking, she was one determined woman. She might have wanted something. Or known something."

She patted the file and then sighed.

"You know, I think the police won't be long ruling out the father. I don't think he had the resources to put the impostor in place and why would he bother? Meg Wynne was out of his life and even if they didn't like each other much, they probably wouldn't need to see each other after the wedding. No need to play happy families. Estrangements happen and they can easily last a lifetime. She could have stayed in touch with her mother, but the father didn't matter. No, I don't think he did it. And as suspects go, he's pretty obvious."

She continued with her train of thought.

"Unless, he was hard up for money. Maybe he was a gambler and owes the wrong people a lot of money and they were threatening to come after him if he didn't pay up."

"Do you think Meg Wynne had a will?" asked Victoria. "If she didn't, and she died before she married Emyr, wouldn't the money go to her parents? Wouldn't that be a pretty good motive?"

"Could be," agreed Penny.

"What about a former boyfriend?" asked Victoria.

"Do you think it was a jealous ex-lover . . . 'If I can't have her, nobody can' kind of thing?"

"Oh I'm sure there are lots of ex-lovers around, but she'd been going out with Emyr for almost two years, I think the bridesmaid said, and if there hadn't been problems of that kind before, it's unlikely someone would come crawling out of the woodwork now," said Penny.

"No, I think whatever happened here, happened close to home. I think this begins and ends at Ty Brith and that's where we should keep digging."

She glanced at her watch, stood up, and looked over at Victoria.

"I've got to get back to work so I'll leave you to it. Do you think you'll be comfortable in here?" She looked around the tiny space. "It's not much, I know, but on the bright side, you won't be sharing with a thirteen-year-old."

"I think so," smiled Victoria. "I'm all for the simple life, me. Oh, I'm going over to Bronwyn's to practise this afternoon. She's had an idea for a song to play at the funeral and she's asked me to stop for dinner, so don't wait for me. I'll be back later."

As Penny turned toward the door, Victoria said, "Penny, I know we're all tiptoeing around Emyr because his father's just died, and everyone's feeling very sorry for him, but when you said 'close to home' do you think he could have done it? I mean, really, we've got to consider that possibility, don't you think?"

Penny thought about it for a moment, and agreed. "I think we need to find out why someone would want her dead. And I wish there was some way we could figure out who that woman was who came to the shop for the manicure. She's the key to all this, if you ask me."

* * *

Shortly after eight that evening Victoria let herself into the shop and, expecting to find Penny in the flat upstairs, was surprised to see her sitting quietly in the salon, reading a magazine and soaking her fingertips in one of the silver bowls, like she was her own best customer.

"Hey, look at you!" said Victoria. "What are you doing?" And then, a moment later, a look of realization and understanding passed over her face. "Oh, I get it! He rang, didn't he? He's taking you out!"

Penny's fair, freckled skin pinked up.

"Well, if you must know, I'm trying out a new soak I've just got in. It comes in lavender, and Mrs. Lloyd will probably love it. I usually try out new products before I use them on customers. It's just a good policy. It is nice though. Come on, dip in, there's room here for you."

Victoria smiled, sat in the chair opposite, and gingerly lowered her fingertips into the warm, fragrant water. As the lavender-scented mist rose between them, Penny asked after Bronwyn and Thomas Evans.

"Oh, they're great," said Victoria. "You know what they're like . . . they just rub along together like they've been doing for years, rough with the smooth and all that."

Penny nodded.

"She did say something, though, that I wondered about. She asked if maybe I'm wearing out my welcome and if you are still okay having me here. I said I thought you were, that we've just done up the extra room, but really you would say, wouldn't you, if you wanted me out of here?"

Penny reassured her that if that time ever came, Victoria would be the first to know but in the meantime she was glad of her company and she was welcome to stay as long as she needed to.

"You know, I've been thinking about the shop, Victoria, and wondered if you'd like me to show you a few things so you could help out a bit more. That way, we could get more customers through and make more money. I thought maybe you could take over the managing of it—order in supplies and look after the business end of things. That would free up my time to take on more clients, and we could share the increased profits."

"That's a great idea, Penny, I'd love to," said Victoria eagerly. "Where do I start? What should I do first?"

"Well, I usually go up to Llandudno to see the wholesaler, so I thought we could do that together and I'll show you the ropes and after that you can take it on. But I'll help you."

"Sounds great! When do we go?"

"Well, I was thinking about going tomorrow as we're running a bit low on some things, but as it happens, a certain gentleman *is* taking me to lunch tomorrow."

"I knew it!" squealed Victoria, splashing lavender water on the table as she pulled her hands out of the soaking bowl and spraying water in all directions as she clapped her hands.

And then she asked the question that the supportive good friend in this kind of situation must ask.

"What are you going to wear?"

Penny grinned.

"I'll sort that out tomorrow. For now, what colour polish do you think I should have? I've gone this far, I might as well give myself a manicure. Better yet, why don't you do it? I'll talk you through it. And I think I'll have the Chocolate Shake-speare. It goes well with anything."

As Victoria rose to get the bottle of varnish from the

shelf, Penny placed a wet hand on her friend's forearm and looked intently at her.

"And you know, I've been re-thinking what we were talking about this morning and now I think we shouldn't have been so dismissive of the father. By all accounts, she was making big money in London and had some really serious jewellery. Her estate has to be worth a bob or two, and if she didn't have a will, look who's first in line."

Victoria's eyes widened.

"Dear old dad."

CHAPTER TWENTY-THREE

Wishing she had put more thought the night before into what she was going to wear, and after much trying on, groaning, and tossing of discarded clothes onto a pile on her bed, Penny finally chose a beige pantsuit with a crisp white blouse. The jacket made a small change from what she usually wore and dressed the outfit up a bit, she thought, but not so much that it looked as if she were making a big deal out of the lunch or attaching more significance to it than it probably deserved.

But she did feel oddly nervous and was looking forward to seeing Davies with a mix of excitement and apprehension. She wasn't sure why he had asked her, but assumed he just wanted to talk to her in a neutral environment, like he said, and then, when she was feeling comfortable and relaxed, poke around to see if she could remember any more details about the woman who had visited her salon on the morning Meg Wynne disappeared.

She busied herself all morning with customers, glancing out of the window from time to time as the sky became darker and a soft, warm drizzle settled over the valley.

By noon, she was dressed and ready to go, hovered over by an approving Victoria, who had suggested at the last minute that she needed some jewellery and loaned her a necklace made of large brown beads, with small gold pieces scattered amongst them.

"I thought we'd just pop over to Betws-y-Coed," Davies said when he picked her up. "I have in mind a rather nice restaurant where we can sit outside but from the looks of things, we'll be better off indoors."

"Sounds great," said Penny, smiling at him. "I love picnics but my problem has always been finding other people who like them, too. I think you either like eating outdoors, or you don't."

After a few moments driving in silence, Davies asked Penny how long she had lived in Wales.

"About twenty-five years. Sometimes I can't believe it's been that long."

"And what part of Canada are you from?"

"Nova Scotia," replied Penny, and then after the significance of his question had sunk in, she had a question for him. "But how did you know I'm Canadian? Most British people ask me what part of America I'm from."

"Oh, my nephew went out to Canada to join the Mounties," Davies replied easily. "And there's something about the way Canadians say 'about' that gives them away every time."

Penny laughed, fingering her necklace.

"People have told me that before but I don't hear it myself."

"It's true," said Davies. "Canadians say it so that it sounds like 'a boot'. Actually, I rather like a Canadian accent, but the really funny thing is that most of you don't think you've got one. You think the British do, and the Americans do, but you don't."

"That's right! We don't!"

Davies laughed and a few minutes later they pulled into the car park.

The restaurant had a wonderful view of the Conwy River and Penny could see that on a fine day it would indeed be a pleasure to have lunch outdoors on the terrace.

By the time they had settled, ordered their meals—soup and salmon for him and salad and salmon for her—and handed the menus back to their server, Penny found her initial nervousness was wearing off and she wondered if it would seem rude to ask him why he had invited her to lunch.

"You're probably wondering why I asked you here today," he said.

She smiled and nodded. "That's exactly what I was thinking," she said, "and I was trying to decide if it would be rude to ask."

"No, no, certainly not," he said. "But I hope you know I don't usually invite witnesses to lunch. It's just that you've been very perceptive and I had hoped that if we chatted a bit more, in a friendly, casual environment, we might jog your memory a bit."

Penny hesitated. "I'll try, but if nothing else has come to me yet, I may not know any more, if you know what I mean."

"Oh, I think you do," Davies said with an encouraging smile. "It's my job to help you seek out and recover those memories."

As the server appeared with a basket of warm bread rolls, Davies reached into his pocket and pulled out a piece of paper.

"I'd like to start by asking you to take a look at this and tell me what you think."

"What is it?" Penny asked.

"It's a photocopy of a scrap of paper we found in Meg Wynne Thompson's room. Sergeant Morgan and I aren't sure what it means, and she suggested that I show it to you."

He handed it to Penny and then broke a bread roll in half, buttered it, and sat back while she looked at the document.

"Hmm," she said after a few moments. "Is it MOMA? Could it be a reference to her mother? Or, what about the Museum of Modern Art? That's in New York and one of the bridesmaids—sorry, can't remember which one— told me Emyr and Meg Wynne were going there on their honeymoon. The bridesmaid said she was green with envy that they were going to New York."

"Did she now?" said Davies.

"The handwriting is interesting, though," said Penny. "Very stylized, like something an architect would do. A very fine hand, as they used to say."

Davies nodded. "She was a graphic designer so I guess she would write in that ornamental way. Well, you might be right about the museum. That's probably what it was."

Penny handed the paper back to him, and then took a bread roll.

"I love bread," she said. "I have to really watch it, though, or I'll eat too much of it. I used to bake my own. There's nothing like fresh bread."

"Really?" said Davies. "You baked your own bread? That's really amazing."

"My fiancé loved it, too, actually," said Penny. "It was great fun to bake for someone who really appreciated it."

"Oh, I didn't know you were married," said Davies. "But you're not now, though, are you? I see you're not wearing a ring."

He smiled.

"Not much gets past me!"

Penny shook her head. "He died many years ago in a very sad accident, before we could get married. He was a police officer, too, so maybe that's why I know a little about your work and what you have to do here."

"I'm sorry to hear he died," Davies said simply. "I lost my wife a few years ago."

"Oh," said Penny. "Now it's my turn to be sorry."

"No, it's okay," said Davies. "Don't be. I wasn't much of a husband and we didn't have much of a marriage left. We'd grown apart. If she hadn't got sick, I probably would have moved out, but as it turned out, her cancer wasn't discovered until it was too late and she died within a couple of months."

The two sat in silence for a moment.

"Well, now that I've put such a damper on everything," said Davies, "I wonder if can find something a bit lighter to discuss. Murder, for example."

Penny smiled at him and as their soup and salad arrived, decided she was rather enjoying herself.

He took a few spoonfuls of soup and then looked at her.

"Sorry, but I'm curious to know. Did your fiancé discuss his work with you?" he asked.

"Oh, all the time," said Penny airily. "I loved hearing everything that he did—what he felt he could tell me, of course. I think it takes a really special kind of person to be a police officer. After all, you're not usually mixing with the nicest people, are you?"

"No," agreed Davies. "I always thought my marriage would have gone better if she'd taken more interest in my work but she just didn't want to know. It's often hard for police officers to see the kinds of things they see, and leave it all behind when they head home. But often the people at home don't understand what we're up against, and so we turn to other officers for comfort and support—and that can lead into dangerous territory.

"There was certainly an element of that in my marriage. I was hardly ever home, and just left all the domestic things up to her. She looked after the house and the kids and I paid the bills. And in the end, there wasn't much left of the two of us."

Penny murmured sympathetically.

"With my fiancé, it was just the opposite. We enjoyed sharing everything and were very close. I was devastated when he died. Relationships don't come easy for me. It took me a long time to get close to him and then a long time to come to terms with his death. He was only thirty-two."

"I have to ask," said Davies. "What happened?"

"He'd managed to rescue a child who had fallen into the Conwy River," said Penny. "But the current was too strong and Tim was swept away before the fire brigade could pull him to shore." She shook her head.

Davies reached out to touch her hand and although she welcomed the warmth of the gesture she felt uneasy with it.

"Now then," said Penny. "I've been giving some more thought to this murder of yours and wondered if you've been able to exclude the father.

"It seems to me that he might have had a financial motive, but I can't help thinking there's something else going on here. Something we don't know about yet. Something really big and nasty."

"I think so, too," said Davies as their salmon arrived. "But you're right—we've pretty much eliminated the father. He was either with the mother or at the off-licence when she disappeared. And frankly, I don't think he had the resources or intelligence to pull off something like this. We're focusing on the people who were at the Hall but with the funeral coming up, we've got to be sensitive."

They ate in silence for a few moments, and then Penny abruptly changed the subject.

"This salmon is delicious," she said. "And such a beautiful colour. With the glaze, it's almost red. How's yours?"

"Excellent," said Davies. "And speaking of red. Can you think why a curved piece of red plastic about this long," he held his thumb and forefinger about two inches apart, "would have been found in Meg Wynne's hair?"

"Well, I think we can safely say it wasn't a hair slide. She wouldn't wear anything so tacky, I'm sure of that."

"No," said Davies. "It was a jagged piece of plastic, came off something else. Can't think for the life of me what it could have been."

Penny looked at him intently.

"Was it from the murder weapon, do you think?"

"Could have been," Davies said carefully. "There was blood and hair on it. But people don't usually try to kill someone with something made of plastic."

"Unless that's all there was to hand," said Penny.

Davies started forward slightly, and then, as if reaching a decision, leaned forward in his chair.

"Look," he said. "To be honest, we're at a bit of an impasse here, and I'd appreciate hearing your thoughts. Why don't I tell you what I think happened and when you know a bit more, you might start to see something that you'd overlooked, or didn't think was important, in a new light.

"But first, how about another glass of wine?"

CHAPTER TWENTY-FOUR

Penny sipped the last of her wine and shook her head as she set the glass down.

"That's a lot to take in," she said. "So what you're saying is that Meg Wynne Thompson was killed twice, that either the strangulation or the blows to the head would have been enough. And then there's the needle. What to make of that?"

Davies nodded. "Exactly. I had a word about this with my nephew Martin," he said. "You know, the one who emigrated to join the RCMP. Martin's been sent to America to take a course in profiling and he told me that overkill like this can mean a couple of things.

"First, it sometimes means that the killer hasn't killed before, so doesn't know what he's doing—doesn't know how much force he needs to use to get the job done, so to speak. Second, the frenzied nature of it probably means that the killing was personal. So for some reason, Meg Wynne had antagonized the killer to the point where there's so much emotion embedded in the attack that whoever killed her used far more force than he needed to."

Penny nodded. "Right. I can see that. Killings like this are usually domestic, aren't they? Close to home."

"That's right," Davies agreed. "They are."

After a few moments, as Penny pondered what he had told her, he looked at his watch.

"Almost time we were heading back," he said. "But there's plenty of time for coffee, if you'd like one. Or pudding. I don't eat sweets much anymore," he said as he patted his middle, "but you go ahead if you want something."

"I think not," said Penny, patting hers. "I need to be getting back, too. I've left Victoria on her own running the salon and I told her I wouldn't be gone too long. She's my new apprentice!"

She placed her napkin on the table and smiled at Davies.

"Thank you," she said simply. "I enjoyed that."

"So did I," he replied, and after a brief pause added, "What have you got on over the next few days? Will you be available if I need to speak to you again?"

"Oh, I think so. When you have a business, you're pretty well tied to it, but Victoria and I are planning to go up to Llandudno for the afternoon to get some stock at the Cash and Carry. I'm making some changes to my business plan, you see. I've been thinking for a while about getting in someone to take over more of the day-to-day running of things so I can grow the business, and with Victoria there now, it just makes sense for her to do that."

"Really?" said Davies. "Good for you. Hope it works out."

"Speaking of Victoria," Penny said, "she's going to be playing at Rhys Gruffydd's funeral tomorrow. Apparently most of the wedding party is coming back to be there. Thought you'd like to know."

Davies nodded and looked up from his wallet where he was sorting out his credit cards.

"Please remember what I told you about getting involved in this, Penny. Whoever he is, he's dangerous. When you've killed once, why not kill a second time, or even a third?"

While they'd been having lunch, the weather had started to improve. The sky had lightened and the drizzle was letting up. The air felt fresh and charged, and Penny felt an unexpected lifting of her spirits.

They drove in an easy silence for a few minutes, until Davies tapped her on the knee and pointed at something outside his rain-spattered window.

"Look!" he said. "Ordered especially for you."

Leaning forward to see past him, Penny gasped.

A magnificent, shimmering rainbow arced across the sky stretching from Snowdon across the valley. As its bright red blended into a spectrum of colours ending in vibrant violet, it gave off a subtle glow that transformed the view into a surreal glimpse into a magical world. A gentle mist rose from the green fields and Penny felt a rare and welcome sense of well-being.

"Oh, wow," she said. "And look again now! There're two of them! See! Over there! To the left!"

Davies slowed the car until he found a spot where he could pull over safely. He reached into the glove box and pulled out a digital camera.

"Let's get some photos. We might want to remember this."

"For sure!" called Penny as she jumped out of the car. "Hurry, Gareth, before they disappear."

She slowed as she reached the top of a small embankment and as Gareth photographed the rainbows for her, she breathed in the freshly cleansed air that smelled so sweetly of recent rain.

"Well?"
"Well, what?"

"Well, how did it go?"

Penny took her jacket off, hung it carefully on the coatrack, and turned to face her friend.

"Well, if you mean did I have a good time, then yes, very nice, thank you. We went to Betws-y-Coed and saw the most beautiful double rainbow on the way home. It was spectacular. The kind of thing you're really lucky to see once in a blue moon, if that isn't mixing up too much freaky nature into one thought.

"But if you mean did I find out anything, then yes, I did, a little. He told me how Meg Wynne died and it was pretty brutal I can tell you. Oh, and he warned us off again. Says whoever it was killed Meg Wynne could easily kill again.

"What happened in the shop while I was gone? Did you get the list made of the things we have to get in Llandudno? Are you ready for the funeral tomorrow? Should we have a chat about what you might look out for?"

Victoria laughed.

"You must have had a good time. You're positively ranting. How much wine did you have?"

She gave Penny a hug and then stood back to look at her.

"I'm glad you had a good time. Will you be seeing him again, do you think?"

"Later in the week, possibly, depending on how his work goes. Might go out for a drink." After a moment she added, "I think he's just interested in me for now, because of what he thinks I know. When all this is wrapped up, we probably won't see him again."

She shrugged and raised her hands in a what-can-you-do gesture.

"Anyway, why don't you fill up the kettle and tell me how you got on in the shop. Did you get a chance to sort out the inventory and make a list of the things we need?"

The next day, Victoria returned from the Gruffydd funeral to find Penny restlessly poking about in the kitchen.

"It was all very tasteful," she said, in reply to Penny's raised eyebrows. "Everything had been planned down to the tiniest detail."

She paused for a few moments and watched as Penny opened the door to the fridge, peered at its contents, then closed the door and moved on to the cupboard where the biscuits were kept. She shook her head in response to Penny's offer of one.

"No, I couldn't eat another thing," she said. "There was so much food in the church hall afterward. Gwennie had done it all, I heard—sandwiches, little cakes, pastries, everything. She did a beautiful job. It was all just perfect."

She eyed the biscuit box and held up a hand.

"Mm, tempting, but I mustn't. Anyway, I was all psyched up to suss out the wedding girls, but they were pretty obvious. In those clothes, and looking so smart and Londonish, they really stuck out."

"Were they wearing their high heels?" Penny asked.

Victoria laughed. "Oh, absolutely. You should have heard Mrs. Lloyd go on about them. In her day, girls knew the difference between town shoes and country shoes. You have to admit she's got a point, though. So impractical. Not to mention uncomfortable, I shouldn't wonder. Still, they say you get used to it but why on earth would you want to, I ask myself.

"Anyway, I had a little chat with them and told them you and I were working together now in the shop. They said you gave them the best manicure—better than anything they get in London. Said it lasted for a week, with no chipping and if they can, they'll ring for an appointment. I gave them a business card.

"Which reminds me, should we think about updating the cards? I thought maybe you could come up with a new design—put a spectacular red fingernail on it, or something. Jazz them up. Splash of colour."

Penny nodded. "We need to sit down and go over everything. I'm updating the business plan, so we can certainly add that in. We'll use up the old ones first, though. No point in wasting them when we haven't changed phone numbers or moved or anything. But we're getting off topic. Let's go back to the funeral. Who else did you talk to?"

"Oh, right. Well, Emyr, of course, and his friend, David Williams. It turns out that I knew David's family many years ago, when I used to spend my summers here. He was just a cheeky lad, then, always up to something but so charming he always got away with it. He was called by his Welsh name, Dafydd, back then. Apparently he's done really well for himself in London. He's got a big life there, bags of money, by all accounts.

"Oh, and a pretty fancy girlfriend. A woman picked him up after the funeral in a BMW. I didn't get a good look at her, though, and don't know if I'd recognize her if I saw her again. She was wearing big sunglasses and a head scarf like a 1960s Italian movie star. La dolce vita."

"Be nice to know who she is," said Penny. "As for David, he was Emyr's best man at the wedding. Apparently very supportive and helpful, he was, by all accounts, when Meg Wynne went missing, but I think we've already been over that.

"Was the other one there? Robbie? I wish we knew more about him."

Victoria thought for a moment.

"I don't think he was, but I'm not sure I would have known him. The good thing about playing at the funeral, though, was that I had a really good seat at the front and got to see the faces of the people who were there, as opposed to sitting in a pew and looking at the backs of their heads."

"Oh, sorry!" exclaimed Penny. "I should have asked—how did your playing go? What songs did you do? Were you a hit?"

"Do you know," said Victoria, "I think I was. I did John Lennon's 'Beautiful Boy' and Emyr started to cry. Is that good or bad, do you think? I can never tell."

"I think it's good," said Penny, "although just thinking about it makes me want to cry, too."

She thought for a moment.

"Well, since you've already eaten, why don't you get changed and we'll go for a walk? I've been cooped up here all day and the exercise will do us both good. And I'd like to pick up a few things on the way back."

Victoria cheerfully agreed, telling Penny she might want to put on a jumper as the wind was cool.

A few minutes later they set off, and rounded the corner into the town square.

Penny stopped short and placed her hand on Victoria's arm.

"What is it?" said Victoria, looking at her. "You look as if you've just seen a ghost. Are you okay?"

Penny slowly lifted her hand and pointed in the direction of the town clock at a small woman in a light green spring coat, with a carrier bag in each hand, who was making her way toward them.

"Sorry," gasped Penny. "She looks so much like Emma the first day I saw her, I was just taken aback for a moment."

"Oh, that's only Gwennie," said Victoria. "She'll have been tidying up after the funeral. Hello, Gwennie," she called out.

"Oh, Mrs. Hopkirk, I'm that glad to see you!" she said rushing toward them as the bags flopped against her legs. "I was so busy seeing to the refreshments at the reception I didn't have a chance to tell you how much I enjoyed your playing." She looked up admiringly at Victoria and then stole a sideways glance at Penny. "I'm just taking a few sandwiches and cakes home to my sister. They'll enjoy them for their tea, I thought. But tell me, what did you think of the service?"

She paused to catch her breath.

"I thought it was lovely," said Victoria. "Gwennie, have you met my friend Penny Brannigan? Penny does our manicures."

"Oh, Miss Brannigan, how do you do?" said Gwennie politely. "I've often thought I'd like to stop in your shop and have my nails done but then I think what with all the washing and cleaning, what would be the point? I remember you always did them for Mrs. Gruffydd on her special occasions. Like Christmas. Always got them done, then, she did."

Gwennie and Victoria chatted away for a few moments while Penny, in a world of her own, stared at Gwennie's distinctive coat. Undoubtedly the height of fashion in its day, the coat was full-length, unbelted, and unfitted. With a full, generous cut, it flowed straight down from the yoke and featured a stand-up collar, raglan sleeves, and small, brown leather buttons. She would have known it anywhere, because she had seen it so many times on its previous owner.

Finally, she spoke.

"Gwennie, do you mind me asking you where you got that coat?"

"What? This old thing? I bought it years ago at the charity shop, just over there," she said, pointing to the one that faced the square. "But it's very good quality and there's still lots of wear left in it," she said somewhat defensively. And then, eager to continue discussing the details of the funeral, she turned back to Victoria.

"I told young Mr. Emyr that you would do a beautiful job, and you did," she gushed. "He's been through such a lot lately, and is very grateful for all the kindness and support of his friends. I told him we'd had such a lovely chat in the kitchen that day you came by and how concerned you'd been over that awful business with poor Meg Wynne.

"I do hope you'll drop by again for a cup of tea with me, Mrs. Hopkirk. You'll always be very welcome and I do enjoy a bit of company. It looks like I'll be working more hours up at the Hall as young Mr. Emyr needs that much looking after, now that he's on his own. Of course, he's in and out and I expect he'll be off to London or somewhere soon so I don't know what's going to happen, really I don't.

"Well, I must get off or my sister and her husband will be wondering whatever happened to me. They'll have been expecting me long since. Good-bye, then."

"Good-bye, Gwennie," said Victoria, watching as she left and giving a little wave.

Penny made no move.

"Earth to Penny!" said Victoria. "You didn't say good-bye to Gwennie. Are you all right?"

"Sorry, I'm fine," said Penny. "I wasn't really listening. I was thinking about something else."

She watched as Gwennie's receding figure got smaller, turned a corner, and disappeared from view. Shrugging, she smiled at Victoria and pulled herself together.

"A little trip down memory lane. That was Emma's

coat. I didn't realize she'd given it to the charity shop. I'm glad someone's getting some good use out of it. To tell you the truth, I never really liked it at the time, but now I think it's rather smart. Very retro. Vintage!"

Victoria smiled at her.

"That'll be the nostalgia setting in," she said. "It comes to us all. I get that way thinking about glass milk bottles and the lovely, dear men who used to deliver then."

She shook her head and they walked on. As they turned the corner they saw Gwennie further on down the street hoisting her bags into the back of what looked to them like a high-end BMW.

"There's his good deed for the day," Victoria observed. "David Williams giving Gwennie and her bags a lift home. How nice."

CHAPTER TWENTY-FIVE

Penny had always enjoyed daytrips to Llandudno. She could have had her supplies shipped directly to the salon, but she looked forward to closing her shop early once a month or so and visiting the charming seaside town, with its elegant Edwardian architecture, handsome shops, fine restaurants, and half-mile long Victorian pier that juts into Llandudno Bay with views to the famous limestone cliffs.

When they had finished choosing the salon supplies, Penny and Victoria decided to leave their parcel behind to be picked up later, and take a leisurely stroll along the sweeping promenade. They admired the regal, four-storey terraced hotels as they went, and soon found themselves outside the region's best-known contemporary art gallery, Oriel Mostyn.

"This was one of the last places Emma and I visited," said Penny wistfully, "before she became too ill to get out and about.

"I was thinking this morning that I'm going to retire her Altar Ego polish. I can't see myself using it on anyone else."

Victoria nodded sympathetically and put her arm around Penny.

"I'm sorry you lost Emma," she said softly. "But I'm here now. As friends go, will I do?"

After a few moments, she pointed in the direction of the pier.

"Just for fun, should we pretend we're holidaymakers and take the sea air properly? It's been years since I walked along the pier and maybe we'll feel like a cup of tea at the café, if it's open."

"All right," said Penny, "but when we come back I want to have a good look around Marks and Spencer. Be funny if we bumped into Mrs. Lloyd. She always shops there and then treats herself to a nice tea at Badgers. I've just realized that I've got nothing to wear. Must get my hair done and lose a pound or two, while I'm at it."

Victoria smiled to herself as they turned in the direction of the pier, with its decorative turquoise wrought-iron balustrades and lattice-work railings.

"Imagine all the people who have made their way along here over the past hundred and some years," mused Victoria as they stepped onto the pier. "Why do you suppose the Victorians had such a thing about piers? They must have loved them, they built so many of them."

"Like God and poor people," laughed Penny. "Maybe piers served as a safe destination for courting couples and were seen as a wholesome place for families to go, although exactly what people did beyond just hang out for a bit, I really don't know. But look how crowded it is today, and this isn't even a weekend. So whatever the attraction was, it's still going on today, apparently."

They walked on in silence, and then stopped to lean on the railing and admire the views out over Llandudno Bay toward Craig y Don. Seagulls called to one another and swooped over the blue waters of the bay.

After a few moments, they resumed walking, their footsteps making soft sounds on the pier's wooden planks. A gentle breeze, carrying with it the unmistakable smell of the sea, rippled their hair.

Suddenly, Penny placed her hand on Victoria's forearm, stopping her.

"What is it? What's the matter?" Victoria said.

"That woman up ahead, in the head scarf. I think she's the one who came to the shop that morning for a manicure. The wedding day! I think it's her!"

"You're kidding!" said Victoria.

"No, of course I'm not. Why on earth would I kid about something like that? And why do people always say that?" said Penny impatiently.

"Sorry, sorry," said Victoria. "What should we do?"

"Let's turn away so she can't see us," said Penny, as she shifted to face the railing and bent over pretending to tie her shoelace. She turned her head slightly to look up at Victoria.

"She doesn't know you. You stand in front of me here and watch and see what she does and tell me what's happening."

Victoria swayed slightly to the right to get a better view and to block Penny.

"Right. Well, she's just standing there looking around," Victoria said quietly. "She has that anxious look about her that you get when you're meeting someone. You know, have I come to the right place? Did I get the time right? I think she's looking for someone. That's what these piers are good for . . . meeting people. You know, I'll meet you on the pier at two o'clock, that kind of thing."

"Never mind that," whispered Penny. "What's happening now?"

"Nothing. She's just standing there looking around

but she seems, oh I don't know what the word is, furtive. That's it. She seems furtive. Maybe you should back off a bit in case she sees us. She might recognize you."

"Good idea," said Penny as she stood up and sidled a few steps toward shore.

Crowds of people drifted past them in both directions, and a few moments later Victoria let out a small gasp.

"I don't believe it," she said. "It can't be. Don't look now, but I think it's . . ."

Penny turned her head a fraction and watched in amazement as a tall man, wearing blue jeans and a pale green golf shirt, approached the woman. He placed his hands on her shoulders and kissed her gently on both cheeks. As he turned to stand beside her, smiling, Penny recognized Emyr Gruffydd.

She closed her eyes for a second and, heart pounding, turned toward Victoria, who looked horrified.

"They're coming back toward us," Victoria whispered. "Look out over the water."

The two women turned their backs to the pier and then, rotating slowly, saw Emyr and the woman begin to make their way casually back toward the town.

"What should we do?" whispered Victoria.

"We'll have to follow them, and see where they go," said Penny. "If we phone Gareth now it'll take too long for him to get here. We want to find out as much as we can. Where's your mobile?"

Victoria reached into her bag and pulled out her mobile phone. She switched it on, and then groaned.

"I forgot to charge the batteries," she wailed. "It's dead."

"Well, never mind that now," said Penny. "Come on, let's get after them or we'll lose them. We'll ring him later, first chance we get."

They followed the couple at a discreet distance and watched as they left the pier, ambled slowly along the promenade toward Mostyn Street, and then ducked into a pub. The two women stopped in front of a bookstore a few doors down and looked at a towering display of bestsellers.

"Should we go into the pub, do you think?" asked Victoria.

"You look in the window and see if you can see them, while I stay here out of sight," said Penny. "Just walk past and look in as if you're thinking about maybe having something to eat."

A few minutes later Victoria was back.

"They were looking at the menus," she said. "They might be there for a while. Do you think we should try to find a phone box and ring the police?"

"I don't know. I wish we could hear what they're saying, but that would be too obvious. They'd see us and know what we were up to. I don't think one of us can leave, either, to find a phone in case they decide to leave. If one of them leaves, or if they split up, then we've really lost them."

"Argh, I wish I could think this through."

Suddenly, Victoria started to snicker.

"It's just like something in the movies, only we don't have a clue what we're doing."

"Be serious, Victoria," admonished Penny. "We have to get this right. The only thing we can do is wait and see what happens, and phone Gareth as soon as we can."

They kept watch on the pub for what seemed like an eternity, and eventually the couple emerged and stood on the pavement as if unsure what to do next.

Emyr made a faint gesture with his right hand and the woman smiled at him.

She reached up and patted him on the shoulder and then, still smiling, turned and walked away down the side street. He stood there for a few moments looking after her and then ambled away.

The two women were left staring after them.

"What was that all about, then?" asked Victoria. "They're leaving? Is that it? Do you think we should follow her to see where she goes?"

"Well, we don't need to follow Emyr," said Penny. "We know where to find him. But we'd better see where she goes and what she's up to. But if she realizes she's being followed we could do more harm than good so we've got to be careful. Come on, let's get after her."

They followed the woman down the side street at a safe distance and watched as she turned into one of the better hotels.

"You have to admit this doesn't look good, the two of them together, whoever she is," said Penny. "Right. I'll have to wait out here and you get in there and see what you can find out."

Victoria looked mortified.

"Me? Find out what, exactly?"

"Well, who she is, of course! That's what we need to know. Then we'll really be getting someplace with our investigation."

Victoria sighed, took a few steps toward the entrance, and then turned around to look at Penny who nodded encouragingly and gave a little flutter with her hand in the direction of the door.

A few steps later Victoria found herself in a large, old-fashioned hotel lobby, filled with overstuffed wing chairs and sofas, huge potted plants, and a couple of side tables with folded newspapers on them. In the distance, she could hear the steady, back and forth drone of a Hoover.

She made her way across the highly patterned burgundy carpet to the long wooden reception desk where a young man in a dark green uniform was tapping away on a keyboard. Victoria stood in front of him until he stopped typing. He shifted his eyes from his computer screen and gazed at her with an impatient, sullen look as if he deeply resented the interruption.

"Good afternoon. May I help you?" he asked impersonally.

Victoria cleared her throat and smiled weakly.

"I hope so, yes," she began, and then gaining confidence, added, "I think I just saw a woman come into the hotel. She's about thirty-five, well dressed. I believe she was a friend of my, ah, niece's, yes, that's it, niece's from school and I wondered if you could just let me have her name so I can tell my niece I saw her."

She groaned inwardly at how lame and pathetic it sounded.

"I'm sorry, madam, but hotel policy is that we do not give out personal information about any of our guests. I am sorry I cannot help you."

With that, he walked away to retrieve some papers from a pile sitting beside another computer terminal.

"Well, thank you anyway," said Victoria softly. As she emerged from the hotel back into the sunny afternoon she glanced at Penny, shrugged, and shook her head.

"Well, never mind," said Penny. "Let's find a phone and call the police. We'll have to think of something else."

The desk clerk, meanwhile, envisioning a hefty tip from a grateful guest, reached for his telephone.

Two hours later, as they were putting away their supplies, Penny groaned.

"Damn! In all the excitement, we didn't get to Marks and Spencer and now I've got nothing to wear. The next time I see him I'll have to make do with something old and awful. That's if he's still speaking to me, of course."

"Never mind about that," said Victoria. "It's too bad we weren't able to reach him, but we did try. We can't help it if Bethan wasn't answering her mobile and you've left a message. They'll figure it out."

"God, I hope we did the right thing following her," said Penny anxiously. "I'm really having second thoughts about that and I just hope we didn't screw it up. It all happened so quickly and we didn't have enough time to come up with a plan. What if we put the wind up those two and now they're on to us?"

She thought for a moment.

"But we have to find out who she is. You know, we considered that there might have been someone in Meg Wynn's past who didn't want the wedding to go ahead, but what if we got it the wrong way around and the person from the past was connected to Emyr? Maybe she's an old girlfriend and she got very jealous and killed Meg Wynn. And if that's what happened, did he know about it? Was he in on it? Is he covering up for someone?"

Victoria looked startled.

"You know, I might be wrong, but she could be the woman who picked up David Williams after the funeral. How would that fit together? Maybe they were all in on it."

CHAPTER TWENTY-SIX

"I'm old fashioned," Davies said to her a few days later. "I'll call for you. Sevenish suit you? We'll talk about it then."

It was a beautiful evening with hours of daylight left as the two of them made their silent, awkward way in the direction of The Leek and Lily. The street was crowded with townsfolk enjoying the fine summer weather as they did a bit of late shopping or ran a last-minute errand.

Penny and Davies, both dreading the chat to come, didn't take much notice of their fellow pedestrians, least of all a good-looking man wearing a baseball cap pulled down over his eyes who passed them headed in the other direction. He stopped, shifted the cellophane-wrapped bouquet of flowers he was carrying from one arm to the other, and waited under the awning of the stationery store until they turned the corner into the High Street, and then he crossed the street and headed up Station Road.

A few minutes later Victoria, who was just settling in with a magazine and a glass of wine, was startled when the bell in the flat rang to announce someone at the salon door. Thinking Penny must have forgotten her keys and come back to get them, rather than risk waking her up if she returned late, Victoria hurried down the stairs to let her in.

"Oh hello," she said as she opened the door. "What gorgeous flowers! Who are they for?"

Penny entered the pub first, and Davies, ducking his head slightly, followed her in. Two steps down to the right and they were in the large, welcoming main room. Mercifully, it had somehow been spared the modernizing trend of the 1980s, and retained a look from a much earlier period. The low ceiling featured genuine oak beams, the whitewashed walls had lovely old prints of Llanelen's historic ties to the local quarry, and there wasn't a pseudo horse brass in sight. Facing them as they entered the room was a large fireplace, empty and cold now, but when the nights began to draw in, it would provide the welcome warmth, comfort, and soft, flattering light that it had since the pub opened in the 1920s. And best of all, the real look of the place went with the real ale it served.

Along two walls were large tables with bench-type seating and smaller tables were scattered throughout with simple wooden chairs. The pub was about half full, and as Penny and Davies entered, a few regulars stopped their conversations long enough to look at the newcomers and then went back to their pints.

"White wine is it? Davies asked.

"No," said Penny. "Better make it a large G and T, please."

"Right," said Davies. "Be right back."

He made his way over to the bar, spoke a few words to the amiable barmaid, affectionately known as Lily, and returned in a couple of minutes with their drinks. Setting them down on the table, he looked around for a moment before taking a seat opposite Penny.

"Not too many in tonight," he commented.

"No, not yet," agreed Penny. "I don't come here very often, but when I do, I ask myself why I haven't been back sooner. I like it but I'm just not a pub person, I guess. Well, cheers," she added as she picked up her drink and raised it toward Davies.

"Cheers," he replied and then took a sip from his pint of Honey Fayre, the locally brewed beer.

"Mmm," he said. "That's good."

The tension hung in the air between them like thick, acrid smoke.

He hadn't spoken to her since the sighting in Llan-dudno, sending Bethan to interview her and Victoria. You could see the steam coming of out his ears, Bethan had told them, when he'd heard about their clumsy attempt to discover the mysterious woman's identity. By the time the police got there, Bethan said, she'd undoubtedly been tipped off, probably by the desk clerk, and was long gone. Not only that, but Emyr had apparently gone missing. Penny had apologized profusely to Bethan and had been dreading the moment when she would have to face Davies.

Now that he'd had a chance to cool down, he was ready to discuss it. He cleared his throat.

"You did exactly what I asked you not to do," he told Penny sternly. "Not only did you put yourselves at risk, but if you'd done this by the book, we might have had her in for questioning by now. I told you to leave it to us, and I wish you had."

He sighed and took another sip of his beer.

"I can't tell you how sorry we are," Penny said. "We didn't know what to do for the best and we thought we were doing the right thing."

Unable to look at him, she gazed around the pub and welcomed the diversion of a group of regulars calling out greetings to one of their mates who had just arrived.

A short, middle-aged man with a ruddy complexion that gave the impression of long years of outdoor work, waved to a group sitting around a corner table and made his way over to them, leading a black-and-white, medium-sized dog of uncertain parentage on a lead.

His cronies greeted them and slid down the bench to make room for the two of them. The dog hopped up on the seat and the man unfastened the lead, placed it on the table and, announcing it was his round, took the drinks orders from his companions and walked over to the bar.

The man sitting beside the dog put his arm around it and gave it a friendly pat. The dog looked at him and then, its lips drawn back in what passed for a smile, panted lightly and looked happily and expectantly around the room.

Penny watched all this play out and then turned back to Davies.

"That's Mackie, and the dog's called Buster," she explained. "Mrs. Lloyd told me that he rescued the dog from an abusive owner, and they've been together ever since. Mackie does odd jobs, a bit of gardening, clearing out your gutters, that sort of thing, and takes the dog everywhere with him. Just adores him. . . ." Her voice trailed off as she stared at the group.

"What is it?" Davies asked.

"I've just remembered something Gwennie told Victoria."

She got up slowly and made her way to the table. Davies watched as she leaned over to give the dog a pat and then spoke briefly to the man sitting beside him.

She turned around to face Davies, holding the dog's lead. Unlike a simple, old-fashioned leather leash, this one was retractable, designed to give a dog the chance of a bit of controlled roaming. On the business end was a clip that attached to the dog's collar, then a short strip of heavy nylon banding about an inch wide, and then a long cord like a stout fishing line that disappeared into a heavy blue plastic case with a built-in handle. Davies watched as Penny grasped the case in her right hand and taking the clip end in her left hand, slowly wrapped the band two or three times around her hand as she carefully pulled the lead from the case until she had exposed about two feet of heavy nylon cording.

Now what she held was a formidable weapon.

Allowing the cord to rewind inside the case, she made a heavy chopping motion with it.

Davies licked a trace of foam from his top lip and set his glass down on the table. Mirroring his action, Penny set the lead down on the table, nodded her thanks to the mystified men, and returned to Davies.

"Remind you of anything?" she asked softly. "What do you think? Imagine the case is red plastic instead of blue. And Gwennie told Victoria that the dog's lead went missing the morning Meg Wynne disappeared."

"We'll have to ask Gwennie about the dog's lead and interview the wedding boys again," he said. "Find out if the groom had time for a little dog walking." As the frosty, formal atmosphere between them began to thaw, Penny felt a slight glimmer of hope that she might have redeemed herself.

"Too bad we can't just ask Trixxi," said Penny. "She'd know."

"Trixxi?"

"Emyr's dog."

Davis nodded and took another sip. A few minutes later Penny set down her drink and looked at him.

"I don't know why," she said, "but I've got a bad

feeling and I've suddenly started to feel anxious. I need to go home."

"Right," agreed Davies. "Let's be off."

They made their way back to the flat more quickly than they had come, scarcely speaking.

"You've given me a lot to think about," Davies said. "I have to get in touch right now with Sgt. Morgan and prepare to track down Emyr and the rest of them. She's been in London for a couple of days checking out Meg Wynne Thompson's life there but so far she hasn't turned up anything that we think concerns us."

As they approached the salon, they slowed down and Davies looked at Penny.

"Look," he said, "things are going to speed up now, and I don't think this case is going to go on for too much longer. But once it's wrapped up and all this is behind us, I hope that we can, that you'll . . ."

They had stopped in front off the salon and Davies reached out to Penny and putting his arm around her waist, pulled her gently toward him. She reached out to steady herself and as she touched the door to the salon, it opened a couple of inches.

Reacting to the startled look on her face, Davies turned to look at the door and immediately understood.

Gesturing to Penny to stand to one side, he pushed open the door and cautiously looked in.

"Oh God, no!" he said as he sprang through the door.

"What is it?" said Penny as she charged in after him. "What's happened?"

Reaching for his mobile phone, Davies gestured at the floor and a few moments later was speaking rapidly into his mobile.

"It's Davies. I need an ambulance to the manicure salon on Station Road in Llanelen. We have a woman here who seems to be unconscious." He bent down and touched Victoria's forehead. "Her skin is very hot and flushed. Sweaty. Oh, and we'll need officers, too. Quick as you can."

Penny was crouching beside the limp Victoria, stroking her hair, gently lifting her up. A small moan escaped from her lips and Penny bent closer as Victoria struggled to speak.

She looked up at Davies, with tears in her eyes.

"She said 'die'. She told me she's going to die," Penny whispered. "And look."

Mixed in with the broken blossoms strewn across the hardwood floor was a syringe.

CHAPTER TWENTY-SEVEN

After what seemed an eternity but in reality was a very few minutes, the ambulance with its distinctive green-and-yellow markings arrived and paramedics rushed in, followed by two uniformed police officers.

As Victoria, who had lapsed into unconsciousness, was placed on the stretcher, Penny glanced quickly around the salon. Apart from the torn cellophane and scattered flowers, nothing seemed to have been disturbed.

"You go with her," Davies directed. "I'll leave an officer here and follow in the car. Got your keys?"

Penny pointed to her handbag on the floor.

Grasping Victoria's hand tightly, Penny accompanied the stretcher and once it had been secured, clambered in after her friend. As a paramedic closed the vehicle's rear doors, she glimpsed Davies, her handbag under his arm, pulling the door to the salon shut and sprinting off up the street to his parked car.

The ambulance pulled away and she turned her attention to Victoria who lay pale and still.

"They've taken her through to casualty," an agitated Penny told Davies in the hospital's reception area about fifteen minutes later. "They said to wait over here and they'd come and talk to me when they've had a chance to examine her and know more."

She sat down heavily on a plastic waiting room chair and covered her face with her hands. Davies immediately sat down next to her and placed his arm tentatively around her shoulders, and then, when she didn't resist, pulled her in to him.

"We'll get whoever did this," he said soothingly. "In the meantime, you have to stay strong for Victoria. I don't know how serious her condition is, but it has to be good that we found her when we did and the paramedics were no time at all getting to her. And not only that, they brought the syringe with them, so they can find out what she was injected with. They'll run tests.

"I think she'll make it. You'll see."

He gave her shoulders a small squeeze and then stood up.

"I've spoken to Sgt. Morgan. We're still searching for Emyr and we're going to send a team to go over your salon to see if the attacker left anything behind."

Penny nodded and then looked up at Davies.

"Will you stay with me, please?"

"I will. But I've called in another officer, and if I do have to go, I'll make sure you've got someone with you and to drive you home. We can't take any more chances. You could be next."

They sat quietly, looking up expectantly every time someone emerged from the trauma area until, finally, a man wearing hospital greens came out and scanned the crowded room.

As Davies and Penny stood up, he moved toward them. He was middle-aged, with thinning grey hair and over the years seemed to have figured out how to completely hide his emotion. Unfortunately, his mask of neutrality ended up giving him an uncaring, stone-faced look. As he approached them, Penny had no idea if he had bad news or good but realized she had taken an instant dislike to him.

"You're here for the woman who was brought in with the overdose?" he asked, looking at Davies.

"Yes, we are," Davies replied. "This is her friend, Penny Brannigan, and I'm Detective Chief Inspector Davies, North Wales police."

"Well, she hasn't regained consciousness, and we're not sure yet of her cardio status, but the good news is that she seems stable and she's breathing on her own. We've got her on a drip and we're running blood tests. The next twenty-four hours will be crucial to her recovery.

"That's about all I can tell you at this point. You can wait here, if you like, or leave a number at the desk over there, and we'll call you if there's any change. Okay? Right then." He nodded in a businesslike way and disappeared down the hall.

"I hate that!" said Penny. "Did you see what he did? It makes me furious!"

"What is it?" asked a bewildered Davies. "What did he do?"

"You don't get it, do you?" Penny flared. "He completely ignored me, and talked only to you because you're the man and I'm just the silly woman. She's *my* friend, I'm the one who cares about her, and he should have spoken to me! Oh, I hate this getting older. Victoria was right—people treat us as if we're invisible." She paused for a moment and then added, "Or worse, imbeciles."

Davies seemed taken aback by this outburst and knew he had to be careful not to seem patronizing or dismissive of Penny's charged feelings.

"I hadn't thought of it that way, but you're right," he

said. "You are her friend and he should have spoken to you. It was insensitive of him and I'm sorry that happened." He smiled at her. "Would a really bad cup of machine-made tea in a nasty styrofoam cup help, do you think?"

Penny shook her head.

"I think I'll wait until I get home, whenever that might be," she said, stifling a yawn. "I feel very tired all of a sudden. Really drained. I hope they'll know soon if she's going to be okay."

A few moments later, Davies's mobile rang.

He listened, nodded, said "right" a couple of times and then ended the call.

"That was Sgt. Morgan. She's on her way here. She's been up at the Hall again and there's no one there except the housekeeper."

"Gwennie," said Penny mechanically.

"Yes, Gwennie. She's moved in to look after the dog, apparently. Emyr hasn't been home for days and she hasn't heard from him. But Gwennie has confirmed that the dog lead that went missing on the morning of the wedding was a red, retractable one, so well done, you.

"The best thing now would be to leave an officer here with Victoria, and send you home with Sgt. Morgan. You can't be left on your own after what's happened, and if things change, Sgt. Morgan can drive you back here.

"Does that sound like a good plan?"

Penny nodded and they sat down to wait for Bethan Morgan. When the three of them left the hospital some time later, there had been no change in Victoria's condition and night had fallen.

Sometime after midnight it started to rain and as she woke to a grey, dreary day, Penny felt the stirrings of resentment. She felt weighed down by all that was going on in her life, things over which she had no control. She also realized that for some time she had felt a creeping sense of boredom. How many times could she paint the same pastoral scene? The same fingernails? It had crossed her mind that it might be time to sell the business, but then what? Where would she go? What would she do?

Shaking off the feeling, she slipped on a turquoise bathrobe that had seen better days and stepped out into the living room. Morgan, who had spent a restless, uncomfortable night on the couch, was dressed and drinking tea.

"Good morning," she said brightly. "There's been no news from the hospital, so we'll take that as a good sign. I'm waiting to hear from himself about what our next move is going to be. I thought he would have called by now, actually."

She looked at the rumpled, grumpy Penny and smiled.

"You look like a woman who could use a nice cup of tea. Hope you don't mind, but I brewed up," she said gesturing at her cup, "but let me make some fresh for you."

"I think I'll have a bath first," said Penny. "And then open the shop. And I think I'll have coffee this morning, for a change. But thanks."

"No problem. Oh, the rector called and he and his wife are on their way to the hospital."

The morning dragged on endlessly as Penny waited for news. She dreaded having to answer customers' questions and most of her clients showed a polite restraint in not asking too many. Everyone, of course, had heard about the attack, and all her regulars were deeply anxious to know if Victoria would be all right.

"I don't know. I hope so," was all Penny could tell them.

Morgan had made herself at home with the magazines in the waiting area and was catching up on all the latest news of has-been pop stars, obscenely rich athletes, and actors with really bad taste in just about everything.

Finally, just before noon, her mobile rang.

With an emery board suspended in the air, Penny and her customer turned anxious eyes toward Morgan. They held their breath and watched as Morgan's expression changed from concentration and concern to relief and her shoulders relaxed as she ended the call.

"She's come around," said Morgan. "They think she's going to be all right, but she doesn't remember anything about what happened to her. She's asking for you, though. I'll drive you up as soon as you're ready to go."

Excusing herself from her customer, Penny went to check her appointment book.

Nodding, she turned to Morgan.

"Mrs. Lloyd is coming in after this lady," she said, "so I'll do her. As for the others, would you mind ringing them and asking if I can reschedule them until, say, this evening or tomorrow, in view of what's happened? I'm sure they'll be fine with that. Oh, and you can always tell them Victoria's better, if they ask. They'll like being among the first to know."

Penny returned to her customer and the two of them began to discuss the good news.

Twenty minutes later, while Morgan was finishing up her calls, Mrs. Lloyd arrived for her Thursday manicure.

"Oh, my dear," she said. "I was shocked when I heard what had happened. Not surprised, mind you. I know how these things go. There's never just one murder. Oh, no. These people never stop at one. It has to go on and on until they're caught."

Looking at Morgan, who had moved on to tidying up the rows of nail varnish, Mrs. Lloyd asked pointedly, "And has he been caught?

"No offence, Penny dear, but I would have thought police resources would have been better spent catching the person who did this dreadful deed rather than assigning one of their officers to be your salon assistant."

Penny laughed.

"Now, Mrs. Lloyd, the sergeant hasn't been sent here to help me. They just thought in light of what happened I shouldn't be alone. But now that you mention it, as she is here, perhaps we could ask her to make a cup of tea for you, if you'd like that."

"Oh I would. You always see that in the movies, don't you, where the nice lady policewoman gets sent off to make a cup of tea while the clever men solve the crime."

"Mrs. Lloyd, don't get me started!"

"Me, neither, Mrs. Lloyd," laughed Morgan.

Half an hour later, they had come to Mrs. Lloyd's favourite part of the manicure. What colour to choose? After much dithering and deciding, she finally opted for Windy City Pretty.

While Penny was applying the last few brushstrokes of top coat, Morgan announced she was going up to the flat to make sandwiches so they could have a quick lunch before setting off for the hospital.

A few minutes later, Mrs. Lloyd was admiring her new nails as she prepared to leave.

"I'm not sure I'd have that colour again, Penny," she said. "But you do need to try out new things, don't you?

Sometimes they work out for the best and sometimes they don't. And, if they're really good, you wonder how you ever managed without them."

Penny accompanied her to the door, and Mrs. Lloyd stepped out into the street. As Penny prepared to turn the shop sign to CLOSED, Mrs. Lloyd held up a finger.

"Speaking of trying out new things, Penny, Morwyn has given me a mobile phone. Got it at the post office of all places. Imagine! I never dreamed the post office would one day be in the telephone business, but who knew?

"Anyway, just pull it out of my bag for me, will you, dear? I'm still not used to carrying it around, but I need to have it handy in case someone calls. Otherwise, there's no point to having one, is there? My nails are still a bit tacky and I wouldn't want to ruin your beautiful handiwork."

Mrs. Lloyd held out her bag for Penny to open and then stepped back.

"Oh dear me, I know that look! You've just remembered something and now you'll be off to ring that policeman of yours. Well, this time at least you've actually finished my manicure. Honestly, Penny, sometimes I wonder about you."

"You're absolutely right, Mrs. Lloyd. Thanks to you, I've just remembered something really important. At least, I think it might be. Oh, I could hug you. Oh, what the hell!"

She gave Mrs. Lloyd a quick hug, said a hurried good-bye and ran back into the shop.

"Sgt. Morgan! Bethan!" she called as she raced up the stairs.

And as she turned into the High Street, Mrs. Lloyd was fiddling with the call button on her new telephone.

"Morwyn!" she said when her niece answered.

"I've just said something that's set that Penny Branningan off again. She could hardly contain herself. But the funny thing is, I don't know what it was. But I think it was something to do with my mobile phone."

CHAPTER TWENTY-EIGHT

A little while later, Davies beside her, Penny emerged from the small incident room that had been set up at Llanelen Police Station for his use during the investigation. As she wiped her inky fingertips with a tissue, she looked up at him and smiled.

"You'll let me know if they match, won't you?"

"Oh, you'll be hearing from me, ma'am, I assure you." They walked down the hall in an easy rhythm, their footsteps making soft padding sounds on the green linoleum.

"I figured that you knew more than you thought you did and sooner or later you'd remember something really critical."

She looked at her fingertips that were still lightly covered in ink and then held them up to Davies.

"Those tissues are useless," she said. "You might want to invest in some wet wipes."

"Right, well, don't let me keep you. I know you're anxious to see your pal." Davies smiled at her. "Oh, and do give her my best."

Penny poked her head around the door of the hospital room and caught sight of Victoria sitting up in bed.

"Well, you look pale and interesting, but altogether much better than you did the last time I saw you," she said as she entered. "How are you feeling?"

"Not too bad, really," said Victoria in a weak voice. "A bit weird though. Almost myself but not quite there yet."

"I'll bet," said Penny. "They told me you don't remember anything about what happened. So you don't remember someone showing up with a lavish bouquet of flowers?"

"No, I don't. I think I remember pouring myself a glass of wine, and after that, nothing, really until this morning. I was quite shocked when they told me where I am. They said I might remember more in time but that often with traumatic events you just block the whole thing out."

"What was it like when you regained consciousness?" Penny asked as she settled herself on the chair beside the bed and placed a modest bunch of carnations in Victoria's lap. Victoria smiled her thanks, sank back into her pillows, picked up the cheerful pink flowers, and gazed into them.

"It was like waking up from a deep sleep, but I was very disoriented," she said. "It was like being beneath the surface of awareness, if you know what I mean, while I tried to figure it out. Am I awake? Am I asleep? What's happening to me?" She paused and looked very subdued. "I even thought, 'Am I dead? Is this what it's like to be dead?' I don't know how long that part lasted, but I was glad when it was over and then I knew I was alive, just like I used to be."

"Wow. That's really something."

After a few moments of silence, Penny looked at her friend.

"I was really worried about you," she said simply.

"When we found you, you said you thought you might die."

"Did I really?"

A thoughtful look, punctuated with puzzled confusion, crossed her face.

Sensing she had caused some distress, Penny tried lightly to move the conversation on.

"Well, something like that. Anyway, you're on the mend, and that's what counts," she said briskly. "Did they say how long you'll be here?" She looked around the small, clean room "At least you've got a room of your own. That's got to be worth something."

"Mm. The room to myself is because of the policeman who has to sit outside the door. He's very young and very dishy, one of the nurses told me. Fancies him like mad, she does!"

Penny looked toward the door where Bethan Morgan was now occupying the chair.

"He's not there now, but we did see him when we came in. I guess Sgt. Morgan gave him a break and he's gone off in search of the loo.

"Anyway, they told me I wasn't to stay too long. But don't worry, we'll find who did this to you. And I guess you know, it is connected to Meg Wynne's murder. So, all things considered, we're very lucky to still have you with us."

She stood up, patted her friend on the shoulder, and leaned over to give her a little hug.

"I miss having you about the place," she said. "You kind of grow on people."

Morgan swung around in her chair to look at the two of them and then got up and entered the room.

"Sister asked me to pop in and tell you that your time's just about up, Penny. Hello, Mrs. Hopkirk. Glad to see you're looking a bit better."

As they prepared to leave, Penny reached into her bag.

"Almost forgot to give you this," she said, handing over a greeting card in a pale pink envelope. "It's from Gwennie. She's really taken a shine to you, and was terribly cut up about it, when she heard what had happened. You made a deep impression on her. Oh, and Gareth sends his best."

Victoria nodded and took the envelope.

"I'll open it later," she said, letting it drop beside her. "I'm too tired right now. But there was one thing I wanted to tell you. They told me I'd been given a heavy mix of street drugs. Where would anyone get filthy stuff like that around here?"

"Unfortunately, everywhere," said Morgan. "People think street drugs are just a big-city problem, but they're in every nook, cranny, and schoolyard of this country."

As Morgan drove Penny home, her mobile rang. She pulled over to answer it, spoke briefly, and then tuned to Penny.

"You were right," she said. "Your fingerprints were on one of the phones we recovered from the Meg Wynne burial site. There's yours and another set we've still to match."

They looked at each other.

"So let me just make sure I've got this straight," said Penny. "Whoever that woman is, the one who came to the salon that morning pretending to be Meg Wynne, somehow her phone ended up in Meg Wynne's grave?"

"That's almost right," said Morgan. "She had that phone in her possession, and that's the one you pulled out of her bag for her, but the phone originally belonged to a kid in London. So technically, it wasn't her phone."

Penny nodded.

"I see, or at least I think I do. So when you find the woman whose fingerprints are also on the phone, you'll have the accomplice. The woman who came to my shop that morning."

"Right," said Morgan as she checked to make sure the road was clear and then pulled smoothly back into the driving lane.

"He said something else, too. He told me to 'get some wet wipes, whatever they are.'"

Penny laughed and looked at her fingertips.

"That's all very well for your next villain, but doesn't do me much good!"

Two days later, at lunchtime, Rev. Evans and Bronwyn drove Victoria home but declined to come up, saying they'd stop by in a day or two after Victoria had had a chance to rest up and settle in.

"Gareth and Sgt. Morgan might drop by later to bring us up to date," Penny told her when she was settled on the couch. "How are you really?"

"I'm fine," Victoria said, "unless I move too quickly. Then I get dizzy. I'm supposed to take it easy for a few more days. But I still don't remember anything about that night, if that's what you're wondering."

"Well, never mind that now," said Penny. "Come with me, I want to show you something. There's a surprise for you in your room."

Victoria made her way gingerly to the former box room, peeked in the door, and then squealed with delight.

The formerly windowless room had been freshly painted and transformed by a painting on one wall that looked like an open casement window with a view onto a windswept New England beach, complete with tall, waving grasses and a brilliant blue ocean. On each side of the painted window pale green curtains fluttered cheerfully in an imaginary breeze.

"Oh, it's wonderful, Penny," said Victoria.

"It's a trompe l'oeil," said Penny, "and rather good if I do say so myself. Thought it might transport you when you're lying in bed. Might make the room seem a little more like a proper bedroom."

"I love it!" said Victoria as she sat on the bed and looked gratefully at her friend. "But would you mind awfully leaving me to enjoy it? I think I'd like a nap now. Get a bit of rest."

Penny nodded. "I'll leave the door open, shall I? Just call me if you need anything. I'll be here for an hour or so and then I'm going downstairs to work for the afternoon. I'll sort something out for supper later."

As she was speaking Victoria lay down and by the time she had finished, she was talking to herself; Victoria was sound asleep. Penny draped a light blanket over her, left the room, and sat down at the kitchen table.

We're not nearly there yet, she thought. We don't know the why, . . . why was Meg Wynne killed and Victoria attacked? When we know the why, we should know the who. And was the assault on Victoria meant to kill her or was it a warning? So many unanswered questions, so many pieces still to be fitted together.

She remembered how she and Emma had solved their jigsaw puzzles, each with her own way of doing it. While Emma would sift patiently through the pile looking for a piece of just the right shape, Penny could tell just by looking at the colour whether or not a piece would fit. This green one might look like the right shape, but the colour was just slightly too dark or too light.

I wonder what Emma would make of all this, she asked herself. Emma, with her insightful wisdom, who had seen so much of human nature in its purest, rawest form—the unguarded behaviour of children. As she thought of her dear old friend, an idea began to form in the back of her mind.

She glanced at her watch and stood up. Time to open the shop and get the girls ready for their Saturday night dates. As she reached the top of the stairs, the phone rang. Probably Bronwyn, she thought, checking to see how Victoria was doing. She thought about letting the answering machine pick up but then realized the ringing might wake Victoria.

"Hello?"

"Penny," said a soft voice at the other end. "It's Bethan. I'm just calling to let you know they think they've picked up our mystery woman. At a petrol station in Glasgow. I can't say any more right now, but I'll drop by as soon as I can."

The line went dead and Penny slowly replaced the telephone receiver.

The afternoon wore on and just as Penny was getting ready to close up shop, the door opened and Sgt. Morgan entered, looking like the cat that got the cream.

"She was picked up in Scotland this morning, she's been fingerprinted, and they match. We've got her."

She smiled smugly and nodded as Penny gasped.

"Really? Scotland? How did they know it was her?"

"That's the funny thing about policing," said Morgan as, at a nod from Penny she locked the door and turned the sign to CLOSED. "No matter how high tech we get and how clever we think we are, it's always something really simple that blows things wide open.

"This woman—we still don't know her real name—was wearing a head scarf and you don't see many of them around these days, so she fit the description on the memo that had been circulated to all the police services. Anyway, there she was using a credit card with a stolen number in a petrol station and it just so happened that an off-duty officer from Stirling was behind her in the queue. When the card was declined and the kerfuffle started—you know, the woman in the head scarf protesting there must be some mistake—he got curious."

Penny opened the door to the flat and led the way upstairs.

"It's uncanny how often you see it," Bethan went on. "First, something has to happen and when it does, there's someone on the scene smart enough to pick up on it and figure out what it means. That's how these cases get solved." She followed Penny into the flat where Victoria was setting the table.

"Anyway, I knew you'd want to know." She looked brightly at the two of them. "Room for a little one at dinner? We could order in Thai. My treat!"

"Does Inspector Davies know you're here?" asked Penny.

"Of course he does! He knows I like being here and he thought it might be a good idea if I kept an eye on the two of you while he's away."

"Away?"

"It's his case, remember? So he's gone to Scotland to question her. She's got a lot of explaining to do, and we're pretty sure she'll tell us who she was working with."

By the end of the evening they had their answer.

On Monday, Rev. Thomas folded the morning newspaper, set it beside his wife's breakfast plate, removed his reading glasses, and placed them in their case.

"There's something very wrong here, Bronwyn," he said as he wiped homemade marmalade from his fingers before reaching for the cafetiere to pour himself the second cup of coffee he sometimes allowed himself. "This makes no sense to me," he said, gesturing at the newspaper headline.

LATE LANDOWNER'S SON SOUGHT IN BRIDE'S SLAYING

"I know," said Bronwyn as she picked up the newspaper. "The whole village is in shock. No one can believe it."

"Yes, well, there's that, too," said Rev. Evans. "But no, what I'm referring to is that headline. It makes no sense. 'Late Landowner's Son'. Emyr is the landowner now. Why not just say 'Landowner Sought in Bride's Slaying'? Still, what's it matter? The point is that they're after the wrong chap. I saw his anguish that day when Meg Wynne went missing. Either he's a very fine actor or he had nothing to do with it. And my money, what there is of it, is on the latter. There's something not right here."

"But that woman, that accomplice, what's her name, oh, where is it?" said Bronwyn scanning the newspaper, "Here it is . . . Gillian Messenger, she's given police all the details and she says Emyr put her up to it and that he killed Meg Wynne. That's what the police are going on."

"Well, they're wrong," said Rev. Thomas as he pushed himself away from the table and took a couple of steps toward his wife. Bending over, he kissed her upturned face.

"Lovely breakfast as usual, dear, thank you. I'll be in my study if you should want me."

A few minutes later he settled himself behind his desk, switched on his computer, and started to check his e-mail. Sometimes, on a Monday, there would be a special note from a parishioner telling him how much he'd enjoyed Sunday's sermon. It didn't happen often, but the rector enjoyed getting a friendly little note from time to time. This morning, though, there was just the usual rubbish that comes in overnight.

When he was finished with the delete button, he turned away from the computer, folded his hands on his desk, and gazed out the window. Usually he found the gentle view over the ancient green hills a great comfort as they restored his sense of calm. But not this morning. After a few moments he opened the top drawer, pulled out a small sweets tin, and gently lifted the lid. He looked at the green plastic cigarette lighter inside, then took it out and rolled it around in his fingers.

No, I mustn't, he thought. Tempting, but I mustn't.

A few moments later, deep in thought, he walked over to his bookcase, reached in behind a dusty anthology of Edwardian sermons, and pulled out a cigarette box.

Well, just the one, he told himself as he opened the window and leaned out. Just a few puffs. He inhaled deeply. Ahhh. He watched the grey smoke drift away on the light morning breeze.

But the business about Emyr weighed heavily on him all day and by evening he had decided to go around and have a word with Penny and Victoria.

"I'm just going to pop out for a little while, dear," he told his wife. "I'd like to see how our Victoria's doing. You'll be all right on your own here for a bit, won't you?"

"Yes, of course, Thomas," she replied. "I've got in a new library book I've been looking forward to, so off you go."

She helped him on with his jacket, and then stood at the window, pulling back the curtain slightly, as she watched his familiar figure set off on the short walk to Penny's flat.

When she was sure he was well on his way, she poured herself a small sherry, settled into a comfortable chintz chair, reached down the side, and pulled out the latest in a popular series of Regency Romances. She smiled at the cover image of the heroine with her flowing hair and luscious, pushed-up breasts. With a contented sigh, hoping the story would include a handsome earl with a smart carriage, she opened the book and was soon whisked away to the Assembly Rooms in Bath where a candlelit ball was about to begin.

"It's not settled until it's settled right," Rev. Evans was saying to Penny and Victoria. "Believe me, Emyr just doesn't have it in him to do these dreadful things and I think the police are making a terrible mistake. Why would they take any notice of that awful woman?"

Penny and Victoria nodded.

"It does seem hard to believe," Victoria said, "but apparently she told them lots of details that only someone involved in the crime could possibly know, and she says Emyr was in on it." She looked at Penny. "And we did see them together in Llandudno that day and you have to admit, they were looking awfully chummy."

Penny looked from one concerned face to the other.

"I agree it doesn't seem right. I don't know Emyr very well, but this does seem completely out of character to me. It doesn't sound like something he'd be capable of, does it?"

They sat in silence for a moment.

"Listen," said Penny. "I don't know what you'd think of this idea, but I've been wishing that Emma was here because she knew Emyr and the other two when they were lads, and she always used to say, 'Show me the boy and I'll give you the man.'"

"Yes, she did," agreed Rev. Thomas. "Very wise, was Emma. Then again, she might have been paraphrasing Wordsworth. You know, the child is the father of the man."

"Well, wherever it came from," continued Penny, "the thing is, she kept notebooks in which she wrote down her comments on how the school year was going and her observations about her pupils, especially in their last year or so with her. She often jotted down where she thought they were headed, and loved when they proved her right. She found the notes handy when talking to parents about their child's progress or planning for next year, especially as she got older. There are dozens of these books, going back years. Anyway, if we could see what she wrote all those years ago about the men in the wedding party, back when they were kids, that might give us some insight into their characters now. Might show us what direction we need to go in. Who should be on our radar."

She looked from one to the other.

"What do you think? Should we go and get them?"

"Are you suggesting what I think you are?" asked Rev. Evans. "That we should just waltz over there, break into her cottage, and help ourselves to her notebooks, wherever they are?"

"Well, no, not exactly," said Penny. "It's not as bad as it sounds. I know where the key to the back door is hidden and where the notebooks live, so it wouldn't exactly be breaking and entering . . . it would be more, well, just going over there and letting ourselves in and borrowing them, really." She thought over what she had just said. "Yes, that's all it would be. And then, of course, we'd return them," she added.

Victoria and Rev. Evans glanced at each other and then turned their attention back to Penny.

"Let me think about this," said Rev. Evans. "I must not do, or be seen to be doing, anything that could possibly be considered illegal or unethical. I have to be mindful of my position, see."

He folded his hands together and leaned on them. After a few moments he sat up straight.

"I suggest we look at it this way. If she were here, Emma would be glad to help. Indeed, she would want to help. But as she's not here, if this is the only way she can help, then this is the way it has to be.

"Perhaps I could just wait here?" he added hopefully.

"No, sorry, Rector, we need you to hold the torch," said Penny. "Victoria will be the lookout. It's getting dark now, so let's get ourselves sorted and then be off."

They walked silently through the back streets to Emma's cottage, located on a quiet lane backing onto a gently wooded area. With a quick look around to make sure they were not being observed, they edged their way around to the back of the cottage, brushing aside some overgrown foliage as they went. Reaching under a stone urn filled with dry, dying geraniums, Penny pulled out the key to the back door, placed it in the lock, and turned it.

A few moments later they were standing in the small kitchen. The air was close and musty, heavy with the empty smell of abandonment and recent neglect.

"I should have come around and checked on things," Penny muttered. "I should have made sure everything was okay. You know, with all that's happened, it never occurred to me. Emma would be so upset if she—"

Rev. Thomas put his hand on Penny's arm.

"Don't think about it now," he said softly. "Let's just get through this as quickly as we can and we'll talk about all the rest of it later."

Penny nodded and led the way into the small sitting room that lay in front of them. Victoria knelt on the small sofa in front of the window and pulled the curtains shut.

"I saw that in a film," she said. "The first thing you do is close the blinds."

"Right," said Penny. "Let's switch on the torch and shine it over here," she said, motioning to the bookcase. "Victoria, twitch the curtain open a crack and watch to make sure nobody comes."

Penny and Rev. Evans made their way to the bookcase where rows of small red notebooks, with the years embossed on the spines in gold, were neatly lined up. By the light of the small torch she ran her fingers along the books. "Nineteen seventy-six . . . that would be too early. They're about thirty-two years old now, so we should be looking at—

"Try 1981," said the rector.

Penny pulled out that year and flipped through it.

"No, don't see anything. I'll try the next one."

The only sound was the rustling of pages as she checked the entries.

Sensing her rising distress, the rector tried to comfort her.

"Don't think about the handwriting, just keep going."

Penny stepped back.

"I can't touch them. You look."

The rector handed over the torch and Penny tried to hold it steady.

"Sorry," she muttered. "I wasn't emotionally prepared for this."

The rector didn't reply but kept leafing through a small notebook.

"Here we are. This is the one we want! Let's take it back to your place and we'll read it there."

Victoria let the curtain drop and once the torch had been switched off, opened the curtains again. By the soft glow from the streetlamp they made their way to the back door which Penny locked, and then replaced the key under the urn.

The rector tucked the notebook into his jacket and as quietly as they had come, they melted away into the night.

CHAPTER TWENTY-NINE

"Should we have a cup of tea or a glass of wine?" Victoria asked.

"Wine, please!" said Penny and the rector in unison.

"Right, here you go," said Victoria, plunking down three glasses and a cold bottle of Chardonnay.

"Let's hear it, then."

"I'll start with Emyr," said the rector over the sound of wine gurgling into glasses. "She writes and I quote: 'A quiet, gentle boy, easily led. Eager to please and anxious to be liked. Helpful in the classroom. Comes from secure home. Much-loved only child of wealthy parents. Will feel he has position to uphold and may resent expectations placed upon him because of inheritance.'

"This was"—he turned the book so he could see the spine—"1983. Sounds a lot like him today. How perceptive Emma was," he said admiringly. He nodded his thanks at Victoria for the wine and took a sip.

"Right. Let's see what she had to say about Robbie Llewellyn.

"Sharp-witted. His work is careful and sustained. Solitary and studious. Would do well in profession where work is detailed and requires careful thought and planning. The law, perhaps. Suspect he is homosexual but not yet aware of it."

"Careful thought and planning," repeated Penny. "That would describe Meg Wynne's murder. Emma was right, he did become a lawyer, and a good one, by all accounts. Didn't know he was gay, though. I guess he keeps that hidden."

She fingered the stem of her glass and looked at Victoria.

"How are you holding up? Are you okay?"

Victoria nodded. "I want to hear what she says about David."

"David?" asked the rector.

"David Williams."

"There's no David, here," said the rector, scanning the names and then turning the page. "Oh wait, this must be him. He looked up at them. "Or should that be 'he'?" He shrugged. "Anyway, Dafydd Williams." He read silently to himself. "Hmmm. Sounds like trouble. She describes him as 'Very self-confident. Does not take responsibility for own actions. Blames others when things go wrong. Alarming sense of entitlement. Talks a good game but short on substance. Cannot apply himself to one task for long. Takes credit for others' work. Makes friends easily. Demonstrates leadership qualities but always for own purpose. Will stop at nothing to get what he wants (ruthless). Home life unsettled and violent. Will likely end up in position of some power or in trouble with the law.'"

He closed the book and the three of them looked at one another.

"I knew it!" exclaimed Penny. "It was Williams. It had to be. And if we're going to help Emyr, we'll have to find a way to prove to the police that it's that weasel Williams they want, not Emyr."

The rector started to say something and then looked at his watch.

"Oh, good heavens! Is that the time?" he exclaimed, jumping up from the table. "Bronwyn will be wondering whatever's become of me. I must go." He touched Victoria on the shoulder. "You'll keep me informed, won't you? We're all in this together now, aren't we?" He looked from one to the other. "Oh, and it might be a good idea if I saw you two in church on Sunday. If there's any forgiveness needed for our activity this evening, we'll seek it then."

Penny smiled at him as Victoria reached up and patted his hand.

"Thank you, Thomas," she said.

"God bless you, my dears," he replied. "No, don't get up. I'll see myself out."

Rev. Evans felt deeply troubled but at the same time, strangely exhilarated on the short walk home. The night was calm and clear as he made his way along the deserted street. When he reached the rectory he paused for a moment, looked up at the stars, and silently thanked God for all the blessings in his life.

If he was mildly worried that his wife would be cross with him for staying out so late, he needn't have been. He arrived to find Bronwyn waiting up for him and in a very good mood. She had had a bath and was wearing a new cappuccino-coloured nightdress with a matching dressing gown. Her ensemble showed rather more lace and cleavage than the rector was used to, and as he bent over to kiss her, he noticed that she had dabbed on a few drops of the light perfume he had given her for Christmas.

When he saw that her favourite magnolia-scented

candles had been set out, waiting to be lit, he couldn't believe his luck.

"I'll just go and fetch my lighter, darling," he said in a husky voice. "Won't be a tick."

"That woman is lying to protect the killer," said Penny over her shoulder as she rinsed the wineglasses. "What do you think? Do you think it was David Williams?"

Victoria nodded.

"But we have no proof," Penny continued, turning back to the sink "And we definitely need to find out why. Why would he kill her? Why would he attack you?" She shut off the taps and turning around as she dried her hands, was startled to see Victoria looking drawn and pale. She walked over and rested her hand on her shoulder.

"I can't think anymore tonight, Pen," Victoria said, gazing up at her friend. "I'm too tired and this is doing my head in."

"Mine, too," Penny agreed. "But there's something in that book that I can't quite put my finger on, but it's the key to this whole thing and if we . . ."

Her voice trailed off as Victoria slumped over the table with her head resting on her arms.

"Gosh, you are all in. And here's me going on and on. I'm so sorry. It's all caught up with you. Let's get you to bed."

Penny tried to read her library book for about half an hour, and then, too distracted to continue, took off her reading glasses and set them on the nightstand. She closed her eyes and began to drift downward into sleep but just as she was about to cross the threshold into unconsciousness, was jerked awake.

That's it! she thought. That wasn't what she meant. It

was like the flowers on the Queen Mother's hat from the jigsaw puzzle that she and Emma had done so long ago. You think it's one thing, but when you see it in context, it's something else.

The book thudded to the floor as she threw back the covers and got out of bed. Not stopping to find her slippers, she padded quickly along to Victoria's room. She could hear soft, gentle breathing as she approached the bed and as her eyes adjusted to the darkness she could see that Victoria was lying on her side, facing away from her.

"Victoria!" she said softly, touching her shoulder. "Are you awake?"

"Ohh, I am now," Victoria said sleepily as she rolled over to face Penny. "What is it? What's so important?" she moaned. "Can't it wait?"

"It probably could have, and God, I'm so sorry, Victoria. I should have thought but something's just come to me. It's what you said when we found you after you were attacked. I thought you said you were going to die, but thinking about it now, that seems strange. I don't think someone who'd been attacked would say they were going to die; I think it would be more likely for them to *ask* if they were going to die."

She sat on the edge of the bed as Victoria shifted over to make room.

"Wait," whispered Victoria. "Don't say anything for a moment."

She reached over and turned on the bedside light. As its warm light cast a soft glow over the bed, she placed her pale green pillows against the wall and sat up against them.

Penny got up off the bed to allow Victoria to pull the duvet up over her chest.

"Okay," said Victoria as she tucked her arms under the covers. "I'm ready. Let's hear it."

"I think someone would ask if they were going to die," repeated Penny as she sat down on the edge of the bed. "But you didn't say it as a question; you said it as a statement. And I've just realized, what you said was 'Dai'—you know, the nickname for Dafydd. But of course it's pronounced 'die'."

Victoria let out a small gasp.

"That's what was in Emma's book . . . he's not David Williams—that's his big, fancy London persona. He's Dafydd Williams. That was his name back then and you knew him as Dai. Victoria, I think when we found you, you told me the name of the person who attacked you. And then you blacked out, and lost all memory of what happened."

As the pain and fear of the past few days welled up inside her, and the tears finally came, Victoria pulled up her knees and sobbed.

"Don't you worry," Penny said, jumping up to comfort her. "We'll get the bastard. I'll call Gareth first thing in the morning."

CHAPTER THIRTY

Penny put the phone down and shook her head. Victoria raised her eyebrows over her teacup.

"Well?"

"He's not buying it," Penny replied as she pulled out a chair. "Says the woman has implicated Emyr and what's more, we're his best witnesses because of what we saw in Llandudno that day." She snorted. "His best witnesses! I don't think so!"

She thought for a moment.

"So, we have to find out why Williams did it and some way to prove that he did it. And, we're going to have to be very careful, because we know how dangerous he is. I think he attacked you because he heard, maybe from Gwennie, that we were poking around and asking questions. When you think about it, Victoria, you were present at your own murder. You just didn't die."

Victoria shuddered and then started gathering up the breakfast things.

"What have you got on today?" Penny asked over the clinking of dishes being stacked.

"I'm going to pick up some books from the library. They didn't tell me much when I was discharged from the hospital, and I want to know more about what happened to me and what kind of recovery I'm in."

"Now that you're not using anymore," teased Penny.

"Right," agreed Victoria grimly.

"That reminds me," said Penny. "If you're going to the library anyway, would you mind returning a couple of books for me? I got about three quarters through one of them and decided it was a waste of time. I could tell what the ending was going to be, so I read the last few pages, and sure enough, I was right. Too predictable.

"Oh, forgot to mention. Gareth said he'd drop by later to see how you're doing.

"Right, well, best be off. Those nails won't paint themselves."

The door to the flat rang after dinner and a few moments later Penny was showing Gareth into the sitting room where Victoria was curled up on the couch, a small blanket over her knees, engrossed in one of the library books.

"Hello, Victoria," he said. "Just wanted to drop by for a few moments to see how you're getting on. All right, are you?"

She smiled up at him.

"Getting there. Feel a bit more like my old self every day."

"That's the ticket," he said, and then, turning to Penny, asked if he could have a quiet word in the kitchen.

"There's this retirement do on Friday," he said, "and I wondered if you'd like to go with me. I know I should have asked sooner, but with all that's going on . . .

"Should be a good night out. Old Roddy's been with

the force a long time, and we're giving him a proper send-off. Nice meal, a few drinks, and we're even laying on a dance."

"And will there be speeches?" Penny asked innocently. "Can't beat a good retirement speech, I always say."

Davies laughed. "Oh, I think I can safely say that you won't be disappointed. And with us being Welsh and unable to stop ourselves, there might even be singing."

His smile faded.

"Just one thing, though. I wondered if we could see this as just a night out. Let's not discuss the case. Let's just enjoy ourselves. Deal?"

"Deal," Penny agreed. "Is it a formal do?"

"Not too dressy, but it's at the golf club, so you know, something nice but not too formal." He smiled at her.

The phone rang just as he finished speaking.

"I'll get it," called Victoria. After her hello, there was silence.

"We'll call you back," she said, then added in a low voice, "give me your number."

An awkward silence hung over them as Victoria entered the kitchen.

"Well," said Davies, looking from one to the other, "best be on my way, then."

Penny showed him out of the flat and then returned to find Victoria looking at the piece of paper in her hand.

"That was Gwennie," she said. "Emyr's just turned up. He's been in Cornwall and didn't know the police are looking for him. Gwennie's beside herself. She wants to know what we think she should do."

Penny thought for a moment.

"Call her back," she said, "and tell her that Emyr should call Robbie Llewellyn right away. He may not be the right solicitor for this, but he might be able to recommend someone. And tell her we're coming over and we'll explain everything we know to Emyr."

And as an afterthought, she added, "Oh, and make sure she tells him we know he didn't do it and that he's been framed and we think we know who by."

Accompanied by Robbie Llewellyn and another solicitor, Emyr turned himself in the next day. A photo of him, looking glum and despondent, appeared in the next edition of the newspaper.

"I wouldn't be feeling too confident, either," said Penny, "if the best I had going for me were two middle-aged women with no resources or experience in this kind of thing."

"There's that," Victoria replied, "but he did seem genuinely touched by our belief in his innocence."

"And it's not just us," agreed Penny. "No one in the village thinks he did it.

"You know, it's going to be hard not to say anything to Gareth about this on Friday night, but I sort of promised not to go there. He just wants a nice night out, without any of this rearing its ugly head."

"Well, you can understand that," said Victoria. "To him, it's just his work. He wants to forget about all that and enjoy himself with you.

"Have you thought about what you're going to wear, by the way?"

"No, not really. Any suggestions?"

"I was thinking . . . have you got a little black dress? You can't go wrong there. With the right shoes, maybe some pearls—"

"You're right!" said Penny. "I feel a trip to Marks

and Spencer coming on. Maybe get a sexy new slip to go with it. I've got shoes and a bag that'll do. Great!"

As her last customer left on Friday afternoon she heaved a sigh of relief and made her way upstairs for a bath. She dressed slowly and carefully. Her new dress, on a pink satin hanger, hung on a hook on the back of the door. She liked the way it draped easily from the shoulders, with a small cap sleeve to just cover the upper arms. Feeling excited about the evening ahead, she held it against her face and breathed in the newness of it. It had been a very long time since she'd had the right occasion and the right man to justify a new dress.

She liked her sexy new black slip, too. Do young women still wear slips, she wondered. Goodness knows, she'd seen lots of them about who should have been wearing one. Maybe that was just her, showing her age and generational thinking.

She glanced at the clock and realized she'd better get a move on. Gareth would be here any minute.

She walked over to the closet and reached up to the top shelf to bring down the little black handbag she rarely used. In fact, the last time she'd had it out, she realized, was Emma's funeral. The bag was wedged in between a couple of boxes and as she tugged on it, the boxes shifted and threatened to fall. She dropped the handbag to grab the heavier, bigger box and steady it. As she touched the box, the unzipped handbag fell to the floor, turning over in mid-air and spilling its contents. A packet of photographs tumbled out and several of them slipped out of the envelope and skittered across the hardwood floor.

Oh no, thought Penny as she bent over to pick them up. Those were the photos Alwynne from the sketching group wanted me to look at and I completely forgot about them. What was it she wanted to know? Something about different views of the high pasture and sheep and a dog and how she could blend the two views into one picture, was it?

Penny glanced at the photos and slowly sank to the floor, where she sat, legs tucked under her. She looked closely at the photos and then, holding her breath, pulled the others out of the packet.

"Penny! Gareth's here," called Victoria.

"Tell him to come in!"

"Are you decent?" Victoria asked as she pushed the door back and showed Davies in.

"It doesn't matter," said Penny. "He needs to see these," she said.

"What do I need to see?" he asked.

"These!" she said, handing him the photos. "They're those old-fashioned ones with the date stamp on them. Look at the date. It's the Saturday that Meg Wynne disappeared. Look at where it is and look," she said, pointing to the photo, "look there. It's Trixxi, Emyr's dog. Not just any old black Lab. She's wearing that red bandana. It's definitely Trixxi. She was up on the high pasture that morning. And look at this one," she said, fumbling to find another photo. "Down here, in the corner. There's a figure. See? You can get it enhanced and that'll tell you who was there, with the dog! And I'll bet you anything, it's David Williams."

Davies nodded, gathered up the photos, and put them in the inside pocket of his suit coat.

"You look very nice," he said unable to resist giving her lightly freckled décolletage a quick once-over. "Is that what you're wearing, though, or is there something else that should go over it?"

Penny looked down, placed her hand on her chest, and started to laugh.

"Stop looking and help me up," she said, "and I'll finish getting dressed."

"Good," said Davies. "And then you can tell me where you got these."

"I thought we had a deal that we weren't going to discuss the case," teased Penny.

"We aren't," said Davies. "Not after you've told me where you got them, who took them, and why we're just seeing them now. And then we won't discuss it anymore."

The retirement party was in full swing when they arrived. As they made their way through the crowded room several older men called out to Davies, who smiled broadly as he led Penny to a table where Bethan and three others were seated.

Bethan's face lit up when she saw Penny and she gestured to the empty seat beside her. Davies pulled out the chair and when Penny was seated, took his place on her other side.

"Bethan likes you very much," Davies said, leaning closer to Penny to be heard above the background din of crowd noise. "I think she'll be sorry when this case is wrapped up and she might not get to see so much of you." Penny smiled at him, and then turned to Bethan.

"You look really nice tonight, Penny," Bethan said. "That black dress really suits you!"

When the dinner and speeches were over, and as the upbeat sound of Rod Stewart's "Maggie Mae" started up, Davies led her onto the dance floor. As they danced, they sang the familiar words along with the rest of the dancers. After a few upbeat songs, the opening piano sequence of Carly Simon's title song from *The Spy Who Loved Me* slowed down the pace and they turned toward each other.

He put his arm around her waist and as they moved gently back and forth in time to the music, she looked up at him.

"I was thinking during dinner that it's rather fun to be in this company," she said, gesturing around her. "Almost everyone here is a police officer and yet everyone looks so normal and ordinary. You'd never know."

Davies pulled her closer and she relaxed in his arms, closed her eyes, and enjoyed the moment. She breathed in the scent of him, a masculine blend of a garden after the rain and cigar smoke.

Around midnight, they said their good-byes and drove home. As they made their way along the quiet deserted road, Penny looked over at him in the pale light from the dashboard.

"It was a great evening," she said. "Thanks for taking me."

He nodded and reached for her hand.

"I was really proud to walk in there with you," he said. "You looked," he took his eyes off the road for a moment and glanced at her, "really lovely."

They pulled up in front of the shop and Davies switched off the ignition. They sat for a moment and then turned to each other.

"Are you coming up?" Penny asked.

"Stay where you are for a second," he replied. "I'll get the door for you."

Penny looked at her watch and groaned. Seven-thirty on Saturday morning and the shop had to be open in an hour and a half. She rolled over and then, as memories from the night before tumbled into place, she threw back the bedclothes and smiled. She thought about the longing in his eyes when he looked at her, the warmth of his embrace and the way he had kissed her, at first gently and then, with insistence. She realized how excited she was at the thought of seeing him again, but just as she was mentally getting ready to reach for him, she heard the sound of running water and was jolted back to the reality of Saturday morning.

She pulled on her dressing gown and walked into the kitchen where Victoria was filling the kettle.

"Morning," she said.

"Hi," said Victoria. "Well, you certainly look like a woman who had a good night!"

"It was great," said Penny, leaning on the counter. "Remember when you were eighteen and having the best night of your life and you just didn't want it to end? It was like that. I didn't want it to end, and I don't think he did, either."

Victoria opened the tea caddy and held out a tea bag to Penny who shook her head.

"No, coffee, please."

"What time did he leave?" asked Victoria. "I didn't hear a thing."

She broke into a grin. "Or did he leave? Maybe you're hiding him in your room!"

"No, sadly, he went home about two," said Penny. "They'll have a busy weekend. He said they'd be talking to Alwynne and Bethan will have to go over everybody's statements and of course, they'll have to get the photos enhanced. I guess all we can do is await developments."

The morning dragged on slowly and Penny found it hard not to keep looking at her watch. Every time the door opened she looked up expectantly, and hoped she had managed to hide her disappointment when each new arrival turned out to be the next client.

* * *

A few streets away in the incident room, Bethan was repeating herself to Davies whose mind seemed to be elsewhere.

"Emyr, sir! What do you want me to do about him?"

Davies looked up at her.

"Sorry, Bethan. Not quite with it today. Emyr. Right. Let's keep him where he is for now, because if we release him, Williams will know we're onto him.

"Look, here's what I want you to do. You know that woman's phone—the one we recovered from the grave? The tech guys must be finished with it by now. I want the passwords and then you and I are going to set a little trap."

Bethan broke into a broad smile.

"Sounds good. I'll be back."

By lunchtime, Penny was more than ready to call it a day and wondering how she was going to make it through the afternoon, went up to the flat. She shook her head when Victoria asked her what she wanted for lunch and plopped down on the sofa.

"Not hungry," she said. "I feel like there's something I should be doing, but I don't know what it is. I feel all wound up . . . can't concentrate."

"Have you heard from him this morning?"

"No, but I didn't think I would. I know he's got a lot on. He says this is all going to be over soon, one way or another."

"Good," said Victoria. "It's frightening to think that Williams is still out there.

"Sure you don't want a cuppa, or anything?"

"Okay, a tea would be great, thanks," said Penny as she reached over and picked up one of Victoria's library books from the coffee table and idly started leafing through it.

She sat back and thumbed through the pages, glancing at the names and descriptions of the different kinds of drugs available on the streets of Britain, each one easily capable of destroying every life it touched.

She turned the pages slowly and then stopped. Turning back a page or two she read the description closely.

Users of the drug face many of the same risks as users of other stimulants such as cocaine and amphetamines. These include increases in heart rate and blood pressure, a special risk for people with circulatory problems or heart disease, and other symptoms such as muscle tension, involuntary teeth clenching, nausea, blurred vision, faintness, and chills or sweating.

In high doses, it can interfere with the body's ability to regulate temperature. This can lead to a sharp increase in body temperature (hyperthermia), resulting in liver, kidney, and cardiovascular system failure and ultimately, death.

"Methylenedioxymethamphetamine," she muttered, underlining it with her finger as she stumbled over the word. *MDMA. More commonly known as Ecstasy.*

She tore a piece of paper off the small pad beside the telephone and printed MOMA. Looking at it critically, she printed the letters again, this time flattening the O.

"Victoria," she shouted. "It's all about drugs! And Meg Wynne must have known it! That's why he killed her. It's drugs!"

Teapot in hand, Victoria peered into the sitting room to see Penny jumping up off the sofa with a book and scrap of paper in her hand.

"What time is it? Have I got time to go and see him

before the first appointment this afternoon?" Penny asked.

She glanced at her watch.

"Look, just call the first couple of appointments and see if they can come in later, would you? I've got to go and see him. I'll explain later."

Victoria watched as Penny flew out of the flat and shook her head.

"Tea for one, then."

Penny arrived at the incident room, out of breath and barely able to speak, just as Bethan was returning with the accomplice's cell phone.

"It's all about drugs, Bethan," Penny panted. "I have to speak to him."

Davies looked up as Bethan entered his office and when Penny followed a few seconds later, he stood up. The smile that was just starting to form faded quickly when he saw how agitated she was.

"It's all about drugs," Penny said. "Here, look at this," she added as she pushed the piece of paper across his desk. "It wasn't MOMA, to do with the Museum of Modern Art, it's MDMA. Ecstasty. He's into drugs, probably in a big way, and Meg Wynne must have found out about it. That's why he killed her."

Davies picked up the paper and handed it to Bethan. "Sort this out later with the paper we took from her room," he said.

"Let's have the phone."

He gestured to Penny to sit down.

"Williams poses a huge flight risk," he said, "so we've got to reel him in carefully. We'll keep Emyr where he is for another day or two."

As Penny started to protest, he held up his hand.

"It's okay. He understands. If we release Emyr, Williams will know we're onto him. So we've just made Emyr a bit more comfortable. Upgraded his accommodations, you might say. Told him it won't be for much longer."

He pointed at the phone on his desk.

"Right, now Bethan. I want you to text him, pretending you're Gillian, and ask him to come and see you. Tell him you've got important information he needs to know. Tell him to come to Llandudno. Say visiting hours are Monday from two to four. Tell him to get back to you."

Davies and Penny watched as Bethan picked up the phone and using two thumbs deftly entered the message, read it over carefully, showed it to Davies, and when he nodded and handed the phone back to her, sent it. Exhaling quietly, she put the phone on the table and sat back.

They waited and a few minutes later came the text-speak reply: C U

"Right," said Davies. "Let's get our welcoming party ready."

On Monday afternoon, Gillian Messenger, looking pale and exhausted, was led into a visiting area in the Llandudno jail. Dressed in jeans with a dark green turtleneck pullover and wearing the bright yellow vest that identified her as a prisoner, she looked about her uncertainly and then sat down at an empty table. A few moments later, David Williams was ushered in.

Impeccably dressed as usual, he made his way slowly over to her, taking in every detail of the room, including the guard who stood with his arms folded beside the heavy door.

The room had about a dozen small tables in it, and

almost every one was occupied. The female prisoners were of all ages, some young, wearing their hair in ponytails, others middle aged or even approaching retirement age.

Their visitors included young, fit men and grey-haired older men. They talked quietly and calmly.

Gillian's face lit up as David approached her table.

"David!" she said. "Am I glad to see you. My solicitor is trying for bail, and I can't wait to get out of here. How have you been? How are things?"

He glared at her.

"How could you let yourself get caught, you stupid bitch!" he whispered. "What the bloody hell were you thinking?"

"I know, I know," she said. "It was that credit card you gave me. When it was declined, I just started to freak out."

"Anyway," said David. "Let's get to it. What did you want to tell me?"

"Me?" said Gillian. "Nothing, I . . ."

David shot a glance around him.

"You didn't text me to come here?" he asked.

"No," she said. "How could I? They took my phone. They don't let you use your own phone. You have to use the one in the hall and there's always a queue."

Bewildered, she tried to read the look on his face.

"What is it? What's the matter?"

"Right. I'm getting out of here," he hissed as he pushed back his chair and began to stand up.

Across the room a young woman in a prisoner's visiting vest also stood up, walked over to him, and placed a firm hand on his shoulder.

"Sit down, please, Mr. Williams," she said.

He pushed her aside as complete quiet fell over the

room and all eyes turned to him. Then, several other prisoners and their visitors stood up.

"Sit down, please, Mr. Williams," she repeated.

As he reacted to the unmistakable authority in her voice and sank slowly into his chair, a guard approached Gillian, touched her on the arm, and then led her, sobbing quietly, out of the room.

Williams watched her go.

"Look," he said easily, "I don't know who you are or what's going on here, but there has to be some mistake. I just dropped in to visit an old friend. I'm sure we can clear all this up."

"Oh, I'm sure we'll get to the bottom of it," said Bethan, who, wearing glasses and a blond wig was unrecognizable as the policewoman who had interviewed him.

As she produced her warrant card Williams tried to stand up again but was pushed back into his seat by the fit young visitor at the next table. He, too, produced a warrant card and ordered Williams to sit down and put his hands on the table.

"We're going to start by giving your car a good forensics once-over," Bethan told him.

"You can't do that!" he shouted.

"Oh, I think you'll find it says in here," she said, sliding a piece of paper across the table, "that we can. In fact, we've already started.

"But don't worry, sir, we've arranged a comfortable ride for you. Of course, you won't be going home, sir. No, probably not for some little while. But as you say, sir, we'll get this cleared up."

As the other prisoners and guests prepared to leave, Bethan signalled to a guard to take Williams away.

"It's over, David," she said. "Doesn't it just feel over?"

CHAPTER THIRTY-ONE

"Everyone in the room was a police officer?" asked Penny at dinner that night in the Red Dragon Hotel where they had all gathered to go over the events of the day.

"Yes," said Gareth as he offered Victoria a second glass of wine. "It was an idea I got from something I read once about the Queen Mother wanting to have dinner at a certain restaurant in Paris. When her security detail told her it couldn't be arranged in time, she said nonsense, she wanted to go anyway. So the royal party went, she had a lovely time, and afterward told them all, 'See, I told you, nothing to worry about.'

"But what she didn't know was that the police had arranged to close the restaurant for the night to the public and everyone dining there was actually a police officer, so she was surrounded by security."

Penny and Victoria exchanged glances and smiled.

"Not the Queen Mother!" said Victoria.

"What?" said Davies. "What about her?"

"Nothing," said Penny. "Don't mind us. Do go on."

"With Williams, I thought it best not to take any chances. People involved in narcotics will do whatever it takes to protect their investment, so this way, we were prepared for anything."

He looked across the table.

"And you, Bethan," he said, "were wonderful when the pressure was on. Well done!"

Penny offered the bread basket to Gareth, took one for herself, and then passed the basket on.

"Is he a psychopath, do you think?" she asked.

"Probably," Davies said. "He's smart enough, but they have one fatal flaw that trips them up every time. They're very arrogant, and think they're that much smarter than us poor plods. It's always their undoing."

"Have you put all the pieces together yet?" asked Victoria. "Can you tell us how it all happened?"

"Scotland Yard's looking into Williams's business affairs, but it looks as if he's one of the biggest up-and-coming drug lords in Britain. Got operations all up and down the UK, Ecstasy, meth labs, grow ops, heroin, and cocaine importing and distribution. There's not much he isn't into. It's going to take some time to unravel everything, but not only have we arrested a murderer, it seems we've uncovered a huge drug operation. That's apparently where his money came from—and there was lots of it, I can tell you.

"Now, from talking to Meg Wynne's mother, we learned that her son—Meg Wynne's younger brother—died last year of a drug overdose at one of those rave parties. Meg Wynne found out about Williams's business and was blackmailing him. We think they'd had a falling out and she might have been planning to turn him in but the timing was dead wrong—she just wanted to get the wedding over with, so as not to upset Emyr and more importantly, his father. But Williams knew that he had to act.

"This Gillian Messenger—the woman who came to your salon the morning of the wedding—was his business partner, and while she was taking Meg Wynne's place at the manicure Williams simply lifted his victim off the street. They knew all the details of the appointments because Williams had heard the bridesmaids making the plans.

"He was one cold killer. He drove her out to the woods, presumably to find out what she intended to do, and then he killed her.

"He tried to inject her with a lethal drug, probably in the car, but she wrenched away from him, snapping off the needle. She got out and tried to run away, but she couldn't escape in the shoes she was wearing, and when he caught up with her he bashed and strangled her—with the dog lead as Penny suspected."

He paused for a moment, took a sip of water, and continued.

"He was the one who had taken the dog out that morning. We've taken the dog's bed away for analysis; it probably contains soil or leaves similar to what we found on Meg Wynne's clothing. And when it was over, he and his accomplice put Meg Wynne's body in the boot of his car.

"And here comes the really nasty part. The body stayed in the car all Saturday. At least he had the decency, if you can call it that, to pretend that he was having car problems so Emyr wouldn't have to ride to the church with his dead fiancée in the boot."

Penny and Victoria groaned and looked at each other.

"I know," Davies agreed. "It's an awful image.

"So the body stayed in the boot of his car until the Sunday night when the opportunity arose to dispose of the body. We tracked down the nurse who was looking after Emyr's father, who told us that she was up late that night preparing medication in the kitchen and saw a vehicle leave the car park at the back of the house with its lights off, as if the driver didn't want to attract any attention. When we asked her which car, she confirmed it was Williams's BMW. It was a full moon that night, so she had no trouble making it out. Emma Teasdale's grave had been opened and was ready for the funeral on Monday, and they saw their chance and took it. And if it hadn't been for Penny's intuition, the body probably would never have been found. You have to admit, hiding the body in a grave was very clever."

He looked at Penny, then Victoria.

"So there you have it. We think it's a pretty tight case."

"I wonder," said Penny. "What do you think Meg Wynne was going to do about Williams and his drug operation?"

Davies was silent for a moment.

"That's a good question, and I've wondered about that, too. I'd like to think that she was going to report him, and he knew if he wanted to keep his business going he had to get rid of her. I think she was starting to realize just how filthy drug money is—they don't call it laundering for nothing—and she didn't want to be on his payroll any longer.

"Anyway, she was about to marry Emyr and she didn't really need Williams's money anymore.

"And speaking of money, it turns out that Meg Wynne left everything to her mother, who has finally found the courage to leave her husband."

The women nodded and smiled.

"And now, a toast. To Victoria," he said, raising his glass, "and to Penny."

As they raised their glasses, the manager approached their table carrying a large bouquet of flowers.

"This has just been delivered for the two ladies," he

said, lowering it into Victoria's arms. "I met him earlier today in the bank and told him you'd be dining with us this evening."

Victoria looked at the card and smiled.

With heartfelt thanks, Emyr.

And then she handed the bouquet to Penny.

"No more presentation bouquets for me, thank you very much!"

A few days later an official-looking envelope arrived from Jenkins and Jones, solicitors, requesting that Penny contact them to set up an appointment.

When she arrived, she was immediately shown into the office of Richard Jones, the senior partner.

A small, tidy, bald man approaching seventy, he had looked after many of the townsfolk's legal affairs for decades.

"Ah, Miss Brannigan," he said, standing up as he held out his hand to show her to the chair facing his old-fashioned oak desk. "Thank you for coming. Yes, indeed. I have some rather good news for you."

"Oh, yes?" said Penny cautiously, sweeping her skirt behind her as she sat down.

After a few moments of settling back into his chair, Mr. Jones picked up an important-looking document comprised of several pages, with red stickers and seals attached in strategic places, and leafed through it.

"Yes, here we are.

"It's to do with the last will and testament of Emma Teasdale. She was a good friend of yours, I believe?"

"Yes, she was," said Penny.

"Well, it turns out that she has left you her tea service which you had always admired," he said, raising his eyes from the page and peering at Penny over his glasses. After a moment he lowered his eyes and added, "And, it says here, and I quote, 'and also that which holds them'."

"Oh, she's never!" exclaimed Penny. "She's left me her beautiful Welsh dresser! Where will I put it? How will I get it up the stairs?"

"No," laughed Jones, enjoying his little joke. "She's left you Jonquil Cottage and all the contents! And a tidy sum to go along with it.

"Do you know, it never fails to impress me that these wonderful, elderly people, who were always of fairly modest means, were such careful savers and wise investors. You wouldn't believe the size of the estates some of them leave behind, and after having only worked at fairly humble jobs all their lives. The young people of today could learn some very important lessons from them about living within their means.

"'The road to financial hell is paved with credit cards,' I always say. But that's neither here nor there.

"Now that I've told you the main points of the will, I can also tell you that Miss Teasdale spoke very highly of you to me, and you were very dear to her.

"See here, she refers to you as her 'beloved friend.'

"Oh my dear girl, I've upset you. I'm sure this has all come as a terrible shock. I'm sorry about the delay in telling you. There were one or two complications and other bequests we had to sort out before we could turn this over to you."

"Please, have a tissue. On second thought, better have two."

One week later, Gareth drove Penny and Victoria, with a few suitcases, to Jonquil Cottage. What had begun its life as the humble home of a worker in the old slate quarry had become what estate agents were now referring to as "a desirable period property with many original details."

Built of fine Welsh stone, the two-bedroom cottage waited to welcome its new owner. Although the garden had become overrun with weeds, Davies had assured Penny they'd have that put right in no time.

Carrying a couple of cases each, they walked up the narrow path between small beds of pink and white roses to the front door.

As Penny prepared to put the old-fashioned key Jones had given her in the lock, Davies and Victoria waited a few feet behind her. She looked back at them, then turned the key, pushed open the door, and entered what had been Emma's home, and was now hers.

Davies set the cases down in the entrance hall.

"We think you'd probably like some time on your own," he said. "We'll see you tomorrow. But call if you need anything."

"Right," agreed Penny. "Probably best. Thanks for being so understanding."

She closed the door behind them and after taking off her shoes, turned to look around. She had been to the cottage many times before, of course, but Emma had usually been there to welcome her.

She felt the hot sting of unshed tears as she slowly made her way through the familiar sitting room with its comfy furniture and crowded bookcases. The table in front of the window where they had done their jigsaw puzzles stood empty. She entered the kitchen and smiled when she saw the Welsh dresser with the charming Sweet Violets tea set.

The floor was of beautiful Welsh slate, taken from the very quarry where the original owner of the house had spent his entire working life. Large French doors off the kitchen opened onto a kitchen garden, sheltered by mature trees and framed on two sides by a brick wall.

Carrying the brown envelope of legal documents Jones had given her, she slowly went upstairs and entered what had been Emma's bedroom. She walked over to the window, opened it, and peered out at the garden. The sweet sound of birdsong rose to greet her.

She sat on the edge of the bed and smoothed out the coverlet. She gazed thoughtfully at her hand for a moment, then placed the envelope on the bedside table.

Slowly, she lay down on the bed and crossing her hands on her chest, turned her head to look out the window, and watched as a gentle breeze tousled the treetops in her garden.

Mrs. Lloyd's words, spoken soon after Emma died, came back to her.

I think there was someone once, though, but nothing ever came of it. They certainly never married, did they?

Who was he, Penny wondered. Had he visited Emma in this house? Had he ever been in this room? Did they make love in this bed?

Unanswered questions and unbidden images crowded into her mind. She shoved them away and in the peaceful serenity of her new bedroom, closed her eyes and drifted off to sleep. On and on she dreamed. The afternoon turned into early evening and the sun's last bright rays slanted through the window kissing everything in the room with a warm, golden glow. Finally, they came to rest on a small glass globe in which delicate purple flowers hung suspended for all time.

Read on for a look ahead to

A BRUSH WITH DEATH—

the next Penny Brannigan mystery from
Elizabeth J. Duncan, available in
hardcover from Minotaur Books!

Penny Brannigan awoke disoriented and confused. What on earth was she doing in the old-fashioned spare bedroom of Emma Teasdale's cottage? Why wasn't she at home in her own bed in the small, tidy flat above her manicure salon?

And then, through the just-woke-up muzziness, it all came back to her. She had recently inherited Jonquil Cottage, today was Sunday, and she had just spent her first night in her new home.

She kicked back the rumpled duvet, sat up and looked about. The subdued light of a cheerless, rainy late summer morning revealed an outdated pattern of orange poppies on yellowed wallpaper that had started to peel away from the ceiling and a substantial layer of dust on shabby, mismatched furniture. The room gave off a musty feel of neglect and the air was so close and stale that she leaned over to turn the latch of the small, leaded window beside the bed and pushed it open. When the first breath of cool, damp air from the garden filled her lungs she felt her spirits lift as a feeling of excitement and anticipation began to creep in. She hopped out of bed, found her slippers and padded across the hall to the loo.

A few minutes later she was standing at the bottom

of the stairs. In front of her was the door that led to the street, to her right, the sitting room and dining area and adjacent to that, toward the back of the cottage, a small kitchen which gave access to a partially walled garden, now somewhat overgrown but well laid out with mature pear trees espaliered along the south-facing brick wall.

With her hand resting on the banister, she surveyed the sitting room. What little light managed to filter through the closed curtains on this gray morning bathed the room in a soft, desolate luminosity, giving it the abandoned look of a place someone had once loved but would never be coming home to.

Although Penny had realized that the charming Welsh cottage would require major renovations to shift it out of the 1960s, she had decided to live in it before undertaking any drastic changes so she could get a feel for it, get to know it and discover what she liked and what she didn't. She wanted to modernize it, but in a way that would respect its history and the memory of its previous owner.

But there are too many memories crowded in here, she thought, memories not mine. Other people, from other times, living other lives.

A Canadian in her fifties, Penny had met Emma when she arrived in the Welsh market town of Llanelen decades ago. Over the years, their friendship had grown and Penny had been deeply saddened when Emma had passed away. To Penny's astonishment, the retired schoolteacher who had never married and had no close relatives, had bequeathed the cottage and its contents to her, along with a substantial amount of money.

Although she had visited the cottage many times, it was different now. When you're a guest in someone's home, you don't see the precious, secret things that have been carefully preserved and hidden away, to be held, savored and reflected upon in quiet, private moments.

Emma, who had been ill for some time, had made a will and funeral plans, but had not got round to dealing with her personal effects. Perhaps she thought she had more time to wrap up her affairs, Penny thought. And don't we all?

Today, she would have to start clearing out Emma's things, but first things first. Facing the centre of the sitting room window, she reached above her head and grabbed a curtain in each hand. With a smooth, sweeping motion, like tearing off a bandage, she ripped them apart and as they swooshed along their rail, a soft, moist light filled the room.

That's a bit better, she thought. And now, she must find the kettle.

Her friends Victoria Hopkirk and Detective Inspector Gareth Davies had dropped her off at the cottage yesterday and she was well provisioned with the basics. A few minutes later, carrying a steaming cup of freshly brewed coffee and a bowl of cereal on a tray, she made her way back to the sitting room and sat down on the faded, sagging sofa.

Opening a new notebook, she crossed her legs, looked around and began to make a list:

Internet (and computer)
LR—New curtains
New furniture
Paint—pale green/white trim?
No wallpaper!
Carpet?

She crossed that out and then wrote underneath it.

Hardwood floors

Pen poised above the page, she gazed critically about her, taking in the overflowing bookshelves that filled one wall, side tables, a small walnut writing desk and a pair of matching wing chairs that had once been 1950s brown but had been recovered in a 1970s floral chintz. Then, setting the notebook down, she wandered over to the writing desk.

She picked up a small figurine of a stooping man clad in a brown robe and turned it over. Royal Doulton. Scrooge. She set it down, smiled and inclined her head slightly. Emma had loved Christmas and had always been generous with her gifts. Scrooge of all things!

She tugged on a drawer and heard a slightly metallic, rattling sound as something inside shifted. The drawer moved a couple of inches and then stuck. She pulled on it again, harder this time, and under protest, it slid all the way out. Sitting on top of a dog-eared Reader's Digest, beside a magnifying glass with a tortoise shell handle, was a scratched and dented tin pencil box. Wondering if it was a gift from one of Emma's long-ago pupils, Penny picked it up and turned it over. The bottom was painted a distinctive green and the cream-colored top featured a sketch of St Paul's Cathedral with a pencil in the same shade of green as the base of the tin. The Harrods logo occupied pride of place on the top left corner of the lid.

Noting the box was missing a hinge, she pried it open. Inside, she found a tattered ten-shilling note, a National Westminster Bank plastic bag containing a commemorative coin marking the 1981 wedding of the Prince of Wales and Lady Diana Spencer, a key, a concert ticket stub, a square key fob featuring the octagonal red MG logo and a black and white photo.

She set the box down, picked up the photo, moved closer to the window and turned slightly so the light fell on the image she was holding.

Gazing back at her was a young Emma wearing black eyeliner and what had to be false eyelashes. She smiled shyly at the camera, but with a secretive, subtle confidence, her eyes slightly closed against the sun. Her blonde hair had been elaborately styled in a towering bouffant, with curls trailing down her cheeks and she was wearing a sleeveless mini dress with two rows of white buttons down the front. In her arms she cradled a black and white fox terrier puppy. Penny's lips moved slightly as she noted the dark nail polish Emma was wearing and then turned the photo over. In Emma's precise, school-teacher handwriting was written With Winnie, Menlove Avenue, Woolton, 1967.

Penny replaced the photo in the tin, snapped the lid shut and set the battered pencil box back in the drawer.

What am I to do with things like that, she wondered. This was going to be harder than she'd thought. Not only prying into every nook and cranny of Emma's life but also having to sort through it and probably get rid of most of it.

She took a sip of lukewarm coffee, had a spoonful of soggy cereal and then headed upstairs to get dressed.

At the top of the stairs she paused at the doorway to Emma's old bedroom. The day before, emotionally drained and physically exhausted, she had taken a long nap on Emma's bed, but now, in the cold light of morning, knew she would never sleep in the bed in which Emma had died. Getting rid of it would be easy. As part of the cottage makeover she had promised herself a fresh, serene new bedroom.

And that pleasant thought brought her to Gareth. She wondered what he was doing and decided to ring him to see if he could come over and give her a hand. The job might go better with two and he'd be much more objective. None of Emma's stuff would mean anything to him, and in his line of work, he'd had plenty of practice going through other people's belongings in a detached, clinical way.

Just as she was about to duck into the spare room in search of her mobile phone, it rang. She smiled when she saw who it was.

"Oh, I was just thinking about you," she said, "and wondering if you'd give me a hand sorting out all this stuff."

A few moments later she laughed and ran down the stairs to answer the door.

He bent his head to enter the cottage and then, in one easy, wordless moment they wrapped their arms around each other. He held her for a few seconds as she rested her head against his chest. They stepped back and he smiled at her upturned face.

"Right, then," he said, turning around to retrieve a large bouquet of red and white carnations and two bottles of white wine he'd set down on the front step. "These are for you."

Penny smiled as she accepted his gifts. "I'll find a vase and put the wine in the fridge," she said.

"The flowers are for us," he said, nodding at them. "Red and white flowers for you. Canada, see? And then the red flowers and green ferns for me. The colours of Wales!"

Penny grinned at him.

"Oh, very charming! Did you think that up yourself or did you have a bit of help?"

Gareth gave her a sheepish grin.

"Well, Bethan did say I was not to arrive empty handed, but I figured out the bit about the colours myself."

"Well, they are lovely and it was very sweet of you. And Bethan," she added.

Bethan Morgan was Gareth's energetic young sergeant; the three had come to know one another over the summer as Penny helped the two police officers investigate the case of a missing bride.

Gareth stepped into the sitting room and looked around. "Doesn't seem to me that you've got too far. What have you done?"

She winced and waved a hand in a vague flap of defeat.

"Ah, like that, is it?"

She nodded.

"You do surprise me. Your old flat was so uncluttered and I would have thought it would be easy to get rid of someone else's things because you've got no attachment to them. Unless, of course, you just happen to like something. Anyway, I've brought a few boxes so we can make a start. We'll sort it all into piles—one for the charity shop, one for the rubbish and one for the things you want to keep. I think we should pack up as much as we can so the decorating will be easier. Let's start with the walls. You're an artist, so dealing with the paintings shouldn't be too difficult."

"You're right," agreed Penny. "I know what I like and what can go." Besides her manicure business, Penny painted scenic watercolours featuring the beautiful landscapes around Llanelen. She loved rambling through the valley, with easel and paintbrushes, capturing the timeless beauty of the deep greens and purples of the ancient, majestic hills that cradled the town.

She pointed to the small watercolour that hung over the desk.

"See that one? It's the first painting I did when I came to Llanelen. I gave it to Emma to thank her for being so good to me when she gave me a bed for a night or two." She smiled at him and opened her arms in an expansive gesture that took in the whole room. "And now look what she gave me!"

He removed the painting carefully from its hook and set it on the small table in front of the window where Penny and Emma had spent many hours solving jigsaw puzzles.

"Right. What's next?"

She pointed to a pair of Monet prints.

"Charity shop."

She walked across the room and took down a painting.

"But this one, I've always liked and I definitely want to keep it."

She turned it to show to him and then looked at it again.

"Funny, all the years I've seen it and liked it but never had a chance to really look at it up close. It's rather well done, in my opinion, although it does need a good cleaning."

The painting was oil on canvas and showed two people at a picnic, a red and white checkered cloth spread out on the grass between them. She could make out what looked like a still life on the tablecloth . . . glasses of wine, a bowl of fruit, a cheese plate and half a loaf of bread on a cutting board with a bread knife beside it. The people were facing each other, the woman in a flowered summer dress with her legs folded away to the side as she leaned on one hand. The man lay on his back with his feet towards the viewer, his hands tucked under his head. Behind them was a large bank of purple flowers.

"The perspective on this is really excellent, you see," said Penny, pointing at the male figure. "With him reclining like that it would have been too easy to have him look flat and out of proportion but the artist has got it just right. I used to ask Emma about this painting but she wouldn't tell me anything about it. Just turned away and changed the subject."

She squinted at the signature. A. Jones.

Davies walked over to her, put his hand gently on her arm and glanced at the painting.

"Well, I don't know anything about art, but if you like it, that's good enough," he said. "Now, what do you want to do about that one?" They turned their attention to a large water colour of blowsy pink roses as Penny set the painting she held in her hand in the keep pile.

She wagged her head back and forth while she thought about it. "I think I like it," she said finally. "Let's keep it for now. I can find a place for it. Maybe in the new guest room."

Then, as Emma had always loved music, they started in on her rather extensive record and CD collections.

"We'll get rid of the old vinyl records," Penny said. "I don't want them and I don't want the old record player or hi fi or whatever it's called. But I'll keep the CDs. They don't take up too much space. They're mostly classical but as I recall there's some good old pop stuff in there. She loved The Beatles, Emma did."

They moved on to the bookcases and started sorting out the contents. Most went into the charity shop pile, although Gareth kept a couple of thrillers for himself, and by late morning they had filled several boxes. Penny hesitated when they came to the row of Emma's notebooks and personal journals. Emma had kept detailed commentaries on the day-to-day details of her life, including observations on the personalities and characters of hundreds of her pupils over the years. Her assessment of one student in particular had helped in the investigation of the missing bride.

"What's the matter?" Davies asked.

"I don't know what to do about the journals," Penny replied. "It seems a shame to bin them but there are so many and I doubt I'd ever need them again. I certainly don't want to read them."

She looked at him as if asking him to make the decision. Gareth pulled out a slim red volume marked 1982 on its spine and riffled through it.

"Do you think you'll want to know what she wore to a coffee morning at the church on October first or what she had for dinner a few days later?"

Penny shook her head and together they pulled the little books off the shelves and boxed them up for the rubbish.

"Oh, look," he said a few minutes later, holding up a Scrabble game with two elastic bands wrapped around the box holding the tattered lid in place. "I like a game of Scrabble every now and then. Do you? Might as well keep it. Could come in handy on a long winter night. As long as all the letters are there, of course. We could count them out later, maybe. Let's keep it for now, shall we?"

As Penny murmured her agreement he set it down then picked it up again at both ends and gently tipped it back and forth.

"Feels a bit heavy."

Penny glanced at it, and then went on with her book sorting.

"I expect there's a dictionary in the box. Some people keep one with the game so they have it handy for the challenges. I haven't come across one on the shelves, and Emma must have had one, so I expect it's in there."

"Happen you're right."

Penny tucked her hand under her chin and pursed her lips.

"Odd, that game of Scrabble, though. We used to do jigsaws together but she never brought that game out."

Davies grinned. "Maybe she thought you'd be too much of a challenge for her."

Penny gave a little snort.

"The other way round, more like."

Finally, Davies stepped back and assessed the boxes they had filled.

"That wasn't so bad, now, was it? Why don't we drop the charity boxes off at the shop, just to get them out of the way, and then I'll take you to lunch?"

Penny nodded.

"Just give me a few minutes to wash up and get changed. Won't be long." She touched him lightly on the arm as if to reassure herself, and then turned towards the stairs.

As she disappeared, Davies sat down on the sofa to wait. The place really did have lovely bones and he had no doubt that when Penny was finished with it, the cottage would be beautiful. Light and airy, in soft, modern colours with all the right accent pieces and looking like the cover spread in an interior design magazine.

A few minutes later she was back and they began shifting the boxes out the front door.

"You know," he said as Penny locked the door, "this business of clearing away old stuff gets better as you go along. At first you don't know what to keep but once you start chucking things out, it gets easier to toss it than to keep it. At least, that's the way it was for me when my wife died."

Penny grimaced as she put her key in her handbag.

"Let's not go there today," she said. "Dealing with Emma's death is quite enough for one morning."